A Frightfully Fatal Affair

Hannah Hendy lives in a small town in South Wales with her long-suffering wife and two spoilt cats. A professional chef by trade, she started writing to fill the time between shifts. She is the author of The Dinner Lady Detectives series, published by Canelo Crime.

Also by Hannah Hendy

The Dinner Lady Detectives

A Frightfully Fatal Affair

HANNAH HENDY

CANELO CRIME

First published in the United Kingdom in 2023 by

Canelo
Unit 9, 5th Floor
Cargo Works, 1–2 Hatfields
London SE1 9PG
United Kingdom

A CIP catalogue record for this book is available from the British Library.

Print ISBN 978 1 80436 471 0
Ebook ISBN 978 1 80436 470 3

Cover design by Ami Smithson

Cover images © iStock, Shutterstock

Look for more great books at www.canelo.co

Printed and bound in Great Britain by Clays Ltd, Elcograf S.p.A.

1

For Alan Baker. Thanks for comparing me to Charles Dickens, but I think I've got a long way to go!

Prologue

It isn't always so dark in Dewstow woods. Usually, during an autumn day, light streams through every branch of every tree, as it does in the summer. The short grass and dead leaves on the ground glow gold and orange, like they are on fire. But today the sky is smothered in a gloom and the sun doesn't reach far enough through the trees to make even the slightest difference. It may as well be night.

It's not always so quiet in the woods either. Most days you would meet at least one person if you were to walk the easy few miles through from the little town of Dewstow to its neighbour, Ittonvale. Bump into an acquaintance, or nod agreeably at a dogwalker coming the other way down the well-trodden paths. That is not what today had in store.

Today the air is cold and the breeze whistles through the creaking tree, beneath which the body lies. A dead weight under dead leaves. No longer a person, growing colder and colder. Just a vessel that used to hold something much more. Useless now. Legs and arms draped at horrible angles. Lungs empty. Eyes still open and staring in a terrible unseeing way, waiting for the flies that will surely come and eat them. Buzz over and land on the face that can no longer brush them off. Crawl inside nostrils and lay eggs inside the skin. The circle of life.

Worse still than any of that, the body lies terribly, terribly alone. Though, can you feel lonely when you don't exist anymore? Some questions don't have answers, couldn't possibly have them. Or are only known by those that can no longer tell.

There's a bark of laughter down the path, disturbing the peace, and the sounds of tramping through the trees gets closer and closer. Not long ago there would have been someone here, for it hasn't been long. Still, it lies there, waiting to be found.

Chapter One

'What on earth's wrong with that marrow?' Clementine asked. 'Did you feed one of the Year Sevens to it?'

Margery chuckled as they watched Summerview School's deputy head and drama teacher struggling to place the vegetable on the trestle table, which creaked horribly under the weight of it. Rose ignored them both, brushed down her smart trouser suit, turned on her heels and swooped away across the hall, back out through the fire escape to her car. Probably to get another hideously large vegetable, Margery thought. Staff member Seren, Rose's unlikely best friend, tottered along behind her with her own arms full of misshapen potatoes.

'She's got six more sacks of them in the car,' Seren whispered to Margery as she put them down on the table. 'I've told her she can't win if she's a judge, but she keeps saying that rules were meant to be broken.'

Rose barked Seren's name across the hall and she jumped to attention, scuttling back the way she came.

'Gosh, we've got some competition if even Rose is joining in.' Margery smiled at her wife.

'Well, I don't think we're going to win anyway.' Clementine gestured at their own trestle table, with its autumnal-leaf patterned tablecloth and very sparse selection of ugly parsnips and long stringy carrots. They had tried their best, but neither Margery nor Clementine had ever been particularly green-fingered. The best Margery had ever managed was a few sad strawberries in their garden and a house plant they had managed to keep alive for a few months. Until it had been put on the same schedule as Clementine's dusting, that is, and died sadly of dehydration, forgotten on the windowsill next to the ornamental cats.

'You speak for yourself.' Gloria, Margery's second-in-command, had snuck up behind them both with a basket of her homemade jams. 'I fully intend on winning something this year. I didn't slave over the stove all last night for nothing.'

Summerview School's yearly harvest festival was, as always, being held in the sports hall of Dewstow Leisure Centre. Though that meant that it was open to the public and so members of Ittonvale Comprehensive School were more inclined to show their faces to laugh at the paltry selection the Summerview staff were presenting. This year Mrs Blossom, Head of Drama at Ittonvale, had also managed to force herself onto the judging committee, along with Margery and Clementine's neighbour Dawn Simmonds, and their vague acquaintance and school council member, Mr Fitzgerald. Joining them were the food tech teacher, Mrs Plum, and one of the science teachers, Dr Roberts.

It was a motley crew at best and they were all taking it much too seriously; Clementine had sworn she had seen them all in the library first thing, sharpening pencils and printing elaborate score sheets. Mr Fitzgerald always started his scoring at zero for the first item and then scored everything else around that, meaning that sometimes his sheet was a baffling arrangement of fractions and minus numbers. He said that the first score was the benchmark for all the other scores to be arranged around, but Margery was convinced he just enjoyed seeing all the confused faces each year. Last year's winning pumpkin had hung in the balance for an extra hour until the cryptic score card had been decoded. It hadn't helped that Mr Fitzgerald had taken a liking to the blackberry wine a teacher in the English department made.

Margery and her team of Education Centre Nourishment Consultants had been dragged into it all again this year, as they were every year, to supply refreshments as well as their own special harvest festival table. Though she always tried to explain that being a dinner lady and a cook didn't mean you necessarily cared about the harvest festival. Their little plot at the bottom of the school grounds had never produced much more than a few sad vegetables and the odd accidental blackberry. In fact, the Year Eight's patch of vegetables towered over it. Margery was sure that nothing could have grown in the shadow of their tomato plants.

The hall was beginning to fill with students, parents and staff members, all of whom looked particularly annoyed to have been kept after work hours for school business, the first term of the year always being the hardest. Once they got back it would be a steady downhill run to Christmas, taking them all with it like a runaway snowball. The first frost of the year had settled in comfortably and it made the town look marvellous.

All the nastiness of the summer holidays was long over – the seaside poisoning case she and Clementine had solved was all neatly squared away. A silly harvest festival seemed a much better prospect than being dead, and besides, she had finally had the plaster cast on her leg removed the week before and was still enjoying the freedom of movement without a crutch. Before any of the events of the summer, death had been planned for in a very theoretical sense, in the same way that Clementine bought packs of Christmas cards in the January sales. Now that she had somehow managed to evade death, life seemed as real and as close as the paper coffee cups in front of her. There would be far fewer moments to be alive than she would like there to be, even if she lived to one hundred. When she did finally go, she wanted to be able to say, 'I had a great time, thanks for inviting me, I think I'll be off now,' rather than clawing to stay in the world like so many recently departed had.

'We ready?' Part-time dinner lady young Ceri-Ann wandered over with her own basket of dried herbs and lavender, a tray of cakes in her other arm. It was unusual for her to be free to stay behind after work – she was always so busy flitting between her make-up and graphic design businesses, her second year of college and doctor's appointments, but she had managed it today. Margery was glad, they needed all the help they could get.

'You can't carry that in your condition!' Gloria whisked the basket away from her, nearly stumbling at how light it was and plonking it down on their vegetable table. Ceri-Ann put the cakes down on their hot drinks serving table.

'I've got months yet, let me lift stuff,' Ceri-Ann scoffed, but she put her hand on her stomach unconsciously, as though checking the baby was still there. Gloria gave her a stern look that Margery had only seen used on her own children, who were less than half Ceri-Ann's age.

'Good afternoon, everyone!' came the booming voice of the headmaster across the hall. They all turned in surprise. 'Welcome to Summerview School's annual harvest festival!' Mr Barrow was tall enough to stare over most of the gathered crowd. He smiled at them all. 'We've got some lovely things on sale today, and all proceeds will go towards the new school minibus for school events and tournaments.'

Mr Evans, the PE teacher, looked particularly pleased beside the headmaster, his large face beaming from ear to ear like a smug frog. His muscular neck seemed non-existent in a bright-yellow football top that seemed to be two sizes too small. His arms hung at his sides like two huge baseball bats. 'Well, enjoy and don't forget to enter the raffle!'

There was a brief round of applause, then people began to swarm around the hall. Gloria turned to her in a panic, her black plait whipping around and nearly hitting Clementine in the eyes.

'Oh god, we aren't ready!' Margery cried. Clementine and Gloria began to rearrange the table, nearly folding it shut again in their haste as Ceri-Ann turned on the plug for the soup kettle, which Seren had filled with their homemade butternut squash soup. Sharon and Karen were trying to open the little money lockbox on the harvest table in a panic as Mrs Mugglethwaite, the town gossip-monger, lunged forward with her gang to buy parsnips.

'Gosh, why does he never give any warning before he opens anything?' Gloria said as she grasped for the paper cups. 'Remember when he started the hundred-metre relay before any of the students had even arrived?'

'Yes, and the first student to get there won.' Clementine tutted as she rearranged the plastic teaspoons and single-serve sachets of sugar. 'I think he does it on purpose to keep us on our toes.'

'Hello, ladies.'

Margery looked up from where she was desperately trying to fumble open the packets of plastic teaspoons and into the face of one of Summerview's newer staff, Mr Weaver, who merely looked amused by their panic. He flipped his wavy hair back from his face, looking more like a film star than a secondary school maths teacher. Margery could see Ceri-Ann and Gloria swooning at the sight of his chiselled jaw and dark hair. Luckily, she and Clementine were immune to his charms or the service in the canteen would collapse into chaos every time he entered to buy his lunch.

'Hello,' Margery said back, hoping her smile didn't look too much like a grimace and the stress was not showing outwardly. 'Would you like some soup, or a coffee?' She waved her arms towards the portable water jugs in front of her. He smiled at her, avoiding looking at the scar that ran through her right eyebrow, past her eye and down over her cheek, like most polite people did since she had acquired it during the summer.

'What've you got milk-wise?' Mr Weaver asked, pointing at the milk jugs with his left hand, his wedding ring glinting in the light. 'I don't really do cow's milk anymore.'

'We've got oat, soya as well, will either of those do?' Margery asked, but he was not looking at her anymore, his eyes drawn across the bustling hall. 'Mr Weaver?'

He finally turned back to her, his eyes wide and startled. 'Oh, no thank you, Margery. I'd better...' He gestured towards the other side of the hall and then strode away as fast as he had arrived.

'Why'd you chase him away, Margery?' Gloria chastised her, beginning to serve drinks to the queue of people that had built up behind Mr Weaver.

'I didn't!' Margery said, as the perpetually track-suited PE teacher approached the table. Today's sweatshirt and matching trousers had the logo of the town centre's weightlifting fitness centre embroidered to the front of them.

'Did I just see Liam over here?' Mr Evans asked them, looking over in the direction that Mr Weaver had disappeared. He didn't wait for them to answer before storming after him but Mr Weaver saw him coming and picked up his speed, almost running over to the other side of the hall. The crowd was too packed for him to escape, and Mr Evans caught up to him easily. Mr Evans was red in the face, spit flying from his mouth as he spoke. His hand reached out to grasp at Mr Weaver's sleeve, Mr Weaver gesticulating madly before he slid through a parting in the crowd to escape. Margery watched Dr Roberts from the science department staring at them, her eyebrows raised.

'What's that all about?' Clementine asked, but any thoughts Margery had about an answer were quickly washed away by Mrs Mugglethwaite's scream.

'Fire!' she shrieked, stabbing her finger towards them.

Margery swung her head around and gasped at the soup kettle billowing with smoke. Ceri-Ann lifted the metal part containing the soup out of the kettle with a cloth as Gloria tried to stop her lifting anything and a plume of smoke followed.

'We're actually just announcing a new pope,' Clementine said, giving Mrs Mugglethwaite a frayed smile. 'Completely intentional, no need to update the risk assessments.'

'Seren must have forgotten to put water in the bottom of it,' Ceri-Ann said, peering into it as the smoke continued to curl out.

'She's got to be distracted by something, hasn't she?' Margery groaned. Seren suddenly forgetting how to do her job was not what was needed this early in the school year.

'Yeah, she's been weird since term started, she keeps rushing off as soon as we finish work. I'm running out of excuses to give Rose when she comes to pick her up,' Gloria agreed. Gloria had been watching over the kitchen management duties while Margery recovered, but Sharon and Karen also nodded vigorously.

'Well, we can't worry about that now.' Margery sighed over the crowd continuing to bray for coffee. She looked over to where Mr Weaver and Mr Evans had been arguing and found that they had both disappeared.

Chapter Two

Margery breathed a sigh of relief that it was finally Friday. Packing everything up after yesterday's festival had taken almost as long as it had to put everything together and Margery was still exhausted. Clementine insisted that Margery sit on her special 'feeling lazy on a Friday' chair to do the till today, even though she usually liked to wander about and manage everything. Privately, Margery felt as though she had done enough sitting down lately. Since her broken leg, she had been taking it easy, or as easy as you can take it when you're the manager of a busy school kitchen, and she was ready to get back to normal.

Today's dinner ladies' Friday lunch selection included a purple coleslaw, made from the last of the batch of cabbages the greengrocer had dropped in on Monday, and Karen's speciality spicy potato wedges, smothered in cheese and bacon. A Friday lunchtime was a lovely thing indeed: a nice easy day where the dinner ladies served the week's only allowed portions of fried food; fish and chips and mushy peas with 'snacky bits', as they called them, alongside. 'Snacky bits' being whatever Margery and Gloria had left over to use up from the rest of the week's menu.

Amazingly, they had managed to sell most of the weirder vegetables and Margery thought they might be able to use the rest up in school dinners. Their meagre contribution to the minibus fund was nothing in comparison to the gardening clubs, who had managed to sell a veritable feast of seasonal vegetables – though Karen and Sharon were convinced that they had bought them from the supermarket. Karen swore she had seen them smuggling the plastic wrappers from the courgettes into the bins at the back of the school.

'Two pounds fifty, please.' Margery presented the contactless card machine to the next student with his tray of sausage rolls, just as Rose swept up behind him and gently nudged him out of the way with her own tray, a surprise guest peeping out from inside her bag.

'Charge me for my jacket potato, please, Margery.' Rose sniffed, slamming the tray down in front of the till, her debit card already on it waiting to pay. Margery stared at the dog with a tiny ponytail glaring out from the top of Rose's handbag. 'I've had a horrendous morning. I've been covering other teacher's *lessons.*'

She hissed the words, as if the very idea of teaching was beneath her.

'Why have you got Mrs Blossom's dog with you?' Clementine asked, appearing behind Margery. Margery held the card reader out again and the student tapped his card on it and then ran off. Rose leaned against the counter and sighed heavily, looking down at the spoilt Yorkshire terrier Ada Bones in surprise as though she'd just remembered she was in her handbag.

'Rhonda's gone to visit her mother, tricked me into looking after it.' She glared down at Ada Bones. 'Tomorrow can't come soon enough.'

'Whose lessons are you covering?' Margery asked and Rose tutted.

'Mr Weaver. He didn't show up today, no one knew until after the first period,' Rose explained, picking at the jacket potato she hadn't yet paid for with her plastic fork and slipping Ada Bones a piece of chicken mayonnaise. The dog chomped it down. 'Of course, the Year Nines didn't tell anyone, just ran riot for an hour. It wasn't until Year Seven arrived for their lesson that anyone thought to tell the SLT.'

'Where is he?' Margery asked. 'Is he ill?'

'Oh, Christ knows. Don't you dare tell me not to swear, Mrs Butcher-Baker!' Rose pointed the plastic fork at Clementine threateningly before continuing. Clementine held her hands up in faux surrender. 'We tried his wife, but no answer, as per, and he's not set any cover work so I've just had to try and pull two Maths classes out of nowhere and I've got another two this afternoon. Do I look like I know anything about Maths?'

Margery opened her mouth to speak, but shut it again when Rose glared at them both and pointed her fork at them again.

'As if that's not enough nonsense for one day I've got Mr Knight moaning that his art room cupboard is missing supplies,' she said. 'What can I do about that? He needs to look after his inventory better. Look, the real reason I want to talk to you...' Rose's voice suddenly became conspiratorial. She leaned forward over the counter so only Margery, Clementine and Ada Bones would have any hope of hearing her. 'I need you to find out what Seren is doing.'

'What do you mean?' Margery asked. Seren was in the back of the kitchen fighting the endless mountain of washing up. 'What's she doing?'

'I don't know,' Rose said secretively. 'I need you to find out.'

'That's incredibly vague, even for you.' Clementine said. Rose huffed.

'She's going somewhere after work and giving me all sorts of stupid excuses to not come in the car home with me,' Rose explained, poking with the jacket potato with her fork. It was fast becoming a pile of mush. 'She said she's at Gary's, but why would she spend so much time there when she could be at home watching *The Crown* with me and James?'

'Because he's her boyfriend, maybe?' Clementine suggested. 'And spending all her free time with you and the headmaster is weird.'

Rose scowled at her. 'Just try and work it out!'

She turned on her heels and sauntered out of the canteen without paying. Margery let her go, it was not worth fighting with an angry Rose. Seren was almost certainly spending time with her boyfriend, Gary Matthews, and Rose was probably just jealous. Seren continued living with Rose even after Mr Barrow had moved in. Although it certainly was a large house, Margery was sure Seren would need a break from the headmaster and his deputy head once in a while. It was much more of a mystery for Mr Weaver not to show up for his lessons, she thought. Obviously, teachers sometimes call in sick or have other reasons not to arrive at work, but it was practically unheard of for a teacher to go AWOL. Margery thought back to the last time they had seen him, yesterday at the harvest festival. Maybe he needed a break from Mr Evans, perhaps they had fallen out so severely that he had needed a day off to recuperate? Mr Evans was here today though, helping to supervise the dinner hour, which meant leaning against the wall reading a fitness magazine and drinking a protein shake that was so thick it could have probably been used to cement walls. He couldn't feel badly enough about whatever they'd been arguing about to not come to work.

The lunch hour finished quite quickly after that, and Margery was distracted by other things to worry about for a while after. She got to work on the following week's ordering in her office while the rest of the team cleaned down and packed up ready to go home. She had developed a rolling two-week menu that changed each term, to keep it all seasonal and fresh. But she liked to keep room for any special dishes just in case the butcher or greengrocer had anything on offer.

'Oh no, Margery, is this everything that was left over from yesterday?' Gloria asked, appearing in the doorway of the dry store where Margery was sat writing the prep list. She was holding the big shopping bag they had kept the leftover food from the harvest festival in.

'There might be something more in the kitchen, why?' Margery got up and followed her back into the main room. Gloria searched through the boxes of leftover food waiting to be picked up for donation by the walk-in freezer.

'Oh no, I thought there'd be some left...' Gloria said, scrabbling through the bags.

'What are you after?' Margery asked.

'My husband asked me to save him a blackberry jam and I forgot, it's his favourite!' She stood, kicking the bag gently in frustration. 'Christ! I haven't even got any wild blackberries to make some. Where am I going to pick them now? It's the end of October. The town will be picked clean.'

'The woods?' Ceri-Ann shrugged from across the room, tapping away at her phone, not bothering to look up. 'Loads left in there, late-season ones. Nice they are. I'd get you some, but Sy is picking me up in a minute.'

'Is there really?' Gloria said. 'Oh, but I haven't got time for that. I've got to pick the kids up from school.'

'We can go,' Margery offered. Clementine gave her leg a stern look. 'It's fine! I'm supposed to get the strength back in it.'

'You ought to sit down again, that's what you should be doing,' Clementine said, but then she rolled her eyes. 'Where in the woods, Ceri-Ann?'

Ceri-Ann beamed and took one of the paper bags that they had been using to dole out pieces of lunchtime Victoria sponge cake. She picked up a Biro, drew a rudimentary map on one of them, and handed it to Margery.

-

It was just before three when they left school for the day. The afternoon was still light and the breeze fresh as it whipped around them bringing the leaves off the ground and scattering them across the playground. Margery was glad for her coat, pulling it closer around her, but it was a perfect autumn day. The air was crisp and light, the leaves lining the playground crunching underfoot as they sauntered along easily. Margery felt the weight lifting from her shoulders, happy to be on the walk and ready to enjoy the weekend. Friday afternoons were her favourite, for obvious reasons. It was not always easy managing the kitchen – feeding 1200 students, teachers and support staff daily could be hard work – it was good to find time to relax in between.

'Ladies!' someone shouted and they both whirled around to see who was calling them. Rose had opened the window of her office and was frantically gesturing at them. 'Where are you going?' she yelled, as Margery and Clementine made their way over to her. 'That's not the way you walk home.'

'We're going to pick blackberries for—' Margery began, but Rose interrupted by picking Ada Bones up and holding her out through the window.

'Can you please walk Ada while you're there?' Rose said, not waiting for an answer before thrusting the dog into Clementine's arms and then handing Margery a lead. 'I've got so much admin to do here and I'm covering detention in a minute. There are so many students in there today it's a wonder if any of them will pass their exams at this rate. Just take her to yours after and I'll pick her up on my way home. Thanks!'

Before either of them could even open their mouths, she closed the window. Through the glass they watched her sit back down at her desk and purposefully ignore them. Clementine rolled her eyes.

'Well then, Ada,' she said to the dog kindly, 'looks like you're with us.'

Ada didn't look particularly pleased at being passed on to yet another stranger, but seemed to cheer up once she realised that they were going for a walk.

They crossed the playing fields at an easy pace, the dog's tiny legs rushing to keep up with their lazy stroll. The paint lines on the grass were wearing out and they stamped over them until they reached the entrance to the woods. Slipping through the kissing gate they made their way through, following the path. Clementine took

Margery's arm in her own as Ada pulled on the lead in her excitement.

'Did you see Mr Evans shouting at Mr Weaver yesterday?' Clementine asked while they wandered along. 'What on earth was he thinking, in front of all the students and parents?'

'It was quite hard to miss,' Margery agreed. 'I'm surprised the headmaster didn't step in.'

'Do you think that's why he didn't come in?' Clementine said. They wandered deeper into the wood, the trees a gorgeous thick canopy above them. 'Maybe they had a fight, and he couldn't face it?'

'Well, that does seem strange, doesn't it?' Margery said, waiting for a moment so Ada could stop and sniff a particularly interesting bush. 'Not very normal at all.'

'No.' Clementine took her hand as they strolled, giving it a squeeze. 'But then none of that with Seren is either, is it? Where's she off to?'

'She's got to be with Gary,' Margery said. 'Rose is just being overprotective.'

Clementine hummed in agreement. Margery took Ceri-Ann's hand-drawn map out of her pocket while they waited for Ada. From the looks of the neat line drawing they were close, but the bushes had all been picked clean as Gloria had feared. The woods lay behind and before them, the trees winding around the worn path formed by other walkers.

'Should we go back?' Clementine asked Margery, giving her a worried look. 'It's getting dark.'

'Let's just go a little bit further and then at least we can say we had a proper look,' Margery said, putting the map back in her pocket and taking Clementine's hand again. 'No harm in that, is there?'

They began to walk again, pushing their way through the cold undergrowth. Clementine did not look convinced. 'Fine,' she said as they strode. 'But then we're going to go straight home and I'm going to make you a cup of tea and we're going to watch a nice spooky Halloween film.'

'Please don't make us watch *The Little Mermaid* again,' Margery smiled. 'It's not a Halloween film at all.'

'It's got a witch octopus who can sing, Margery!' Clementine exclaimed, reaching out to hold back a branch. 'And it's set underwater.'

'You're just scared of the sea!' Margery laughed. 'Remember when Ceri-Ann lent us that slasher movie and told us it was the newest Disney?'

Clementine laughed too. 'I didn't think you'd ever come out from behind the sofa cushions!'

Margery opened her mouth to remind her that Clementine was the one who had nearly jumped out of her skin at the first scare, but she was stopped midsentence as Ada began to bark madly. The tiny dog was yapping so ferociously that her body was practically vibrating with effort.

'What's the matter?' Clementine asked the dog.

Ada gave a hard pull on the lead and escaped as it whizzed out of Clementine's fingers, rushing off towards the centre of the clearing where a huge tree sat – locals called it the Devil's Yew. Its leaves and branches blocked out all the light that was left in the day. Ada continued to bark and bark at a pile of leaves at the foot of the tree, underneath a strange mark that Margery had never seen before. It was painted onto the bark in what looked like green spray paint a few feet above the ground.

Margery stared where Ada was growling, gasping in shock at the sight of a piece of cloth. Was the pile of fabric a forgotten coat?

Lying on the ground in the pile of autumn leaves and moss, with his mouth wide and eyes unseeing, was Mr Weaver. Margery tried to say something, but all that came out was a shriek of horror.

Chapter Three

'Back again, ladies,' Officer Thomas said gruffly. 'I hoped we'd never meet like this after the last time.'

They were sat in their usually comforting living room. Officer Thomas had escorted them home after the scene had been secured by the rest of Dewstow's tiny police team and then Ittonvale police force had arrived as back-up. The headmaster remained on school grounds as he tried to call Mr Weaver's emergency contact, again and again, to no answer so far. An ambulance had arrived to transport Mr Weaver, but it was many hours too late. He had died hours before, of natural causes, the police seemed to think – a heart attack or a stroke. It was hard to tell before the autopsy had been carried out. Margery kept wondering why he had been out there, lying in the leaves. The thoughts rose up inside her and she felt sick with it, horrible waves of nausea filling her mouth with saliva.

Margery could feel an unpleasant sense of déjà vu crawling up and down her spine at the memory of them all sitting in the canteen last Christmas. The poor music teacher, Mrs Large's, murder had been solvable though. This was different, another awful thing in a world plagued with awful things, but still, a heart attack was not a murder. She pulled the dog onto her lap, closer to her chest for comfort. Ada did not seem to mind; she leaned into

Margery's arms, almost certainly used to being smothered in over-affection from her real owner.

'I can't believe it,' Clementine gasped again, off in her own world. She had been since they had seen Mr Weaver lying there. Margery didn't think she'd ever be able to get the sight out of her head. His handsome face had been twisted and stained a ghastly purple colour, his tongue hanging out of his mouth. She hadn't been able to stop staring at him even while Clementine had wrangled Ada Bones back onto her lead and called for help.

'We should have done something,' Margery said, suddenly panicked. 'We should have stopped him from dying.'

'How?' Clementine asked. 'We don't know how he died, and they think he was dead hours before we got there. And we barely knew him.'

'Maybe that was the problem.' Margery could feel the hysteria rising in her chest. 'He's been here since last September, and we've only spoken to him in the canteen.' She turned to Clementine with a dawning horror. 'I charged him double for his salad last week because he'd overfilled the tub!'

'I don't think that will have anything to do with this,' Officer Thomas said kindly.

He sat back in the comfortable armchair and stroked his moustache, deep in thought as well.

'Right, Mrs Butcher-Bakers…' Officer Thomas said as he wrote both their names on the top of the interview form. 'Another terrible thing, and hardly any time's gone by since that horrific poisoning you dealt with in the summer.'

'You heard about that?' Margery asked, failing to hide her surprise. She hadn't thought that many in the town would know, aside from the dinner lady team and some of the teachers.

'Of course,' Officer Thomas said. 'Mrs Mugglethwaite, do you know her? From the post office?' They nodded. 'She told me all about it, sounded like you did a good job there.'

The mental image of Mrs Mugglethwaite stopping Officer Thomas in the street to tell him the newest gossip about Margery and Clementine brought her a tiny smirk of cheer, which disappeared as soon as it arrived.

'I wish we didn't have to do any of it really,' Margery said shrugging. They hadn't really had a choice but to help. Clementine had been falsely accused of being involved in a series of murders that had happened decades before and they had needed to clear her name.

'Yes, we're always in the wrong place at the wrong time,' Clementine said, sitting back with a weary sigh. 'Nothing more to it.'

'I don't know about that,' Officer Thomas said, looking at the paperwork again. 'Right, tell me what happened from the start...'

Margery began to explain the walk through the woods, but she was distracted as Officer Symon entered from the hallway.

'The headmaster has got in contact with the next of kin,' he told Officer Thomas, who nodded grimly. 'And the sergeant needs a word, if you've got a second.'

'Well, no,' Officer Thomas said, his eyebrows rising at the suggestion, but then he sighed, putting his clipboard down on the coffee table 'Excuse us, ladies.'

He followed Symon out into the hallway again and Margery could hear him begin to radio the sergeant. She could hear the officers clearly from the hallway door, though she usually did not notice how thin the walls were as it was only the two of them living at twenty-two Seymour Road. Clementine gave her a mischievous look and picked up a glass from the tea tray they had prepared on their arrival home.

'Clem,' Margery hissed, 'what are you doing?'

'I just want to know what they're saying,' Clementine said in a matter-of-fact way that Margery knew she thought excused a multitude of sins. 'Don't you?'

'No, I do not,' Margery began, but Clementine was already pressing the glass against the wood of the door and putting her ear to it. Margery groaned and followed, taking her own empty water glass from the table and joining Clementine.

'Yes, sir,' Officer Thomas said, 'not a problem.'

Whatever the conversation had been about, they must have missed most of it, Margery decided. Officer Symon broke the silence.

'What does he mean about the symbols?' he asked Officer Thomas, who paused before answering.

'There was a symbol above his body,' Officer Thomas said. 'The sergeant thinks it's the same that was painted in Ittonvale last week.'

'Well, what could that mean?' Officer Symon asked. This time Officer Thomas mumbled his answer. Margery and Clementine both listened intently, pressing their ears even harder to the door. The door handle turned, and they both jumped back and rushed to the sofa again. Officer Thomas rolled his eyes at them.

'Listening, were you?' he said, almost amused. 'Didn't anyone ever tell you it's rude to eavesdrop?'

'What does the symbol mean?' Clementine asked. 'We saw it too. Do you know who painted it there?'

'That is police business,' Officer Thomas said.

'But…'

'We'll hear no more of it.' Officer Thomas sat back down in the armchair, picked up the clipboard again and began to continue filling out the form. Margery and Clementine exchanged a worried look.

—

The weekend was stolen by Mr Weaver's death and soon enough it was Monday morning, and they were back in the canteen. When they entered just before eight, the sun barely risen outside, Margery struggled to unlock the kitchen door. The weight of what had happened resting on her shoulders, the whole town knew and the rumour mill was running at a million miles an hour. The bus to school had been full of it. Mrs Mugglethwaite had decided that Liam Weaver had obviously been killed by ghosts and Mrs Redburn had confirmed that the Devil's Yew would have lured him there with its song. She didn't say what the song was, but Margery assumed it wasn't some top forty hit.

The police had left without a fuss, immediately after taking their statement. Though Officer Thomas wouldn't tell them anything more about Mr Weaver's death than they had already overheard. In any case, Officer Thomas had repeatedly asked them to leave it alone. Clementine, Margery knew from experience, had no intention of doing such a thing.

'Symbols!' Clementine kept crying, as though it would explain Mr Weaver's horrible death. All it did though was cause Margery to jump, making the lunch hour even more stressful than usual. Margery kept seeing his face, unnaturally purple, eyes bulging out of his skull. She shuddered at the memory, still fresh and raw in her head.

'What kind do you mean?' Sharon asked. 'Musical or you know... pictorial?'

'Just... symbols!' Clementine said, shovelling potato wedges into the polystyrene containers and tossing them at the waiting children. 'Need I say more?'

'I can't believe Mr Barrow hasn't called an assembly yet,' Seren said sadly as she dug into the high pile of mashed potato with an ice cream scoop. 'Usually, he can't wait to do one.'

'He's probably waiting to find out what happened,' Gloria said, her mouth pulled into a grim line as she brought out a fresh shepherd's pie for the hot counter. 'God, what a nasty thing. Do the children know, I wonder?'

'Well, if they do, none of them seem upset, do they?' Clementine glared at the line of tiny Year Sevens waiting patiently to be served. They cowered under her stare. 'Practically psychopaths, all of them.'

'Oi, miss!' One of the Year Elevens yelled from the back of the canteen. 'Can we get on with it? It'll be exam time by the time we get served.'

Mrs George, Head of English, smirked at that from her spot, leaning against the canteen wall overseeing the lunch hour. Margery tried to ignore her.

'That's Mrs Butcher-Baker to you!' Clementine yelled, but she did start serving chips faster. 'See, what did I just say? Evil, all of them. Look at them with their phones. They'll put us on TikTok again, Margery, just you wait.'

The Year Eleven group were still giggling, and one was still pointing her phone camera at them, Margery suspected Clementine might be right. There was a group of them who had filmed the staff show at last year's Christmas concert and uploaded it online, changing the music to some awful contemporary rock band. They'd never lived it down. It kept reappearing every now and then on students' phones, like the smell from a blocked drain.

'Christ,' Gloria whispered, gesturing across the canteen. 'What happened to her?'

Miss Macdonald had entered the canteen. Her eyes were ringed red from crying, the crumpled paper tissue in her hand soggy with recent tears. She got a tray and began to join the queue, but seeing her tearful expression the students all backed away and let her through first.

'One soup, please,' Miss Macdonald sniffed, not making eye contact with Margery. A tear ran down her nose and dripped onto the tray.

Margery doled out a portion of soup into a bowl and handed it to her.

'Elle, are you all right?' Margery asked as gently as she could. 'Only you don't seem yourself.'

'It's just Liam Weaver dying like that,' Miss Macdonald said, 'so unexpected.'

Tracks of mascara followed the tears down Miss Macdonald's cheeks.

'Did you know him well?' Margery asked. She could see Clementine listening as she slowly served food, the children all jostling in the queue. Miss Macdonald looked surprised at her question.

'We were colleagues,' she said, blushing as she did so. 'So, you know...'

Margery supposed she did. Her Education Centre Nourishment Consultants were distraught when former kitchen manager Caroline had died. The conversation puttered out and Miss Macdonald wandered away. They began to serve lunch again, leaving Margery to think about how awful it all was.

Still, they didn't do anything. If the events of the summer had taught them anything, it was that they should certainly try to stay out of it at all costs. The police could deal with this one, no need for any amateur detectives running about ruining things. They would let them get on with it. Not that they would need anyone on the case really. People had heart attacks all the time. It was a horrible thing still, but a normal, natural cause of death. Of course, they would still have to follow his last hours and see what he had been doing when he died, but Margery thought that the worst thing of it for the police would be having to explain it to his family.

'What on earth is that noise?' Gloria asked, bringing out another large gastronome tray of vegetable lasagne from the prep kitchen to slot into the hot plate. 'It's driving me mad. Margery, is it the fire alarm?'

Margery paused for a moment, listening hard until her ears could filter out the noise of the canteen.

'That's Clementine's new GPS key fob.' She smiled as she explained. Gloria raised her eyebrows. 'She keeps losing our house keys and locking herself out. The battery must be low, Clem, can you change it?'

'I've only lost them a few times,' Clementine called from across the room, taking her plastic gloves off. 'Six, maybe seven times.' She hesitated. 'Well, maybe it was eight before we bought the fob.'

She rushed off to the changing room, the electronic wailing filling the canteen as she opened the door.

–

The week began to skitter by in a haze of work and cooking and cleaning and laundry and the general day-to-day routine of it all, until Margery could almost get it out of her mind before they went to sleep at night. The local paper had reported it, of course, and printed a short memorial statement on behalf of the school. Margery wondered what would happen now. The headmaster, Mr Barrow, finally gave his sombre assembly on the Friday morning, informing the school community that they were all invited to the funeral. His face had been practically grey as he'd read from his notes. He stammered out how sorry he was that another dreadful thing had happened so close to the school grounds, how he had dropped the ball on the school's safety. She didn't see how anyone could blame him, after all, he hadn't caused Mr Weaver's heart attack. 'But had something else?' a tiny voice in her head kept asking.

Margery couldn't wait to leave work and go home. It was easier to forget about it all there, where there was the television and Clementine complaining about the time the post would arrive and various other distractions, where she could escape the niggling feeling that there was something more to it all.

Chapter Four

Margery was dozing off when the doorbell rang, causing both cats to bolt from where they had been sleeping curled together at the bottom of the bed. She wondered for a moment if she'd imagined it, but then it sounded again and again, the noise rattling up the stairs. Clementine sat bolt upright next to her, listening too. They shared a look.

'Should we answer it? It's gone ten o'clock, who on earth would pop round now?' Margery whispered into the darkness. She grasped for the alarm clock, its digital face reading eleven o'clock. Who on earth could be calling for them at that time? She briefly worried that they had forgotten to pay the TV licence bill and they'd be bundled into a van and arrested by the BBC, but she shook the thought away.

'I suppose so?' Clementine didn't seem to believe her own words. Even so, she slid out of bed and grasped for her dressing gown in the dark bedroom. Margery pulled on her own dressing gown and followed Clementine down the stairs, both sneaking down on tiptoes. Before they'd even reached the bottom, the letterbox slammed open and a voice shouted through it, 'Mrs Butcher-Bakers!'

Margery could have laughed in relief at the sound of Rose's voice. She stumbled to the bottom of the stairs and opened the door. Rose was leaning on the letterbox and nearly fell forward with the force of it, Seren following behind her in an enormous men's anorak. Rose and Seren existed in a strange and much too co-dependent world of their own, even though Rose had married the headmaster during the summer and he had moved into her house. She had refused to change her surname to Barrow, reasoning that she had just bought a custom number plate featuring her surname.

They both nearly tripped over the two carrier bags of apples that their neighbour, Dawn Simmonds, had left on their doorstep the previous day. Margery and Clementine were running out of ideas of what to use the harvest surplus for. Clementine kept threatening to go over to Dawn's garden with a chainsaw and chop the trees down, but Margery knew she was far too lazy to go to B&Q and buy one.

'What's happened?' Clementine asked as they all went into the living room. Seren plonked herself into the pink crinoline armchair Officer Thomas had been sat in the day they had found Mr Weaver's body and happily settled into it, not even removing her big anorak.

'Murder!' Rose cried, smoothing her silver bob back behind her ears. 'That's what's happened! Just found out from James. You can't tell him you know; I wasn't supposed to tell anyone. I told him I was taking Seren to the McDonald's on Ittonvale Retail Park.'

'Mr Barrow?' Margery said, trying to shake the confusion out of her head. 'What murder?'

'Liam Weaver,' Rose said, almost smugly. 'Not a heart attack at all. He was murdered.'

Margery sat down heavily on the sofa; all the wind had gone out of her sails.

'I'll put the kettle on,' she said dimly, but she couldn't bring herself to get back up from the sofa now she had fallen onto it, suddenly feeling much older than sixty-two.

'No need.' Rose clicked her fingers. 'Seren!'

Seren jumped up at once and scuttled into Margery and Clementine's kitchen and they could hear her clattering around in there, Rose immediately stole her seat. Pumpkin, Margery and Clementine's elderly tortoiseshell cat, stared towards the noise from her place on the arm of the sofa, her round yellow eyes wide with disapproval. Their younger cat, Crinkles, bolted through the cat flap and disappeared out into the night – unlikely to return until the visitors were safely away.

'Seren can't be in there unattended,' Clementine protested, her grey hair and fringe all over the place from sleep. 'What if she accidentally puts our royal family commemorative cup collection through the dishwasher? She'll ruin the resale value.'

'Shut up and listen, you stupid woman,' Rose said, but there was no real malice in it. She reached over and stroked the cat's tiny head. Pumpkin, evidently sensing that they had much in common, promptly climbed over onto her lap and settled herself down. 'His death? Not just a heart attack, the autopsy results just came back. James has just found out, he's distraught, he keeps blaming himself for it all.'

'How does he know that?' Clementine asked. 'Surely the police didn't tell him.'

'His wife came to the house,' Rose said, a gleam in her eyes. 'Told James everything. Once the police finally got hold of her, that is, God knows where she thinks her husband was all this time.'

'Not a heart attack?' Margery blurted out before she could help herself. She thought back to the events of the summer. 'What was it then? Surely not a poisoning?'

'No,' Rose said, leaving a long pause in which Margery wondered what could possibly be coming before continuing. 'The toxicology report came back clear anyway.'

'So why come here?' Margery pulled her dressing gown closer to her shoulders so Rose wouldn't catch a glimpse of the long nightie underneath. Clementine in comparison had thrown her dressing gown off and sat scratching her head in her pyjamas. Rose looked practically alien in leisurewear of a jumper and jeans – miles away from the starched business attire she wore to school.

'Well, you ought to know, shouldn't you, detectives?' Rose said the last word with a smirk, looking between them almost in amusement.

'Wait, how did he die then?' Clementine asked, rubbing her forehead.

'He was attacked,' Rose said, her mouth twisting in disgust. 'His arms and neck were covered in cuts and bruises, and he had a stab wound on his neck.'

Margery felt sick.

'Definitely not a heart attack,' she breathed. 'Why would anyone kill him?'

'Someone stabbed him?' Clementine asked, her eyes still weary from sleep. 'Have they found a knife?'

'He wasn't stabbed with a knife,' Rose said, sitting back in the pink chair and rubbing her arms as if she was trying to warm herself up. Margery folded her own. Before Rose could explain what she meant, the doorbell rang again, and they all looked at each other in surprise. Seren appeared in the kitchen doorway, her eyes as wide as

Pumpkin's. Clementine got up cautiously, peering around the door into the hall.

'Don't,' Rose hissed, grabbing her wrist as she passed the chair. 'What if it's James? I'm not supposed to tell anyone!'

'Yes, you said that just before you told us.' Clementine rolled her eyes and opened the door, revealing Ceri-Ann standing on the front porch holding an envelope.

'Mate! Let me in, I've only got a minute,' she said, waddling into the living room and taking off her huge faux-fur coat, flopping down on the floor to sit in front of the coffee table. 'I've told Symon I've gone to McDonald's. I'm going to have to lie and say the McFlurry machine isn't working.' She glanced around the room in surprise as she realised it wasn't empty. 'Oh, what! You're having a school meeting and you didn't invite me?'

'Hello, Ceri-Ann,' Rose said, gesturing at Ceri-Ann's stomach with her index finger. 'How's all this going?'

'She's naming it after me,' Clementine said smugly, sitting back down on the sofa next to Margery.

'Mate,' Ceri-Ann laughed. 'You wish! I can't name a baby after a bit of fruit, can I? Er... though it's a nice name for you, mate, just not for the baby. Symon hates oranges.'

'Clement for a boy then!' Clementine cried. Margery despaired at the argument that had been raging between them in the school kitchen since the beginning of term.

'Ceri-Ann,' she interrupted before it could start. 'It's lovely to see you, and of course you're always very welcome, but why are you here?'

'Why are *they* here, mate?' Ceri-Ann looked between Rose and Seren suspiciously as Seren brought in tea on a tray and placed it on the coffee table in the middle of them all.

Clementine nodded in approval at her choice of biscuits and then reached out to pour them all a cup. Seren rushed back in with an extra cup for Ceri-Ann and then realised Rose had stolen her seat. She hovered awkwardly in the kitchen doorway.

'What's in the envelope?' Margery asked Ceri-Ann, who was stirring an enormous amount of sugar into her cup.

'I can't say now,' Ceri-Ann said, throwing her hair back and taking a sip of tea. 'It's about important police business, innit.'

'You know about Mr Weaver?' Rose asked, taking the cup of tea from Clementine. Ceri-Ann opened her mouth to speak, but then just nodded. She sighed and passed Margery the envelope. She opened it, revealing a set of photographs.

'Where did you get these?' Margery gasped. She slid the top one over and revealed another underneath.

'Symon keeps bringing work home, even though I keep telling him it's a sackable offence. He wants to be a detective, keeps banging on about moving forces and becoming a trainee detective constable, but he's mega worried about failing the exams.' Ceri-Ann shrugged. 'Might shop him in to teach him a lesson.'

Margery flicked through A4 blow-ups of the scene, Clementine peering over her shoulder. Margery stopped suddenly short of breath, as she had sometimes found herself after the summer. Sometimes even one of the more gruesome crime television shows that she and Clementine used to enjoy could start the feeling off, and she would worry that the few seconds she had been legally dead had been enough to change the way her brain worked permanently. That if they cut her head open, all the sea water would have rushed out of it and spilled everywhere, ruining all their carpets and soft furnishings.

'Don't worry,' Ceri-Ann said gently, seeming to sense her discomfort. 'There's none of the body. Just look at the tree.'

'The symbol,' Margery said showing the photograph to Clementine, who gasped and leaned closer to look.

It was strange indeed, scratched into the dirt near the bottom of the tree in one photograph and then painted onto the bark in another. A large V shape with a cross through it. Margery tried to decide if she had ever seen it before, but nothing sprang to mind.

'He didn't have a heart attack,' Ceri-Ann explained. 'The autopsy said—'

'Embolism,' Rose interrupted, her mouth pulled thin in distaste. 'He was stabbed with a needle in an artery in his neck and the resulting air bubble killed him.'

'Yeah.'

Clementine gasped and then they sat in silence for a moment. Margery flipped through the photographs again. This was horrible, evil even, if it was true.

'And you're telling us this because...?' Clementine asked finally.

Ceri-Ann looked at her like she had just realised that Clementine was very stupid. 'You're the dinner lady detectives. Murder's kind of your thing.'

Rose and Seren nodded, their mouths drawn in grim lines.

After the visitors had finally left, Margery began the washing up, all thoughts of sleep lost. Her mind kept wandering as she plunged her hands into the soapy water and began to scrub the mugs. It had been unsettling enough when they had believed Mr Weaver's death to be of natural causes. Now it was a murder she didn't know what to think. Poor Mr Weaver, and his poor wife. Who could have killed him? Was there another murderer wandering freely around Dewstow? There had already been so many. How many murderers could one little town possibly possess?

Clementine joined her in the kitchen and sat at the table, moving a bag of Dawn's apples so she could rest her elbow on it. She looked as perplexed as Margery felt. Margery left the clean tea things to dry on the plastic drainer and joined her at the table.

'Clem,' Margery said. She reached over to hold Clementine's hand. 'Look, about Mr Weaver—'

'We're not getting involved,' Clementine said firmly, the fingers of her free hand reaching for the bag of apples and taking one out.

'What? But you always—'

'Not this time,' Clementine said thoughtfully. 'This is too big for us, and if you got hurt again…' She shook her head gravely. 'I don't know what I'd do with myself. I can't lose you.'

'What's too big about it?' Margery asked, thinking back to the numerous dangers they had put themselves in over the last year.

'Well, it's just not worth getting into trouble again.'

'But Ceri-Ann and Rose—' Margery began, Clementine scoffed.

'Ignore them! They just want us to meddle in it so they can find out what happened,' Clementine said, putting the apple back on the table with a thump. 'Let the police solve it all.'

'But what if the police can't solve it?' Margery asked, twiddling her fingers. They couldn't let a murderer go free, even if they had no idea who it was. If the safety of the little town and its residents were in peril and they could do something to help, then surely, they ought to get involved.

'They will,' Clementine said, confidently. 'The first person they'll talk to is that PE teacher Mr Evans, he'll confess to beating him up. Mystery solved.'

'What? Mr Evans?' Margery scratched her head. 'Why are you so certain that it was him?'

'The argument they had at the harvest festival,' Clementine said, in the self-assured manner that she had mastered over the years. 'He followed him outside.'

'Oh yes, I suppose. Gosh, I didn't realise you'd seen them leave. But does that really prove anything?' Margery asked. 'And the police wouldn't know about that, would they? Should we tell them?'

Clementine looked conflicted for a moment before her face settled back to its normal resting state. 'No, they'll work it out. Lots of people probably saw them.'

'I don't think so.' Margery tried to remember; it was a blur, but she did remember seeing a few faces watching. 'I don't remember anyone seeming to care except Dr Roberts, and she didn't do anything about it at the time. Not that I saw anyway.'

'Let's just forget all about it.' Clementine had well and truly made up her mind.

Chapter Five

A dark cloud hung over them all once back at work on Monday. Not helped by the relentless rain splattering on the kitchen windows. The mood in the kitchen was frosty, as much as Clementine and Ceri-Ann tried to lighten the mood.

'What about a mixture of Clementine and Margery for the baby's name?' Clementine suggested as she helped Ceri-Ann chop the vegetables for lunchtime's salad bar. 'Cargery? Or Melontine? Both good strong names!'

'Mate, no,' Ceri-Ann laughed, dicing an onion. 'They both sound like weird seventies desserts.'

'You could call it one of our middle names? A lovely kitchen-family name,' Sharon said, from where she and Karen were peeling potatoes. 'Mine is Louise.'

'Mine too!' Karen grinned. 'All the girls at my school had the middle name Louise, except Louise, of course. Her middle name was Louisa.'

'Margery,' Gloria said, they stood together sorting the display fridge for lunch. 'I don't like the idea of a murderer wandering about and I saw the police on the way in.'

'Well, I suppose it's not a bad thing they're keeping an eye on the school,' Margery said, spritzing sanitiser over the fridge doors.

'No, but I can't see what good it's doing either, they certainly haven't arrested anybody,' Gloria said, pulling the old sandwiches to the front so she could slot the new ones in behind. 'Is Clementine still adamant that you aren't getting involved? I think the case could really use you.'

'She is,' Margery said, looking over to where her wife was still suggesting bizarre baby names to Ceri-Ann. 'But I've got a plan.'

'Oh?' Gloria turned to her with an eyebrow raised.

'We'll need all hands on deck for this one,' Margery said. 'I've just got to persuade Clementine that I'm fine.'

Margery didn't need to worry, because soon enough the problem was solved for her. Lunchtime had passed in a blur and soon another shift was over. The rest of the team departed in a gaggle of laughter, leaving Margery and Clementine alone to finish cashing up. As Margery put the till in the dry-store safe, there was a knock on the door.

'Thought I might find you in your office,' Officer Thomas said, pushing the door open gently with his big hands. 'Sorry to barge in.'

'Quite all right.' Margery said, standing up from the safe. 'Can you tell us what's going on? Is Mr Weaver's murder going to be made public?'

'Yes, seems like you've got another murderer wandering about on your watch.' Clementine raised her eyebrows at him. He dodged the look by suddenly finding something very interesting on one of the dry-store shelves.

'Yes, well.' Officer Thomas sighed. 'Look, I won't beat around the bush, we need a favour.'

'No one knows you're here, do they?' Margery said, the realisation dawning on her. 'What is this? Run out of ideas of how to catch criminals?'

'Let's just say,' Officer Thomas said, twirling his fingers together nervously, 'that it hasn't been going as well as we hoped, and we can't afford for a case like this to go unsolved. We can't have another murderer out there in this town.'

'Sounds like you really need us,' Margery said, folding her arms and trying not to look too smug. 'Do you not have a detective who could question the community?'

She thought of Detective Penfold, who they had met in the summer. She had certainly been able to poke about as much as she wanted.

'We do, but I was thinking of something much more subtle,' Officer Thomas said looking between them both. He looked just as reluctant as Clementine did. 'We need your help.'

'Subtle?' Clementine asked, glaring at him suspiciously. 'You can't mean us? Do you not remember when we crashed a car into a pond?'

'Yes, I do remember that,' he said, giving her a half smile, which quickly faded. 'Nevertheless, Dewstow and Ittonvale police forces could use your help; the whole town really. Things have got very bad, very quickly.' He covered his eyes for a moment with a hand. 'Well, it's almost as bad as anything could be, isn't it?'

'In what regard?' Margery asked curiously.

'In every regard, really.' He looked away again and fiddled with a jar of spice on the shelving unit closest. He took a deep breath, seemingly steeling himself for whatever he was going to ask them. Margery and Clementine shared a look but waited quietly.

'We need you to go undercover.' Officer Thomas's face was turned into a grimace that looked as though he had eaten something much too sour by mistake. Margery didn't know what to say. She looked to Clementine, who was standing silent and still, her hands balled into fists.

'Undercover!' Clearly, whatever resolve Clementine had ever been holding on to, the dam had finally burst. 'What does that mean?'

'We need you to talk to people and find out what the hell is going on,' he said, letting out a harsh breath. 'Everyone in Dewstow knows who we are, no one will suspect you.'

'But people know us too,' Margery reminded him. 'We've lived here for years, we know everyone!'

'Yes, but they won't be expecting you to be working with us this time.' Officer Thomas held his hands out. 'You know the school inside out, you're here all the time on the ground. Look at your kitchen manager's murder, or the one at Christmas. Both solved by you. People see me and the force and put themselves on best behaviour, you might be able to see what's really going on.'

He had a good point. It wasn't the worst plan Margery had ever heard; it was certainly better than most of their own.

'What do we need to find out?' Margery asked him, knowing what he was going to say but wanting him to say it out loud anyway.

'Who was responsible for the murder of Liam Weaver,' Officer Thomas said.

'And you're sure it's a murder?' Margery asked, thinking of what Rose had told them. She looked him in the eye. He nodded.

'Yes, we are.'

'Well then, I'm in,' Margery said. She turned to Clementine, who looked conflicted. 'It will be fine, Clem. We won't be doing it alone, the police will help us, won't you?'

Margery turned back to Officer Thomas, who nodded.

'Of course,' he said. 'Though this will have to be kept very secret.' He coughed. 'Very secret indeed.'

Clementine sighed deeply, looking between him and Margery and then throwing her hands in the air, 'Fine! But the slightest bit of trouble—'

'You'll be out,' Officer Thomas said, 'You have my word. We'll protect you both.'

Clementine stroked her chin. 'Will we be getting to wear wires, like in a film?'

'No,' he said.

'Will we get bulletproof vests?'

'Absolutely not.'

'Can I have a taser?'

'Over my cold, dead body.'

'Well, that's settled then!' Clementine clapped her hands together and then grabbed Margery's to thrust it towards the ceiling. 'We're in!'

'Wait a second,' Margery said, pulling her hand back and cutting the jubilations short. 'You can't tell me that if we went marching into the chief inspector's office that he would know and agree with this plan?'

As much as she wanted to help, something felt off. Why would Dewstow or Ittonvale's police force's willingly agree to let two middle-aged dinner ladies do their dirty work? Officer Thomas had gone pale, like he'd bought something very expensive that he needed immediately online and then realised after ordering that it wasn't going to be delivered for four to five business weeks.

'Well, not exactly,' he said. Margery gave him a stern look. 'I did try and bring you up to the sergeant, but he didn't want to hear it. The thing is,' Officer Thomas sighed, and the bristles of his long moustache fluttered. 'You are beginning to set a track record for this sort of thing and as you'll probably end up involved somehow anyway, why not at the beginning with the full support of myself and Officer Symon?'

'We've solved a few bits by accident, you mean. That can't possibly be your reason,' Margery began. Officer Thomas held out his hand to silence her.

'I'm retiring,' he said with a shrug. 'In a few months anyway, Christmas to be exact.'

'Oh,' Margery said. 'Well, congratulations.'

Officer Thomas gave her a sad smile. 'Yes. Well, the thing is, I can't see this case getting solved before then and selfish as it is, I want a clean slate to retire on. Once I'm out I won't be able to get involved in it anymore, you see?'

Margery nodded and so they reluctantly agreed.

Officer Thomas wasted no time filling them in on what the police knew. Some of it Ceri-Ann and Rose had shared, but there were other things they hadn't known. They had something to fill Officer Thomas in on as well: Margery had been right – the police hadn't known anything about Mr Evans and his fight with Mr Weaver before he disappeared.

They wiped clean the whiteboard on the back of the dry store door and set about planning in marker pen.

'Our first suspect,' Officer Thomas said, underlining the name with his pen on the board. 'Is Mr Weaver's wife.'

'Why his wife?' Margery asked. 'Other than the fact she's married to him.'

'Her alibi for the entire week is very shaky,' Officer Thomas shook his head to reiterate his point. 'She says she didn't realise he hadn't been home until we went to the house and told her he was dead, and Mr Barrow had been trying to ring her all day as he'd missed all his classes.'

'Gosh,' Margery said, though now he mentioned it, they had already known that from Rose. She just couldn't imagine being apart from Clementine and not knowing where she was or checking in at some point. Maybe their marriage wasn't as happy as her and Clementine's, or as co-dependant. 'So, you want us to talk to her?'

'Yes,' Officer Thomas said, tapping his pen to the board. 'See if you can find out what she was really doing. She says she was working from home all week, but I suspect there is more to it.'

'What about Mr Evans?' Clementine asked. 'The PE teacher?'

'Well, when we watched the CCTV Mr Evans does follow Mr Weaver out of the hall. But then they go their separate ways,' Officer Thomas said. 'But obviously, there's no cameras up in the woods or on the school playing fields. He could well have doubled back later, and Mr Weaver wasn't discovered for such a long time. The autopsy found that he didn't die until much later that afternoon, if not early evening.'

'Where did he say he was?' Clementine asked. 'Between leaving the hall and Mr Weaver's time of death.'

'He said he was down the Bell and Hope watching the football,' Officer Thomas explained. 'Symon verified it with the barmaid.'

'Really?' Clementine said, shaking her head. 'I don't remember seeing a television there.'

'I'm not sure,' Margery said, the last time they had visited the pub it had been so packed that she wouldn't have been able to see a television even if one existed. Officer Thomas tutted and sucked air through his teeth.

'He certainly said it was on a television, I'm sure of it,' he said, adding a line under Mr Evans name in the marker pen. 'Well, you may well wish to go and chat with the barmaid anyway, her name is Jessica Davis.'

'Jessica Davis,' Clementine wrote the name down in her little notepad and slipped it back inside her tabard. 'All right then.'

Officer Thomas started to stand. 'We know Mr Weaver was stabbed,' Margery said quickly, her mouth twisting into a grimace at the thought of it. She had to make sure this was a murder before they embarked, and exactly how it was committed.

'Do you now?' Officer Thomas raised his eyebrows. 'Well, yes, that's true. Not stabbed in the way you might be thinking though, he had a puncture wound to his neck. From a needle, or something similar.' Margery and Clementine both winced and he gave them a look of apology. 'It's bizarre, but we think the injection killed him. I've certainly never seen anything like it here. The autopsy came back saying it was an embolism caused by air being injected into the artery. I didn't know such a thing was even possible, something new to be frightened about, I suppose!'

Maybe the killer had tried to hide his body under the leaves, Margery thought, but had not thought it through properly. Surely they must have known that was a well-known dog-walking area in the town. If Ada Bones hadn't found Liam's body, then someone else's pet eventually would have.

'Did you find anything like that at the scene?' Margery asked. If the police had found a potential murder weapon, then the case was almost over before it began. Officer Thomas leaned back against the shelving unit and exhaled.

'Nothing,' he said. 'We pulled the entire place apart looking for something, but we didn't find anything. We've got the bloody Dewstow preservation society on us now for ruining the moss on the tree! They don't seem to understand that we're investigating a murder.'

'Officer Thomas, please do not swear.' Clementine rubbed the bridge of her nose with a hand. 'So, the wife, Mr Evans, what about Miss Macdonald?'

'Who?' Officer Thomas asked, scratching his head.

'She's a teacher here, Elle Macdonald.' Margery explained, though she didn't know what Clementine meant either. 'Why Miss Macdonald, Clem?'

'You've seen her, Margery, coming in here weeping all the time, crying all over the jacket potato warmer!' Clementine held the palms of her hands out. 'Explain that!'

'Her colleague just died,' Margery said. 'Maybe they were close?'

Clementine had never looked less convinced by anything in her life.

'I don't think so,' Clementine shook her head, putting her finger to her lips. 'I've never seen them together at all and I talk to everyone, even if they don't want me to! They've never even stood together at assembly.'

It was a well-known fact that all the teachers stood in their department groups, just as the cleaning team and catering staff did. You'd have never found Rose standing next to Mrs Winkle the receptionist, or Mrs Boch the librarian next to Mr Evans. Mr Weaver attended with the rest of the maths teachers and Miss Macdonald with the English department. It just was not the done thing to mix groups. Once, Barbara, the old manager of the Education Centre Sanitisation and Contamination Removal Experts had tried to get Seren to join them. Former kitchen manager Caroline had thrown a spoon at her and told her to get away from her staff. It was all a bit archaic.

'Maybe it's a lead,' Officer Thomas said he turned to the board considering it again. He looked worried. His brow had creased under the weight of it. When he finally spoke again, it was not his usual booming and jovial voice, but an uncertain whisper. 'We certainly don't have much else to go on.'

Chapter Six

It was all well and good the police involving them, but Margery and Clementine still didn't have much to go off other than a few names and a few weak alibis. Usually they'd blunder along sticking their nose into things until something clicked into place, but this time they had the full resources of the police behind them. Well, whatever Officer Thomas and Officer Symon could provide without the rest of the force finding out about it, which realistically wasn't going to amount to much. They needed to use all the resources the police could give them and get justice for Mr Weaver.

Clementine's first thought had been to ask the head-master about Mr Weaver's last few weeks, but Margery was concerned that they'd accidentally give too much away. Officer Thomas had sworn them both to secrecy; it wouldn't do to lose his trust now at this early stage.

In the end they decided to start at the beginning of the trail: Mr Weaver's desk in the maths teachers' office. It had been a hard task to arrange, without the cleaning team or any fellow dinner ladies catching them. Officer Thomas assured them that they had already searched the office and found nothing much of interest, but Margery and Clementine insisted on seeing things with their own eyes. Once they had finally got inside, however, they realised that he was right.

'God, there really is nothing here, is there?' Clementine scowled, poking through the papers on the desk. 'Look at all this ridiculous arithmetic stuff, I've met all the students at Summerview. None of them will need any of this once they leave. Especially that TikTok lot.'

'I don't know,' Margery smiled at the thought of the group who had spent all lunchtime practising some horrific dance or other. 'I find them quite amazing really. Imagine creating a whole podcast, I wouldn't have any idea where to start.'

Clementine scoffed. After the group had finished dancing, the students had cornered them in the canteen again at lunchtime and demanded that they be on a podcast or a TikTok or some other internet thing Margery didn't really understand but had tried to humour. Apparently, Miss Grant, the Media Studies teacher, had said that they would get extra credit on their coursework for an accompanying podcast. Margery couldn't fathom why anyone would want to listen to them being interviewed and the students hadn't seemed too thrilled about it either. Maybe the youth of today had already moved on from podcasts.

'Where now then?' Clementine asked, looking around the tiny office. It suffered from the same poor design as the rest of the school, more an assorted selection of small rooms stuck together, than a real building. It was certainly very different from nearby Ittonvale Comprehensive, with its large airy classrooms, fully equipped Design Technology department and Olympic-sized outdoor swimming pool. Or so she'd heard from listening to Rose complain about Dewstow's resources. Margery had heard on the down-low that Ittonvale even possessed a fully functional set of badminton shuttlecocks.

'Let's just look through his things at least,' Margery said, feeling as nervous as she normally did in spite of herself. Knowing that they would not get into trouble with the police for nosing around did not stop the voice in the back of her mind from telling her that the headmaster would not like it. She reached out and opened the drawer of Mr Weaver's desk. It wobbled as she did so, knocking a photo frame onto the wooden floor.

'Careful,' Clementine warned, picking it up. 'This must be his wife. Gosh, this frame is ruined, Margery.'

Margery turned to look at the photograph, the corner of the wooden frame was broken, split at one of the corners. It was indeed of the Weavers' wedding. Mr Weaver and his wife stood in a dreary churchyard, neither was smiling or even holding hands. In fact, they actively seemed to be keeping their distance from each other.

Margery looked in the drawer and found the usual bits and bobs a teacher would keep inside one, staples, red pens and pencils. Nothing unusual at all. Clementine went to put the frame back on the table, but the whole thing slid apart as she fumbled with it.

'Oh no,' she said, trying to stick it back together and making it worse. The entire thing was falling apart in her hands. The back came off the frame and the contents fell to the floor, the photograph landing gracefully along with several pieces of pink paper that fluttered down with it.

'What's that?' Margery asked, bending down to pick it up. She unfolded it and realised it was cut into the shape of a heart and it had something written on it in lovely neat handwriting.

my love is for you
it will never bow or break
no matter the road

Underneath the short poem was another paragraph, which Margery realised very quickly was not meant for public eyes.

'Oh my!' Margery dropped the page back on the desk. Clementine picked it up and read it anyway, chuckling and raising her eyebrows.

'Oh!' she cackled. 'How funny!'

'Put it back, Clem,' Margery hissed.

'Who sent him it?' she asked, scanning it again. 'Definitely not his wife!'

'What on earth makes you say that?' Margery asked, looking in bafflement at the papers on the floor.

'Come on,' Clementine snorted, gesturing to the wedding photograph. 'Look at them there, you can see they don't even like each other!'

'I don't think you can really tell from that, Clem,' Margery said. 'There's lots more of them here.' She picked up the other scraps of paper that had fallen alongside the first. 'An eternal bond, we must break the old one, then we can live as new. What does that mean? Oh, and it's signed...'

She stared down at the signature scrawled in pencil that read simply, E, in swirling font and a large X underneath that Margery assumed was a kiss.

'E for Elle,' Clementine said in a smug voice, 'X for x-rated poems!'

'That doesn't prove anything, what's his wife's name?' Margery asked. 'Anyway, there are lots of people with names beginning with E, aren't there?'

'Miss Macdonald sent it, that's obviously her trying to get him to leave his wife,' Clementine said with a smile. 'I'd put money on it.'

'That's… No, I just can't believe that.' Margery said, her brow furrowing as she read another. 'Just because she's upset?'

'This is just the sort of mad wishy-washy nonsense that writers and English teachers prattle on with Margery!' Clementine gave a dismissive wave of her hand. 'Poems and that.'

'Is it?'

'Yes,' Clementine said. 'Look at this one!'

She thrust it at Margery, who read it slowly.

> *You deserve the world*
> *I cannot give it to you*
> *While you stay with them*

'They're poems.' Clementine smiled. 'You can't tell me an English teacher wouldn't know how to write a poem? In fact, didn't Miss Macdonald write one for the local paper at some point? I remember reading it when I was trying to do the crossword.'

'Well, that's certainly something, isn't it?' Margery said as she read the poem again. Maybe there was a lot more to this. Perhaps Clementine had got the situation spot on, and her suspicions about Miss Macdonald were correct.

'We'll cross-examine her handwriting!' Clementine said, abandoning the desk and making her way out into the corridor. 'Come on!'

'What?' Margery asked weakly as she trailed after her, her head still wrapped in her thoughts. 'Where are we going?'

The English department's office was on the other side of the school building, and it took a good few minutes to get there, even in a rush. Margery and Clementine didn't usually venture to this block of classrooms and crept over as if they were trespassing. Fortunately, they saw no one, and were soon standing outside another office door. Clementine didn't wait even for a moment before pushing it open and venturing in, as brazen as always and with no thought of any consequences.

It wasn't empty in the slightest, but before they could realise their mistake they had already blundered into the room. The entire English department turned to stare at them, heads swivelling around in surprise. Mr Coxley dropped his pen and it rolled under his desk. Mrs George raised her eyebrows in shock, taking off her headphones. Miss Macdonald put down her book on haikus and stared at the pink heart-shaped paper in Clementine's hand, her cheeks going the same deep red usually reserved for post boxes.

'Sorry,' Margery said instinctively. She was frozen to the spot by a glue made of social anxiety. Clementine saved them.

'We just wondered if you'd booked a tea trolley for tomorrow?' she asked, addressing Mrs George, the head of the English department. She hid the paper behind her back quickly. Miss Macdonald looked at it and Margery watched her face carefully for any flickering of acknowledgement. 'Only we had a request for one, but none of us can read the signature.'

'I've said it before and I'll say it again, this is why you all need to get online,' Mrs George scoffed, pointing at them both with her headphones. 'The catering department is an anachronism now; you've got to get with the times. We shouldn't be having to find a pen every time we need to order a few sandwiches for an SLT meeting.'

Margery groaned internally. She still did everything on paper, much to the headmaster's dismay and constant badgering to start using the computer that sat useless in the kitchen dry store. Margery only used it to print off the next week's cleaning rota, and most of the time the crotchety printer covered her hands with ink. She didn't want to start using it for everything, it seemed such an easy way for everything to go wrong. But the rest of the school was determined to get her on the system, spending much too much time complaining that they had to hand deliver catering requests. Mr Barrow said that she could have an online calendar for catering, and it would be much easier for her, but Margery thought that if something wasn't broken, then there was no need to fix it. There was worry enough with the imminent arrival of the environmental health inspectors. Mr Barrow had warned her to expect a visit soon because they hadn't been since before Caroline, their last kitchen manager, had died.

'Yes, quite,' Clementine said in a cheery singsong way. 'Well, if it wasn't you, then we'll be off.'

They left quickly and rushed back down the corridor, though not before Mrs George had scowled at them.

'Do you think she saw?' Margery gasped as they made it to the main entrance finally.

'No!' Clementine said, much too self-assured for Margery's liking. 'She would have said something.'

'I think she definitely saw it, Clem,' Margery wrung her hands together. 'We weren't very subtle.'

'Well, we're the dinner lady detectives, aren't we?' Clementine laughed, 'That's why Officer Thomas never should have asked us to help. We don't do subtle.' She stopped in her tracks and looked at the main entrance doors. 'The symbol! Christ, that's not very subtle either!'

The symbol was there, spray-painted all along the inside of the automatic school front doors. The upside-down A that they had seen by Mr Weaver's body, also in green spray paint, and with it, a list of numbers.

Chapter Seven

'And you didn't see anyone?' the headmaster asked for the fifth time since he'd sat them down in his office, glancing between them with a bewildered expression. 'Not at all?'

'No,' Margery replied for the fifth time in return. 'Nobody.'

They were sat opposite him, his desk between them. Mr Barrow looked as though he had not been sleeping well, his red hair unkempt and his eyes exhausted – an all-too-familiar sight now after the last few years.

'I don't know how I'm going to explain it to the governors,' he said. He twisted the wedding ring on his finger round and round. Margery watched it twirl. 'We've had a police officer on watch here since last week. I don't know what else I can do.'

'Is there no CCTV?' Clementine asked. 'What about the cameras in the main entrance?'

'The police are watching it now.' Mr Barrow adjusted his tie and slumped back in the chair. 'But whoever vandalised the doorway was wearing a mask.'

'What kind?' Margery asked. Mr Barrow looked uneasy for a moment.

'A plain mask,' he said. 'The kind you can buy at the art shop in town.'

'Well, that should be their first port of call then,' Clementine said. 'Surely they'll know who they sold it to?'

'I would hope so,' Mr Barrow said. He tapped his fingers on the wood of the desk. 'What a nightmare.'

'Indeed,' Clementine said.

'This really isn't what Summerview needs,' Mr Barrow sighed, then he seemed to realise that they were still sitting there. 'I just mean, well, things have been strange.' He looked over to the cupboard on the other side of the office and then back to them, deciding something as he did so. He glanced at the main door, checking it was still closed, and then leaned towards them so he could whisper conspiratorially.

'A personnel file is missing,' he hissed, his eyes wide. 'I only noticed a few days ago, I've got no idea how long it's been gone.'

'Why are you telling us?' Margery asked in alarm. 'Surely the police could help?'

'No, they can't know.' Mr Barrow shook his head. 'It'll just be another nail for the school. There's so much pressure on us as it is, I don't know how we're going to remain open when terrible things keep happening.'

'Whose file is missing?' Clementine asked.

'Dr Roberts',' Mr Barrow said, running his fingers through his hair in a single agitated motion. 'I knew I should have put a better lock on that door.'

Or a lock at all, Margery thought to herself. She cast her mind back to the previous Christmas when she and Clementine had been able to access the cupboard without even breaking in. The headmaster had never taken security as seriously as he should, maybe that's why they were in this mess now. Still, she didn't want the school to close any more than he did.

'Why would someone take Dr Roberts's file?' she asked him. 'Are you sure it's not just fallen behind another?'

'I took them all out and checked when I realised.' His tapping on the desk became more persistent. 'I needed to update her address, that's why I was looking for it.'

'Gosh,' Margery said. 'But why just Dr Roberts?'

'I've no idea,' Mr Barrow said, looking at them both with pleading eyes. 'Could you use your detective skills? Get it back for me before anyone finds out it's gone?'

He looked between them both with a hopeful look written on his face, which faded as he realised neither of them was going to answer immediately. Their hesitation must have been much too obvious, but there was no way to explain to him that they were already undercover.

'I certainly don't want her to find out about it,' he said. 'I can't have her leaving. She's had a very interesting career path and has good credentials. It sets a good example for all the students.'

He sat back in his chair again and folded his long arms over his chest, looking more like a set of twisted-together pipe cleaners than a man.

'We can certainly try and find it,' Margery said finally, though she felt Clementine turn to look at her.

Mr Barrow breathed a sigh of relief. 'Thank you.'

Margery wondered where on earth the file could be, and who would take such a thing. She wasn't holding out much hope that they would be able to find it.

'Are you ready for the environmental health inspection, Margery?' Mr Barrow asked. 'They won't be long now, I'm sure of it. I notified them that there'd been a change in manager.'

He'd already told her that he had notified them about the change in managers. Many, many times, in fact, and always accompanied by the same twirling, anxious, hand gesture that did nothing to steady her nerves. She knew that in principle it would all be fine. There were no outrageous health and safety violations in their clean and tidy little kitchen, nothing like the sort you'd hear about on the news, but she always worried they were missing something that might get them marked down. Former kitchen manager Caroline had been the very best of friends with the old environmental health officer, who had been just as ancient as she was, and it had made all their inspections under her reign an absolute breeze. That officer had since retired and now the prospect of the unknown was terrifying.

There was a rap on the door. They all sat up straight and the door swung open revealing Officer Thomas and Officer Symon – both looked grave.

'Nothing on the CCTV,' Officer Thomas said gruffly. 'We'll go to the shops when we've finished here and see if they have any record of the masks and we'll get another watch set up for security.'

'What about the numbers written by the symbol?' Clementine asked. Margery had been wondering about them too.

'Some sort of code, we think,' Officer Thomas said, sounding distracted.

'I agree,' Clementine said. 'What were they again? Forty-six…?'

'Four, six, two, seven, one, zero,' Officer Symon said from his spot behind Officer Thomas. He had to read the numbers off his notepad where they were written, there were far too many of them to remember.

'Four, six,' Clementine repeated. Mr Barrow looked between them all in confusion.

'Has something…? Are you…?' He looked between the officers and Margery and Clementine before seemingly deciding his theory was too far-fetched and Margery and Clementine couldn't be working with the officers. Margery could have laughed at how close to the truth he was.

–

Although they had spoken about it all night, neither Margery nor Clementine were any closer to working out what the numbers meant. Work itself was not helping – the kitchen was a swarming hive of activity as they all struggled to get everything ready for today's lunchtime as well as peel several sackloads of roast potatoes for tomorrow's. Wednesday was roast dinner day. Margery had brought in another three bags of apples courtesy of Dawn, which Sharon and Karen were peeling for tomorrow's crumble in irritation.

'Four, six, and a lot of other numbers,' Clementine repeated, through a mouthful of stolen carrots. 'What could that mean?'

'A date?' Margery wondered aloud, knowing immediately that it couldn't be a date. They had been very tired by the time they had finally got back to the house and had gone to bed after a quick supper of cheese and crackers. It hadn't made it any easier to get up in the morning though, not now that it was dark long after they had left the house for work, and they were still exhausted today.

'The fourth of June,' Clementine said, her eyes widening. 'Ooh, maybe!'

'June seems a bit strange, what if it's the sixth of April, the American way round?' Margery said, finishing her ordering list with a sigh. 'And what's the rest of it about?'

'Obviously the year, Margery!' Clementine held the carrot she was peeling up in triumph before looking at the piece of paper they had written the numbers on 'No, that doesn't make sense. That would make the year 2710, and I bet the planet will have plummeted into the sun by then.'

'Four, six,' Margery said again, completely stumped. 'Could it be coordinates to somewhere?'

'Maybe,' Clementine said. 'Wouldn't coordinates need a longitude and a latitude though? That would be two sets of numbers, wouldn't it?'

Margery did not know.

'We need to go and see that barmaid the police mentioned at the Bell and Hope,' Clementine said, changing the subject completely. 'After work. And we need to take Mrs Weaver her sympathy card, you know...' She dropped her voice down to a whisper. 'And have a chat with her like Officer Thomas said.'

'We don't know where she lives,' Margery said.

'I do.' Gloria appeared from where she had been setting up the mid-morning snacks in the hot cupboard. 'Mr Weaver and his wife hosted the church choir practice once last year, before he left Ittonvale School to come and work here. They live next to Caroline's old house on the riverside.'

'Really?' Clementine asked. 'Will you give us the address?'

'Do we really need an address for that?' Margery said with a smile. 'We've been to Caroline's before, it's on the old terrace, you can't miss it.'

'It's better to be safe than sorry, Margery,' Clementine said.

'Depends on whether you're planning on bothering a new widow,' Gloria frowned at them both, interrupting their argument. 'I don't like the idea of you two blundering in and upsetting her.'

'Not bothering,' Margery said weakly. 'Just wanted to chat, give our condolences.'

Gloria harrumphed, but she nodded before going back to work. Margery felt a wave of guilt wash over her. She still couldn't help but feel guilty about the last case they had solved and the young man who had died. Even if they had been on the cliff because of Thomas in the first place, after he had poisoned several townspeople. Margery found herself throwing everything she had into the working week because the quiet nights at home, which had used to be her favourite thing in the world, were now a constant reminder that she had lived and he had not. Sometimes, when they were out at the supermarket or in a busy shop, she thought she would catch an impossible glimpse of Thomas out of the corner of her eye, and then for a split second, she would be back on the cliff or looking at his startled face as she accidentally tugged him off the precipice with her.

It was worse still that Thomas may well have been related to Clementine by blood, though Clementine had refused to do the testing in the end. Clementine reminded her time and time again that it was all Thomas's fault, that he had tried to kill them both, but it was no good. Margery still blamed herself and she was sure that somewhere underneath it all Clementine blamed her for his death too.

In the end she had just stopped telling Clementine how she felt, and her wife must have eventually decided that silence was a good thing, because she had stopped asking. Margery had read all sorts of things in her search for a miracle cure to stop her brain from feeling the way it did.

She knew that lots of people wouldn't have remembered the events at all, but she could see it all in full colour. The heart-stopping moment she had fallen, and finding out how it felt to drown. She replayed them both in her mind. She wasn't sure which was worse. Clementine had been trying to get her to arrange a counselling appointment, but Margery had resisted so far.

'Let's forget Mrs Weaver for the moment,' Margery said, eyeing Gloria warily as she wandered off to get Karen and Sharon more brown sugar. 'We should go to the pub and talk to that barmaid.'

'I hate the Bell and Hope,' Clementine sighed. 'They don't even know how to make a piccalilli Paula.' She saw the exasperation on Margery's face. 'All right, anything for a glass of wine, hey!' She nudged her with a grin.

'Clem, is that your alarm?' Gloria yelled from the dry store. 'Why does it still keep making that horrible noise?'

Clementine rushed off to the changing room to fix the GPS alarm again and Margery returned to her ordering list. Then lunchtime was upon them before they knew it and with it the group of amateur crime solvers, who jovially scuttled up the queue towards them.

'Hello, miss!' the blonde-haired ringleader yelled over the hot counter to Margery who was busily serving sausages and mashed potato. Margery could never remember all their names. Instead, she and Clementine numbered each of them. This one was definitely Number One of the group, the rest of them drawn to her like metal to a magnet.

'Hello.' Margery smiled, moving to the other side of the hot serving counter. 'Sausage roll?'

'Ooh, yes please,' Number One grinned. Margery wrapped it in a paper bag and handed it to her. There was something lovely about seeing the students grow up into real people with lives bigger than the school. She had met so many over the years; sometimes she and Clementine would be doing their weekly big shop and some great tall adult would come marching over, and it would be one of the tiny Year Sevens they used to sling portions of chips and lasagne at, fully grown and with a family of their own. Margery wondered if they would see Number One and her gang of friends in ten years.

Number One beamed at Margery as she took the bag. 'Miss, I posted a video on our true crime TikTok last week about when you solved that poisoning, and it got loads of likes. Look!' She dropped the bag on the tray before her and thrust her phone at them. Clementine put on her reading glasses and scoffed as she stared at the screen.

'What's this heart mean?' She leaned over the counter and jabbed at the screen with her finger as the video showed news clips of their first case overdubbed with Number One narrating. 'And this bubble?'

'That's likes and comments,' Number One said brightly. 'Loads of them!'

'Hmmm,' Clementine harrumphed. 'If you say so.'

'Will you please come on our podcast?' Number Two, a short boy with a red mullet, asked. 'I know you said no before, but we do lots of true crime! It's not as good as TikTok though.'

'No, we will not,' Clementine said. 'Especially not for only one view!'

'That's one million views,' Number One laughed. 'Look again!'

'Gosh!' Margery said in surprise before she could stop herself. 'That is quite a lot of views, but regardless... No.'

'Can we film you then?' Number One asked. 'For TikTok? No one believes we know the real Dinner Lady Detectives.'

'Also no,' Clementine said. 'You obviously don't know us, or you'd never ask us.'

'But you can tell us about yourselves on the podcast!' Number One said excitedly. 'We did a TikTok about Mr Weaver dying and it got loads of views!'

'How do you know about that?' Margery asked in horror.

'The newspaper,' Number One explained. 'My mum said she was thinking of pulling me out of school, making me go to Ittonvale, but all my friends are here. It's sad though, miss, because we all really liked Mr Weaver.'

Margery may have been tempted to do the same if she were the mother of a student. All the terrible accidents and murders seemed to revolve around Dewstow School in one way and Margery and Clementine in another.

'What if we do, say, a very short video, for your social… thing.' Margery couldn't bring herself to say TikTok, the words didn't sound right in her mouth. She'd tried before but had sounded like a broken clock. 'In exchange for one thing?'

Number One gasped and clapped her hands in glee, nearly crushing the sausage roll she was holding, 'Yes! What do we need to do?'

Margery wondered how she could ask for what she wanted without either getting Number One into trouble or revealing what they were up to. A police escort wouldn't help them if anyone realised what they were trying to do. Thinking quickly, she grabbed her notepad from the workstation behind her and scrawled a note, ripping it off the page and handing it to the girl.

'Can you give this to Miss Macdonald and ask her to write back, please?' she asked. 'It's just to see if SLT are likely to need any more tea stations.'

Number One looked confused but seemed elated to be finally getting her exclusive interview in exchange for something so simple. She rushed off, almost forgetting to pay for her sausage roll, until Gloria clicked her fingers at her from the till.

'What was that about?' Clementine asked, arriving at her side as the queue was beginning to die down.

'We need a sample of Miss Macdonald's handwriting, don't we?' Margery said. 'To rule her out. We'll have to do a video though, for the children.'

'Oh God,' Clementine groaned. 'I don't know if that's a fair exchange.'

Margery realised much too late that Elle Macdonald was already in the canteen. Number One hurried straight over to where she was leaning against the wall at the back of the room supervising the lunch hour. Margery watched her take the note, read it, and then look up across the canteen. Their eyes met; Elle's were steely cold. Number One bounced away cheerily, but Miss Macdonald screwed the paper in her hands up into a ball. Margery felt a chill go down her spine.

Chapter Eight

'The look she gave us, Clem,' Margery said as they walked hand in hand along the riverside, the path slippery under the oranges and browns of the fallen leaves crumpled to mush over it. The sky was heavy, threatening rain, and Margery didn't dare take off her raincoat even though she was becoming hot and sweaty. The wind was picking up too, the hanging baskets in front of the bar on the riverside threatening to fly off their chains.

'She must know we want her handwriting. She knows we know about the letter after all,' Margery continued.

'Let her know,' Clementine said, tugging her coat closer around her. 'What's she going to do about it?'

'That's exactly what I'm worried about,' Margery said, squinting against the sudden light mist of the breeze billowing around them from the river. 'What if she murdered Mr Weaver? And then she decides to murder us? We've certainly nearly been killed over less.'

'We definitely don't have a good track record, do we?' Clementine said, cocking her head towards Margery. 'But Officer Thomas promised he'd keep us safe.'

Margery feared that Officer Thomas didn't really know what he was talking about. He certainly hadn't been able to stop Mr Weaver from being murdered in a local woodland and buried under an inch-thick layer of moss and leaves. Who knows how long it would have taken anyone to find him if they hadn't had Ada Bones with them that day? They surely wouldn't have seen him under all that mess. They would have walked right on past, realised there were no blackberries for Gloria and then skipped back home, happy in their unawareness. In a way, she wished that was what had happened. In another, she felt like maybe this was a fitting punishment for what had happened in the summer holiday. Maybe they were doomed to have to keep doing this, again and again.

They finally reached the Bell and Hope and entered the pub through the old wooden door. Margery was grateful for the warmth of the bar area as they stepped down the few old stone stairs into it. The fire was blazing in the fireplace. It was a lovely old building – one of the oldest in Dewstow. Low wooden beams ran across the ceiling and the door frames and required clientele to duck through. It had once served travellers who had come to trade at the bustling market and looked after their horses for the night in the stables, which were now converted to a pleasant separate events space which hosted weekend weddings.

It was only four o'clock and so the pub was empty apart from a single regular sat listening to the jukebox, an elderly gentleman slouched on the chair by the window nursing the last drop of the frothy pint in front of him. They took off their coats and looked around. She wasn't sure if they should sit down or try and find out who Jess was or where she was. For all they knew they could have arrived on her day off. There was no one behind the bar either. In fact, there was nothing but a half-poured glass of frothy beer sitting under one of the beer pump handles. Clementine made the decision for them.

She wandered over to the bar and waited, giving the man sitting by the window a nod. He gave a small smile back then returned to the last of his beer. Clementine tapped her hands on the wooden bar top, recoiling as her fingers stuck in the alcohol residue. Margery peered around to look for help but all there was to see were beer pumps and dusty wine bottles, and huge bottles of spirits hanging on the back wall.

The wooden door behind the bar opened and a young woman whose arms and legs were too long and gangly for her body stepped out, looking aggravated. Her purple-dyed hair could have made her a student at school, it was only her attitude that betrayed that she was older. She wiped her hands on the dishcloth on the bar and then returned to the pumps to pour the rest of the drink she had abandoned. She looked ever so familiar, but Margery couldn't quite place her.

'Here you go, Jeff,' she called loudly to the man slumped in his seat at the table by the window. He got up unsteadily to collect the beer, which she had left at the end of the bar for him. 'That keg was a right bugger.'

She popped herself up on a bar stool and returned to the book she had been reading as Jeff reached the bar, after what felt like an age of him dragging himself across the room. 'Thanks, Jess,' he said, and then began to hobble back to his chair.

Clementine cleared her throat. Jess looked up startled.

'Oh, all right?' she said, looking between them both. 'Sorry, didn't see you there. There isn't usually anyone new here during the day, I know all the regulars' orders off by heart! What can I get you?'

'Just two soda and limes, please,' Clementine said. Jess got to work, plonking the drinks down in front of them a moment later. Margery took her card from her purse to pay, but she shook her head.

'Sorry, love. Cash only now.' Jess grimaced apologetically. 'Landlord's too tight to get the card machine sorted.'

'I'll go and get some from the cashpoint up the road,' Clementine said, after a moment's pause. 'Give me a sec.'

She was gone before Margery could stop her, leaving her alone in the pub with Jess and Jeff, feeling awkward. Jess flicked through the pages of her book and Jeff stared off into space while a Wham! song blared from the jukebox. Margery climbed up onto the barstool and made herself comfortable. Clementine would have to traipse all the way back up to the high street to use one of the notoriously terrible cash machines outside the bank. Hopefully it would spit out something smaller than a fifty-pound note. Then she'd have to come all the way back.

Jess gave her a small smile, then went back to her book again. Margery drummed her fingers on the bar again and then pulled them back into her lap when she realised she was doing it. Without Clementine here, she didn't know what to ask. Clementine would have asked her outright, demanded to know, 'How do you know Mark Evans?' and Jess probably would have been so surprised she might well have told her by mistake. Margery couldn't do that, she just didn't have it in her. She decided that she would start with a small question.

'Do you show the football here?' Margery asked, trying to sound light-hearted.

'You don't look like the type who watches football,' Jess said, not unkindly but Margery found herself bristling anyway, the fuse of the temper that had appeared in the last few months threatening to ignite.

'What is that supposed to mean?' she said, tugging at the sleeves of her sensible cardigan. 'Why can't I like football? Surely anyone can enjoy the sport?'

'I didn't mean anything by it,' Jess smiled, half closing the book before giving Margery her full attention. 'I love football too. Watford's my team, a bit far away but it's a family thing. We all still go to as many matches as we can, even though none of us has lived in Watford for years now, but we still try and get up to Vicarage Road for some home games. Who do you support?'

'Right, yes,' Margery spluttered, wishing to herself that she hadn't began the conversation. 'Well, you know...' She paused.

Jess waited in anticipation.

'All of them,' Margery finally said. 'It's just good to see young people getting a bit of exercise.'

They fell back into silence and Jess returned to her reading. Margery ran her fingers along the wooden grooves of the bar, tracing the outline and trying to think of something else to say.

'So, do you show the games here?' Margery asked again, hoping she sounded less mad this time. 'Football, I mean.'

'No,' Jess sighed, putting her book down on the bar in front of her and using a napkin as a bookmark before she shut the pages. 'No TV. I keep asking the landlord if we can get one, but he wouldn't pay for the sports channel anyway. You'll want to go up to the Swan on the high street for that. They play all sorts, even a bit of horse racing sometimes.'

'That's a shame,' Margery said, trying to keep her voice even. Mr Evan's couldn't possibly have watched the football at the Bell and Hope if they didn't have a television. Jess must have lied to the police, she thought in triumph. Now they just had to find out why. The bell above the door clanged as Clementine entered the room again, stumbling down the short few steps on her way to the bar and waving a ten-pound note happily.

'Got it!' she said cheerily, handing it over to Jess who had left the bar stool and passed her the soda water. 'Oh, sod the soda, we're a long time dead, aren't we?' Clementine laughed. 'Add a shot of gin to that, would you?'

Jess complied and Clementine joined Margery at the bar on a stool, taking the change as Jess slid it to her. She reached eagerly for the drink.

'I ran into Mrs Mugglethwaite,' Clementine said, before taking a large gulp.

'Oh?' Margery said.

'Yes, couldn't get away.' Clementine shook her head. 'She kept trying to tell me about how much it was going to cost the preservation society to regrow the moss where the body was found.'

'Terrible about that teacher,' Jess said from where she had been listening to their conversation from behind the pages of her book. 'Loads of weird stuff happening at the moment though, isn't there? The other night, we'd had a late lock-in because we had a band playing, and then on the way out we saw all these people in costumes running down the road. It was one in the morning!'

'What!' Clementine spluttered. 'Surely they were just Halloween revellers though? Not witches!'

'No idea, but they painted a weird thing on the back wall of the car park,' Jess explained. 'The landlord is still fuming about it; says we're going to have to double the price of the crisps to pay for the cleaning. Tight as anything he is, he didn't even need to pay for cleaning. We just washed it off with washing-up liquid and the beer garden hosepipe.'

'What was the weird thing?' Clementine asked. Margery thought they might already know.

Jess took her phone out of her pocket and tapped away at the screen until she found what she wanted to show them. 'Here, bit strange, innit?'

Margery couldn't stop herself from gasping. It was the symbol again, and in the same green spray paint as they had seen at the school and the murder scene.

'You didn't tell the police about this?' she asked. Jess shrugged.

'No, it was probably just kids,' she said, her voice suggesting this had happened many times before. 'We get them doing their graffiti here all the time. They all think they're Banksy, don't they? The police have never cared before, why would they this time?'

'Did you see who they were?' Margery asked, trying to steer the conversation back on track and wishing that Jess hadn't already washed off the spray paint.

'No.' Jess shook her head. 'They were wearing Halloween costumes, or something like them anyway. All masked and that.'

'What kind of masks?' Margery asked.

Jess shrugged. 'Just some plain white ones,' she said. 'I dunno, it was hard to see in the dark.'

That certainly could be the same group of masked people that had been seen on the school's CCTV, Margery thought.

'Wow,' Clementine said, scratching her chin. 'I wonder who they are.'

'So do I,' Jess said. They lapsed back into silence again while they drank, and Jess returned to her book. Clementine finally broke the quiet before Margery could think of a way to tell her about the conversation she and Jess had already shared.

'Do you know Mark Evans?' Clementine asked brashly, diving in feet first like Margery knew she would. 'He's a teacher? Works at Summerview School.'

'Yeah, he's my uncle,' Jess said, not even bothering to look up.

'Your uncle?' Margery said before she could stop herself.

Jess did look at her then, her eyes sliding from the pages to Margery's face.

'Yeah?'

'Was he here watching the football on Saturday?' Clementine asked innocently. 'Only he's a colleague and we wanted to know what his favourite team is so we could get him a present.' It was not a very good lie and Jess's face scrunched up awkwardly.

'You're with the police,' she said, standing from the stool.

'Not exactly,' Margery said, in as soothing a voice as she could muster. 'We're just trying to find out why Mark lied.'

'Christ, I thought I recognised you,' Jess tutted, pointing at Margery accusatorily. 'You're the bloody Dinner Lady Detectives!'

'Yes! That's us!' Clementine beamed. Jess scowled back.

'If you're not with the police, then why are you here? I've already had them ask me loads of stupid questions.'

'We know he wasn't here the night Mr Weaver died,' Margery said. 'Because he said he was watching football here and you've already told me that you don't show it.'

Clementine looked between them, her jaw dropping as she realised what must have already occurred in the time she was gone.

'Yeah, but...' Jess stuttered, realising she was caught. 'It doesn't matter where he was because he wouldn't have killed anyone!'

'The police seem to think he might have,' Margery lied.

'He wouldn't have.' Jess shook her head. 'I think I know him better than you.'

Chapter Nine

'Do you think she was lying?' Clementine asked as they cut across the grass which ran between the river footpath, along the single road lined with old houses. They were all lit by dim street lamps that were not quite adequate enough to light the way under the night's darkness.

'I don't know,' Margery said.

The visit had given them two things: the symbol had been painted by a group and not someone working alone; and the Bell and Hope certainly did not have a television, meaning Mr Evans had lied about his alibi. Maybe that would be enough for the police to further the investigation. It was a shame that the staff of the pub had washed the symbol away before the police could have a look at it. She made a mental note to tell Officer Thomas about it anyway. If the police had enough reason to suspect Mr Evans then surely they would have arrested him already?

They passed Caroline's house, which was in darkness, as it had been since she had died. Her boyfriend, Seth, had sold it to Seren for just a few hundred pounds in the end, as she had been living there when Caroline died, and he had no need of it. It had taken a while to organise so that Seren didn't end up paying the inheritance tax on the house, but it had all worked out in the end.

Margery sometimes missed their lives before Caroline died. She had never woken up screaming before Caroline died or had to leave the kitchen at work and go outside because she was having a panic attack. Her house brought the memories of her past life rushing back and she began to feel her heart racing. She smiled at the memory of Caroline, tripping people with her walking stick as they walked past her in the school corridors. All the annoyances she had felt about her when she was alive had evaporated with time.

They knocked at the house next door and waited. There was a huge 'for sale' sign in the window. The terraced row was lovely, full of tall three- or four-storey houses that were nearly as old as Dewstow itself. Caroline's house did not look too bad from the outside, almost as though it had been painted recently. She was sure that the last time they had seen it the wood of the windowsills had been cracked and looking worse for wear after all the years they had held the glass in them, now they looked reasonably good.

Mrs Weaver answered the door, interrupting her thoughts. Margery recognised her from school events, though probably not many; maybe the odd Christmas assembly where partners and outsiders to the school were welcomed, and not for a long time. The tall woman with a head of long auburn curls looked them up and down as if she knew them but couldn't quite place them in her mind.

'Can I help you?' she asked, folding her arms and leaning against the door frame. Margery felt as though they were being studied with a careful eye.

'Hello, Mrs Weaver,' Clementine said. 'We came to pass on the condolences from the dinner lady team at Summerview School.' Margery held up the paper bag she was holding, with the bunch of flowers and the card. 'We were all very fond of your husband, he was a nice man.'

Mrs Weaver smirked, raising an eyebrow.

'You can call me Liv,' she said.

'All right,' Clementine agreed. 'Liv. Could we come in? Get out of this drizzle?'

Liv didn't answer. Instead, she stood back and gestured for them to join her inside the house.

They followed her and took off their coats at her request, hanging them on the hooks by the door. Liv sized them up as they did so, her face unreadable, but her eyes flicked up and down slowly, taking them in. The house wasn't like Caroline's, who had kept all of the original features, or their own house, which was drowning under the weight of sentimental ornaments and old birthday cards. The Weaver residence was cool – the old stone floor jarred with the shiny new kitchen Liv led them into. The tiles on the splashback were so shiny and clean that they almost hurt Margery's eyes. An extension had been built at some point as there were floor-to-ceiling windows at the far end of the room that she imagined held the view of a lovely garden in the daytime. At night though it showed nothing but the darkness outside.

'Tea? Coffee?' Liv asked, reaching for the nearest gleaming orange cabinet and revealing the alcohol inside. 'Wine?'

'Tea is fine,' Margery said. The drink at the pub had been enough. Clementine murmured in agreement.

They watched Liv collect the matching glass mugs from another cupboard, fill each with a teabag and then pour the boiling water straight from the tap – Margery almost gasped at the cleverness. Liv put the mugs on the orange counter that matched the cabinets and left them there while she went to the big fridge on the other side of the room. Margery watched the steam rise from the mug as the teabag twirled inside it.

'My favourite bit when we had the kitchen done,' she muttered, almost to herself as much as to Margery, finding the milk and taking it back to the counter. 'You never have to boil a kettle.'

She finished the drinks and handed them over. They stared at each other again in cautious silence.

'Here,' Margery said, remembering herself enough to hand the brown paper bag over, sliding it towards her across the kitchen counter. Liv took it by the string handles and peered inside, her hair flopping over as she bent to investigate it.

'Lovely,' she said, her face emotionless. 'Thanks.'

The silence returned, even more awkward and intrusive than before. Margery and Clementine sipped their tea and looked around the room. Liv observed them watching her house with the same emotionless gaze. Margery wondered if they shouldn't have come at all.

'I didn't kill him, if that's what you're thinking,' Liv said suddenly. Margery felt her neck snap up of its own accord. 'I know that's what everyone probably thinks.'

'We don't—'

'Did the police send you?' Liv hissed. Her demeanour had changed completely, her nostrils flaring as she stared them down. 'Because I know all about your exploits. Don't pretend you're here to help me grieve when you're really trying to find out if I killed him. I don't know who killed him! I told the police that, and I'll tell you!'

Margery felt herself trying to stutter an answer out and failing miserably.

'Well, I didn't think you had killed him until you just said you didn't kill him,' Clementine said matter-of-factly, taking another sip of her tea. She raised an eyebrow as if waiting for an answer. 'Where were you when he died?'

'I was working from home!' Liv glared at her. 'I'm a social media manager, all my work is online.'

'Well, can you prove it?' Clementine asked. 'Get your boss to ring the police or something?'

'I freelance. It's my company,' Liv growled. 'I'm the boss.'

She scowled at them both for a moment before throwing her hands up and storming away. Margery and Clementine shared a look and Margery wondered if they ought to leave before she returned — wherever she had gone, it could not be a good thing. Before she had a chance to say anything, however, Liv was back carrying her tablet in her hands.

'There are cameras all over this house,' she muttered, fiddling with the screen, flicking at it with a fingernail that was almost bitten down to the quick. She pointed at the camera Margery hadn't noticed before in the corner of the kitchen.

'Inside?' Clementine asked in surprise. 'We've got one for our cats in the house, do you have any cats?'

'No,' Liv said begrudgingly. 'Liam's idea when we had the house done up.' She rolled her eyes. 'He was convinced someone would break in. He always hated cats. I suppose I could get loads of them now, if I wanted to.'

She turned the tablet to face them, and they watched the screen as she pressed Play, the skin around her fingers red. The date was clearly displayed at the bottom as the nineteenth of October, the day of the harvest festival. The time was just before four. Mr Weaver must have come straight home after he had left the festival. How did he go from his home to a shallow grave less than twenty-four hours? Margery felt a chill go down her spine.

The screen showed the tall flight of stairs in the hallway from the doorway entrance. For a moment nothing happened. But then an object came tumbling down them, bouncing along each stair and landing at the bottom, followed by an assortment of what could only be clothing, plunging towards the bottom of the stairs. Mr Weaver stampeded down the staircase after them. There was no sound through the tablet speakers, but Margery could see him, red-faced and screaming at Liv, who had appeared at the top of the stairs throwing items of clothing. She disappeared from the scene for a moment before arriving back with a piece of paper, thrusting it into his hands. He took it and stared at it, his mouth opening and closing until he went marching down the stairs again. Mr Weaver disappeared from the screen, and Liv clicked through to show them the outside camera, perched neatly over the main entrance to the house. Mr Weaver stormed across the grass and disappeared from sight. Back inside the house, the screen showed Liv sitting on the stairs weeping.

'Thursday afternoon,' she said simply, though Margery had already surmised that. She turned the tablet off. 'I turned my phone off so I didn't hear anything from him until the police turned up on Friday.'

'Christ,' Margery said. Clementine didn't bother to tell her not to swear. 'So, you were in the house?'

'Working from home, as I said,' Liv said quietly, putting the tablet on the marble butcher's block in the middle of the room. 'And drowning my sorrows.'

They sat for a moment before curiosity got the better of Margery.

'What were you arguing about?' she asked. 'Why did he leave?'

Liv shrugged. Margery wondered what she was hiding. You didn't kick your husband out of the house for no reason.

'The affair,' Clementine whispered.

Liv stared at her with wide eyes. 'How do you know about that?' Liv's lip curled but then her face rearranged itself. The change took only a split second, but Margery noticed it.

'Is that when you found out about your husband's affair?' Margery asked. She couldn't help but wonder why Liv hadn't just shown the police. Surely a moment's embarrassment was better than being suspected of your husband's murder. Liv picked at her fingernails, her hands resting in her lap.

'Yes,' Liv said curtly. 'And if there are no more questions...' She pointed to their empty mugs.

'And you know who he was having an affair with?' Clementine blurted out and then slapped a hand over her mouth at the rudeness of her question.

Liv looked startled like she'd stuck the finger she was picking the skin off into a glass of vinegar. 'Yes,' she blurted out. 'Look, I think you should leave—'

'Well, who?' Clementine asked. She gasped. 'It was Miss Macdonald, wasn't it?'

Liv's eyes were open as far as they would go. Her face had turned a horrible ashen white, her shoulders tense. Margery watched as she balled her hands into fists, the nails must have been biting the skin of her palms.

Liv hesitated. 'How? H-how do you know about that?' she stammered out finally.

'It's okay,' Clementine said kindly. 'We saw the notes she wrote him.'

Liv seemed to gain control of her features and her face was unreadable once again. 'You did, did you?'

'Yes,' Margery said. 'In his office.'

'Well then, you know everything.' She stopped talking then, a strangled noise in her throat.

'Why not show that to the police?' Margery asked, pointing to the tablet. Liv looked away and folded her arms around herself, seemingly more comfortable now that the topic of conversation had changed. Margery decided it must be horrible to learn your spouse was cheating on you, and then even worse for them to die and leave you with the knowledge that the last few weeks you had with them were not happy ones. 'You'd have no problem then.'

'A little bit of embarrassment, I suppose,' Liv said. 'I don't want the entire town to gossip. I've seen what this place is like. It's nothing like London, people don't keep to themselves here.' She gave them both a look as if to prove her own point.

'Yes,' Clementine said grandly. 'We also went to London once. Very different. Underground trains!' She said the words in the same befuddled bemusement she had when they had got lost for three hours on the underground, going around the Circle Line again and again until they finally got off at the right stop.

The conversation fizzled out and became awkward. Margery and Clementine took the chance to leave amenably before Liv could threaten to throw them out again. She ushered them through her front door, and suddenly they were outside the front of the house again, the door slamming behind them.

'Well,' Margery said. They began to walk back up the street. 'I suppose that solves that then, doesn't it?'

'No it doesn't,' Clementine said. 'Her chucking him out doesn't prove she didn't kill him, the footage she showed us was from the day before he died, why didn't she show us anything after he had already died? And anyway, I don't believe she threw him out for the affair.'

'No?' Margery stopped walking and turned to Clementine, who had stopped too and was looking off into the distance across the river.

'No,' Clementine said thoughtfully. 'Why throw him out then if she knew about it for that long? Something else happened, I'd put money on it, and the way she spoke about it was strange. What did she give him? That piece of paper.'

'I'd imagine it was one of Miss Macdonald's poems,' Margery said. 'Going to throw away a five-pound note, are you?'

Clementine smiled and took her arm. 'You'll see.'

Margery looked back as they crossed the street and noted with surprise that there was a light on in one of the upstairs windows of Caroline's old house. There was no time to think about it now – it was way past the cat's dinner time, and they needed to get home.

Chapter Ten

They sat in Margery's makeshift office in the kitchen dry store on their mid-morning coffee break with Gloria. Margery and Clementine had seen no need to keep what was going on a secret from the more senior members of the dinner lady team. Whenever they had done their best to conceal what was going on, typically, something dreadful would happen. This time especially, they would need every brain they could get.

'Well, I can't see Mr Evans' alibi holding any water,' Clementine suggested the next day after lunchtime. 'I don't believe he was really at the pub. Not after all that with Jess the barmaid. Do you think Liv Weaver was telling the truth?'

'I don't really know anymore,' Margery said, tapping her pen against the clipboard on her lap. The security camera footage only proved the Weaver's marriage wasn't a happy one.

'What if Mrs Weaver and Mr Evans were working together?' Gloria asked from her seat on the oil container. 'What if she told him to kill Mr Weaver and then asked his niece to lie about his whereabouts?'

'Yes, there might be something to that,' Margery agreed. 'I've been thinking about the video she showed us, there was no sound on it. Which is strange, and surely she could still have orchestrated his murder? Even if he had left the house. But why would she kill him?'

'I really don't know,' Clementine mused. 'But there were a lot of poems on his desk, weren't there? Liv must have known about the affair for a while, she can't have been that bothered if she let them carry on. Why would she kill him now? Why not kill Miss Macdonald too? There must be more to it.'

'Maybe she was planning how to leave him,' Margery wondered aloud.

'Yes,' Clementine agreed, 'Maybe she was planning to confront him and something went wrong, or she asked Mr Evans to help her.'

'We should go to the PE department and have a look about, maybe?' Margery suggested. 'See if we can find out anything useful?'

'How will you get in there?' Gloria sipped her coffee. 'The school netball team is playing Ittonvale today, so they'll lock it up early.'

'Gosh, maybe another day then,' Margery said, putting the clipboard on top of the chest freezer with a sigh. 'Have the police searched it?'

'They were there a few days ago,' Gloria said. 'I can't imagine they found much if we haven't heard anything about it.'

Margery thought about the cryptic row of numbers that had been graffitied on the school entrance. There was a rap at the door, and they all looked up. Rose leaned against the doorway. Her hair was as perfect as ever, large earrings dangled in front of a neat silver bob and her skirt suit was as pristine as the day she had bought it.

'What have you done to upset Miss Macdonald?' She inspected her fingernails coolly. 'The headmaster sent me.'

Gloria raised her eyebrows at them both.

'Nothing!' Clementine protested. 'We just tried to get a look at her handwriting, but that's perfectly normal, perfectly fine and normal to want to see someone's handwriting, isn't it?'

Rose rolled her eyes. 'Not a single thing you've ever done in your life has been normal, Mrs Butcher-Baker. You're mad as a box of frogs.'

'Well, at least I didn't get disqualified from the harvest festival because I was trying to pass off the pumpkin my gardener grew as my own!' Clementine snapped.

Gloria snorted, nearly spitting out a mouthful of coffee. Rose ignored her.

'Why on earth do you want to see her handwriting?' she asked instead.

'We found a love letter to Mr Weaver,' Margery explained. 'We thought it might have been from Miss Macdonald, so we wanted her handwriting to compare.'

'If I wasn't deputy head then I could have supplied that for you,' Rose said, her eyebrows quirking upwards. 'As deputy head, the best I could do is leave a sample of her marking on my desk.'

'Thanks, but no need, his wife confirmed it anyway,' Clementine finished. Gloria gasped in surprise; Margery and Clementine hadn't gotten around to telling her that little morsel of information yet.

'You know,' Rose said thoughtfully. 'If someone were going to search the PE staff areas...' She took a small ring of keys from the pocket of her jacket and took one off. 'They'd use this key to get into the office inside.'

'How long have you been hanging around outside listening?' Clementine cried in outrage as Margery took the key. 'Creeping around the place like a spider!'

Rose smiled in a knowing way, which confirmed to Margery she had indeed been listening to their conversation in the dry store. She was glad Rose was on their side, the alternative was terrifying.

'See you tomorrow, ladies,' she said, and then she left. They all watched her go, listening to her remind Seren about their autumnal-themed movie night at home in her loudest teacher's voice as she went.

–

Gloria had been right. When they snuck into the cold PE department building the changing rooms were very much locked tight. It was attached to the school by the art department, with its large airy workshop, and teachers could access the entrance from there, but students entered from the outside. Margery realised with a groan that Rose hadn't given them the key to the changing room doors, only the office within. How were they meant to get into the ugly changing rooms?

'You'd think she would've unlocked it for us,' Clementine huffed, folding her arms and glaring at the thick concrete walls as though she might be able to melt them if she scowled hard enough.

'Maybe she doesn't have the key for it?' Margery reasoned.

Clementine huffed again and then walked over to the doors, pulling on them brazenly, the padlock clinking against the door as she struggled with it. She stepped back again, staring upwards at the long windows that ran across the top of the wall. Margery could almost hear her thoughts.

'No, we're not climbing anything,' she said. 'Every time we end up falling off something or getting stuck somewhere.'

'So, what's another time, really?' Clementine said, gesturing to the steep walls of the building. 'Just pop yourself up then, Margery, I'll stand guard.'

They both laughed. Margery folded her arms and joined Clementine in considering the windows.

'There must be another way in,' she muttered to herself. She wondered if they might be better off just going home, surely the police would have already searched anywhere in the school they thought could reveal anything. The conversation with Liv last night had been very strange and Margery wondered whether their efforts might be better placed sat at their kitchen table, going over the conversation again.

'Fire escape!' Clementine said suddenly, Margery jumped at the sound. Clementine was already rushing to the side of the changing rooms where the fire escape door sat flush into the wall. She scrabbled against it madly. 'Oh, this is locked too, Margery.'

'I did think it might be, you can't usually open them from the outside,' Margery said, she scratched her head. 'Come on, let's have another look at the windows and if we can't get in that way then we'll call it a day. We can give the police the key and they can come and do their own dirty work.'

'That goes against the whole point though, doesn't it?' Clementine said, standing back and leaning against the wall to the side of the door.

'Gosh, I wonder if we should have taken this all on. I know you're not right still, even if you don't tell me anything.'

'I'm fine.' Margery joined her as she leaned against the wall of the alley. 'It's just been a strange few months. I'll be all right.'

'Well, I can understand that. It's been odd going back to normal, hasn't it? After the summer,' Clementine said, reaching for her hand. 'But are you sure that's all it is?'

Margery battled with herself, wondering if she should come clean about the flashbacks she was having or the sudden panic that would arrive without notice. But before she could even decide where to begin, the fire door opened quietly, blocking their exit from the side alley. Clementine's hand became a vice around her own for a second and then relaxed as the door swung shut slowly again. They watched Mr Evans skulking away with his gym bag. He hadn't noticed them, and as he disappeared around the corner Margery grabbed the fire door just before it closed. He didn't turn around to see why he hadn't heard the door slam back on its hinges. They waited, their breath misting in the cold afternoon air.

'All right then,' Margery said. 'Problem solved.'

They slid inside through the fire escape door, and it finally swung shut behind them with a soft click. The changing rooms were nothing special, just empty hangers and sad, broken lockers. Judging by the broken elastic hairbands littering the floor, this was the girls' changing room. They crept through, past the showers, and out into the hallway that separated the two changing areas, usually accessed by the main entrance at one end and the art department at the other end of the long hallway. Next to the boys' changing-room door were two others and Margery knew the key Rose had given them must belong to one of them.

Clementine went for the nearest one and tried the handle. It jiggled before the door creaked open, revealing a storage room rammed to the rafters with needless junk. A ladder lay on a bed of deflated footballs, squashed netballs and broken tennis rackets.

'Why does the PE department need a ladder?' Margery wondered aloud.

'To get the footballs off the roof, Margery,' Clementine said earnestly. 'I can't tell you how many Year Sevens I've seen whining about losing theirs on the Food Tech roof.'

Margery wasn't so sure, but they closed the door anyway and decided to try the other room. This time they needed to use the key. The lock turned swiftly with a satisfying click and the door swung open easily, revealing a small and smelly office, the bin of netball bibs lying right by the desk. The room stank dreadfully of artificial strawberries; the bag of protein powder spilling out onto Mr Evans' desk leaving a trail of pink dust.

'Right,' Clementine said. She brought a finger to her lips and kept it there while they looked around. There was not much to see, but perhaps there was something the police hadn't noticed. Mr Evans had a little desk, a very old laptop sat on it, a desk with a set of drawers that looked broken and a bookshelf that contained all sorts of boring physiotherapy books. 'Where should we begin? The computer?'

'I don't think we'll have much luck with that,' Margery said. 'But I suppose we could try?'

Clementine reached over and tapped at the keyboard of the open laptop gingerly.

'It needs a password,' she hissed, her eyes widening. 'Quick, Margery! Before it goes off again!'

'Oh, er.' Margery joined her at the laptop. 'Oh gosh, I'm not sure...'

Clementine tapped at the keys with one finger. 'I'll try P and then, er, E. Yes PE, that's probably. Oh, it hasn't worked!'

'Gosh,' Margery said, wracking her brain for any better ideas. 'Why don't you try physical education?'

Clementine clacked her way over the keyboard slowly with her pointer finger until the computer buzzed at them again. 'Wrong!'

'Oh no,' Margery could feel the panic washing off Clementine and onto herself. 'His birthday?'

'Brilliant, Margery!' Clementine said. 'What is it? I'll type it in?'

'I've no idea.' Margery said. Clementine tapped at the laptop again.

'It's probably April, he looks like he was born then, and at a guess nineteen seventy...five? Oh no wrong again! We've only got one more go!'

Margery looked around the room for the answer, though she wasn't sure it would help. For one, this is exactly what Ceri-Ann had warned them not to do when choosing a password – 'Mate, you've got to pick something random, like eggs, or something like that.' Margery opened the drawers of the desk instead and took out the diary she found.

'Let's look through this,' she hissed to Clementine. 'Forget the computer. We've still got to find Dr Roberts' file for Mr Barrow, haven't we? What if it's in here?'

'We can't forget the computer, that's where the secrets are. What if the file's on there?' Clementine scoffed. 'Wait here.'

Before she knew it, Clementine had left the room. Margery watched her take her phone out of her bag and skulk off somewhere in the hallway as the door squeaked closed. She looked around at the office and at the walls covered in posters featuring athletes and the big wall calendar that Mr Evans had scribbled sporting events onto in permanent marker. There were photos stuck to the walls as well, some of Mr Evans himself. A few of him shaking the hand of a referee while holding a first prize trophy or posing on stage to show off his muscular body to the judges. Several more were of him lifting the sort of weight that would have probably crushed her to death if she had tried to lift it. Margery sighed and flipped the diary open.

It was a large day-to-day year diary with a whole page of space for each date. Most of the entries were quite boring, all considered, but there were a few dotted here and there with pound signs and numbers. More interestingly were what Margery assumed were initials next to the numbers, the most constant being LW, written in ink, over and over again.

The letters were all over the diary, all with numbers next to them each time they were written. Money? It was something to do with money, and sport, judging by the scrawl before the pound signs. There were small events that she recognised, Ittonvale vs Summerview Year Eight football, and larger national ones. She flipped back to the beginning of the diary and began to go through it again, now she knew what she was looking for. The numbers started off low, a fiver here and there, but by September they were in the hundreds. What did it mean? Was Mr Evans running some sort of gambling ring? There were dozens of initials all written in scrawled writing in the margins of the book.

'Come on, Pete, make yourself useful.' Margery hadn't noticed Clementine pushing her way back into the room, followed by the handyman. Margery put the planner into her handbag for later. Surely the police would be interested in it.

'Oh, Ben.' Margery finally noticed the young man who had followed Clementine into the office and then realised her mistake. It was very easy to confuse him for his identical twin, Benjamin, as they all had in the past, but Pete was much better at maintenance than cooking. 'I mean, Pete. How are you? What are you doing?'

'Mrs Butcher-Baker asked if I could help unlock the computer, Mrs Butcher-Baker,' Pete explained with a grin. 'I kept telling her I don't know how to do that.'

'You managed with the headmaster's computer,' Clementine insisted. Margery grimaced at the memory of Pete logging in to Mr Barrow's computer while they hid inside his cupboard.

'Yeah, but I guessed his password, it was just luck.' Pete shrugged, resting his hands on his tool belt. 'What do you want with Mr Evans' computer anyway?'

'We don't know yet,' Clementine said. Pete looked around the little office in interest.

'I've never been in here,' he said. 'I've always wondered what it looked like.'

'Does it live up to your imagination?' Clementine joked.

'I mean, it's quite messy, isn't it?' Pete said. Margery and Clementine nodded agreeably. It really was. 'Hmmm.'

'What?' Clementine asked, following his gaze to the ceiling.

Pete looked up at the suspended ceiling panels. He reached up with ease and tapped the tile just above their heads. It moved.

'I think someone's had this off, you know,' he said, poking it again. 'It's quite loose, it shouldn't really sit like that. I think I'll be able to fix it with my tools...' The tile slipped out of place completely and came crashing down on them.

'Careful, Pete!' Clementine reached down to clean up the mess, grasping at the tile that had fallen to the floor to try and put it back.

Suddenly she recoiled in horror and let go of what she had been holding. It bounced to the floor and landed in between the three of them. Margery's mouth opened of its own accord and they all leapt back. A small gentleman's wash bag landed on the floor, the contents of which had spilled out all over the floor in the fall from the ceiling. Needles and syringes had spilled out everywhere, some used and some not.

Chapter Eleven

Officer Thomas arrived not twenty minutes after they had called him with what they'd found and the entire area had been cordoned off. After their discovery it had seemed likely that the governors might close the school. It was the day before half term began after all, but somehow Mr Barrow had managed to keep it open. When Rose arrived with the headmaster, Margery managed to slip her back the key to the changing rooms without Mr Barrow seeing. Mr Evans had been arrested and taken in for questioning about the needles in his office and Clementine hadn't stopped congratulating herself ever since.

Margery had reminded her that just because Mr Evans had been arrested didn't mean that he would be charged with anything. Yet the police seemed happy enough. Even if he had yet to confess to anything – the DNA would prove his involvement once and for all. It just would take a few days to come back from the lab.

The entire kitchen team were winding down; emptying fridges of anything that wouldn't last a week and deep-cleaning all the equipment. Friday afternoon was always when the stocktake was done anyway, and it had been since the dawn of time, as far as Margery was concerned, though Clementine was always trying to persuade her to skip a week so they could go home early, as former kitchen manager Caroline had often done.

Caroline always tried to count it during the middle of lunch, getting in the way while she individually checked off the sugar sachets, completely disrupting the flow of service. Anyway, Margery liked to do things properly. It would be silly to ruin her good standing now that things were beginning to go well for the kitchen. The headmaster had somehow managed to find more money for catering. Clementine was convinced it was because he was so happy that Margery hadn't died when she'd fallen from a cliff during the summer holidays. Whatever the reason, things were going to be much easier this term now that she had some wiggle room. Clementine always stayed to help her count as there was no point in her going home alone, so they moved in a well-practised dance around the kitchen, its little storeroom and big walk-in fridge and freezer.

Margery still hated going into the freezer to count anything, ever since they had been trapped inside it after Caroline had been murdered. Clementine or Gloria counted the frozen food. This afternoon, however, Clementine was making the job much harder than it needed to be.

'Half a kilo of bacon powder, Margery!' She chuckled to herself in the dry store.

'You mean baking powder?' Margery asked.

'Can't answer, sorry.' Clementine popped her head around the storeroom doorway, waving her hands at Margery. Dried herbs dropped all over the floor. 'I've got too much thyme on my hands.'

'That doesn't even make sense!' Margery groaned, almost throwing the clipboard down in frustration. 'Can we just get on with it, Clem? We spend enough time here as it is.'

'Sorry!' Clementine disappeared again. Margery went back to counting the teabags. For a moment there was silence.

'Margery, there's a leak in the sink!' Clementine yelled from out in the main kitchen. Margery immediately dropped everything and rushed out of the dry store to where Clementine was gesturing at the stainless-steel sink under the kitchen window.

'Oh gosh, Clem, shall I get the mop bucket?' Margery gasped as she hurried over to her, the she stopped dead in her tracks and glared at Clementine's smirking face when she got close enough to see the bunch of leeks in their string bag sat at the bottom of the metal sink.

'What's the date, Clem?' Margery ignored the bag of vegetables and turned back to the stocktake pages on the clipboard, determined to ignore the stupid jokes and get on with it.

'We've been writing it on the food safety paperwork all day, how could you forget?' Clementine smiled at her. 'It's the twenty-seventh though.'

Margery wrote the date at the top of the page and then began to rummage through the spice containers to check their levels. Clementine stood and watched her awkwardly for a moment before picking up the string bag to put it back in the vegetable fridge.

—

It was gone five by the time they had counted the stock and pulled on their coats, the kitchen windows showing nothing but the pitch-black darkness. The clocks had gone back on the Sunday just gone and they had only just managed to stop Ceri-Ann singing '2 Become 1' by the Spice Girls as a result. Margery couldn't help but be annoyed by Clementine's joking around with the stock-take. Now they would have to get the later bus or walk home, and the weather had grown considerably cooler in the past few weeks. The only silver lining was that Mr Weaver's murderer was in custody and they wouldn't need to be fearful on the walk home. She pulled her coat around her in the changing room, readying herself for the cold evening air. Clementine smiled at her in apology, a bag of cake mix that would expire during the break resting at her feet.

'Sorry, Margery,' she said, taking her hand. 'I was just trying to lighten the mood, after all that in the summer and Mr Weaver and Mr Evans.'

'I know,' Margery said, running a finger over the wedding ring on Clementine's left hand. 'Shall we go? We can open that bottle of red when we get in, I'll cook the seabass that's in the freezer.'

'Pumpkin and Crinkles will love you,' Clementine smiled, picking up the carrier bag. The handles stretched horribly under the weight of the heavy dry powders. 'Yes, let's. If we rush, we can make the half past five bus after we drop off the paperwork, and get back in time to watch an episode of that crime documentary we've been watching on the Netflix before dinner!'

'I think we've had enough crime for a while!' Margery chuckled. 'Come on then.'

She opened the changing-room door, and they made their way down the school hallway towards the head-master's office. Everyone else had already left, clearly desperate to get away for the break. There wasn't even a cleaner around, all the hoovering and tidying had already been done. Margery had seen the cleaning team, Louise and Gosia, rushing through it all much earlier in the day. Margery didn't like to be at the school after hours if they could help it. The hallways were too long and looming and she didn't like the way the empty classrooms seemed to be both devoid of life and full of shadows.

'Where do you think Seren is going?' Clementine asked her as they walked, marching at a good pace down the hallway. One mystery solved and straight on to the next, Margery thought to herself wryly. 'Obviously, I'm enjoying Rose's annoyance, but it is a bit weird for Seren to disappear like that. It's not like her, well, not any more anyway, after all that with the cheese they thought she stole last year. She doesn't have anything to lie about now.'

'No,' Margery said. 'It's not. I thought she and Rose were glued at the hip.'

They hurried as fast as they could down the last bit of the corridor, until they reached Mr Barrow's office door. Margery quickly put the paperwork on his desk, glad to rid of it, and began to turn when there was an almighty crash.

'What did you break?' she hissed at Clementine, though she didn't know why she was whispering. Clementine was standing by the door, and Margery realised with horror that she was not next to anything that could have possibly fallen or split or smashed or dropped. In fact, Clementine looked surprised.

'Maybe it's Gary?' Clementine said, looking at the half-closed door they had just entered through. Margery nodded, more as a wish than in agreement. 'But doesn't he finish earlier on a Friday now?'

'Yes,' Margery said, looking around nervously. 'They couldn't afford to keep paying his overtime so now he doesn't do any.'

'An SLT meeting?'

'The next one's not till after the holiday week.' Margery remembered Mrs George being particularly annoyed by having to hand in the form and giving her a long spiel about the benefits of joining the staff intranet again.

There was another crash, and they both whipped their heads around to stare at the door again. Margery felt her face contort into a frown. 'Should we hide?' she asked aloud.

'Maybe?' Clementine said, twisting her hands together. 'Or it might be nothing.'

'Or it might be nothing,' Margery repeated. The school was old enough to have its own quirks and creaks. It could just be the sound from a classroom door that had been left open, or perhaps a teacher on their way out for the break. Though usually, they would have seen someone on their way to the office. To get through to the main entrance, you had to swipe out using your swipe card now. She grasped for her pass on the lanyard around her neck and held it tightly for a moment.

'Oh, sod it,' she said finally, letting the lanyard fall back beneath her coat. 'Let's just go, what's the worst that could happen?'

'Margery!' Clementine said, looking as though she did not know whether to admonish her or cheer on her new-found bravery. 'What could go wrong? We found a body about three feet away from the school playground, remember?'

'It was a good twenty-minute walk from the school, and they're questioning Mr Evans, aren't they?' Margery reminded her. She could feel indignation rising in her throat. It was an unusual feeling; she was so used to going along with whatever idea Clementine came up with.

'I just don't believe that's all there is to it, Margery,' Clementine said stubbornly. 'It seems much too simple. One argument, and you kill a man?'

'You've been the one celebrating that he's been caught!' Margery exclaimed. 'Now you don't think he did it?'

Clementine looked suitably aggrieved. 'I do, but what if he and Liv were in cahoots? Wouldn't she get an insurance pay-out if her husband died?'

'Well, we can't stay in here all night.' Margery gestured around the little office. 'What are we going to do? Sleep under the headmaster's desk?'

'It's half term, it's Halloween in a minute,' Clementine hissed. 'What about the strange graffiti? That was at the school, what if they come back!'

'But Officer Thomas said they were going to have more police on watch, didn't he?' Margery said, trying to sound much less frightened than she was.

'Well, where are they then?'

'Maybe that's them crashing about now,' Margery said. 'Anyway, they're still trying to work out what all those numbers meant, what if they meant something all together? I doubt it would have anything to do with the school, and even if it did there's nothing to suggest today.'

'That's a point,' Clementine said with a sigh that told Margery that she felt it was more of a knife.

The first time she'd snapped at Clementine she had expected nuclear fallout. Instead, Clementine had laughed in surprise and then cheerily got on with whatever it was Margery had asked her to do. In some ways, she wished she had started standing up for herself years ago.

'Maybe you're right. Maybe they're doing a round, or whatever it's called.'

'Maybe?' Margery said. In truth she wanted nothing more than to leave the room, it was becoming claustrophobic with its small window and shut door. 'Come on, let's just get to the bus stop, we're not far from the entrance here anyway. Gosh, I wish we'd brought the car.'

Clementine still didn't seem convinced. She blew out a breath, her white fringe fanning into the air for a second before returning to her forehead. 'All right.'

They peeped their heads out through the headmaster's doorway, the door creaking under their weight. The hallways of the school were shrouded in darkness, no sounds except the complaints of the door they were leaning against. Margery wondered if she wouldn't rather stay in the office, the journey to the reception seemed to stretch on for miles from here, they could just about see the strip light that lit it at the end of the hallway to their right.

'Coast is clear,' Clementine hissed. 'Come on.'

She scuttled away from the doorframe and began to rush down the dark hallway as fast as she could, laden under the carrier bag of kitchen goods. Margery followed behind her just as clumsily, her handbag swinging and hitting the wall as she dashed along, propelled by her fear. She wasn't sure that the hallways, with their worn carpets and faded paint, were really any better prospect than the office now they were out in them. They were exposed out here in the open space. Her well-worn kitchen shoes were not the best for running and she could feel them catching on every piece of uneven carpet.

They quickly marched all the way down to the wooden set of doors that led to the main entrance, the glass throwing shapes as the artificial light streamed through it. Clementine had stopped dead with her free hand on the wooden bar, her face a horrible ash colour, her eyes wide. Margery watched the light glint in them for a half second before she turned to see what she was staring at, realising instantly that unless the police officers had recently changed their uniform dramatically, that there was no police watch taking place.

Through the glass was a group of people standing together in silence. Margery's brain struggled for a moment before she realised that they were all wearing the same thing. A black cloak tied tightly at the neck that concealed whatever was underneath, and a white mask over their face, the hood of the cloak pulled around it to cover any hairstyle. She had seen that very mask in the window of the stationery shop in the town centre, a cheap papier-mâché sort of thing. It was the sort that children stuck glitter glue and feathers on and painted for art classes. Without colour there was something miserable about them, even frightening. She counted five of them as they turned to stare blankly at her, no sign of movement through the eye holes or mouth. If the figures had not been different heights, you could have convinced yourself very easily that they were clones or ghosts, or some other awful and fantastical entity. The closest to the door strode to it, the bottom of the cloak skimming the floor and making the figure appear to float towards them. Margery found herself holding her breath.

'Run,' Clementine whispered. Margery didn't need to be told twice.

Chapter Twelve

They rushed through the corridors and flung themselves down hallways, barrelling away from the masked strangers as quickly as they could, but it was no use. Margery's bad leg was still weak, she could feel the power going out of it the further they tried to go. Her breath came in shallow bursts, her lungs burned, and the bones in her leg ached so much she found herself stumbling. Clementine was not faring much better. Margery could hear her frantic breathing, the wheezing coming much too thickly. Her shoes were even worse than before, betraying her as they almost tripped her, and she stumbled along, willing herself to keep up with Clementine. If they could get to the doors that adjoined the school building with the steps that led into Dewstow leisure centre reception, they would be safe.

She turned her head and caught a glimpse of them as she and Clementine rounded a corner, they were still following and with ease, the black fabric billowing behind them, all still masked. They weren't even running, just swooping along, as though this was a game. Their feet stomping on the thin carpet as Margery and Clementine struggled along in their kitchen shoes. Margery's weak leg trailed behind the other, forcing her to drag it down the hallway, able to ignore the pain for a moment with sheer adrenaline.

She could almost feel the cloaks as they whipped around the corner seconds behind them, the breeze they caused blowing at her hair. They miraculously reached the end of the hallway, the doors that led to the leisure centre and to safety. Finally, marvellously, she reached her arms out to push them open and enter the safe haven of the reception. Clementine got there first.

She slammed into the door and fought with it for a moment. It was locked from the other side, shut for the evening, Margery felt the panic rise in her throat. The latch rattled as Clementine clawed at it. Her shopping bag forgotten on the floor by her feet. Margery reached the door and leaned her whole weight on it, for a moment feeling as though their combined efforts might cause the door to suddenly give way. But to no avail. They were trapped. She turned to face the strangers, who had caught up to them with ease.

Clementine began to wheeze again, scrabbling in her pockets for her inhaler. Margery turned to her desperately as she found it. The strangers began to advance again, slower this time, no need to rush now they had cornered them. Margery held her breath, rooted to the spot. She couldn't have moved if she had wanted to. The tallest of the group stepped forward, Margery tried to stare into the eye holes of the mask. They were breathing heavily underneath the mask. Before anyone could say or do anything Clementine took the matter into her own hands.

'Get away from her!' she cried, picking up her shopping bag and waving her arms at the figure, who recoiled in surprise and toppled backwards as plumes of powder entered the air, coating everything in a fine mist of dust.

They strangers bolted, covering their masked faces with their cloaks, all bravado gone as the one who had fallen tried to drag himself back up, the bottom of the costume riding up to reveal ugly black plimsol trainers underneath. Clementine continued to pelt them with the cake mix from the shopping bag until they had all scarpered back the way they had followed them, the air thick and sweet with powdered sugar.

Clementine took her inhaler from her pocket again, the dust in the air not helping her situation. Margery leaned back against the door to support her leg, taking the weight off it and feeling the relief that brought.

'What on earth?' she whispered to herself. 'What just happened?'

'Who were they?' Clementine puffed, slumping down on the floor, still holding the box of cake mix. She was as covered in it as the strangers had been, it coated her arms and cardigan in a thin mix of powder. 'Oh, Margery, I won't get to make that chocolate sponge cake now!'

'We need to call the police.' Margery said. 'We should have done that when we heard that noise.' Clementine reached for her phone, pulling it out of her pocket with aplomb and dialled the number. She held a very brief conversation with Officer Thomas as Margery tried to focus on anything but the pain in her leg. She reached down to touch her shin, to try and massage the pain out of it. It didn't work, but she put her weight back on it anyway, wincing as she did.

'He's on his way.' Clementine hung up the phone and put it back in her bag. Her eyes were drawn along the hallway.

'Look,' Clementine said, pointing at the ground in front of them with flour-coated hands. 'Footsteps.'

The dry cake mix had left footprints all over the carpet as the strangers escaped. Like the rest of their costume,

Margery could see with ease that they were all wearing the same shoes. Maybe the imprints could help the police find the culprits. Clementine stood again, wiping herself down. She took a step forward and Margery grasped for her arm gently to stop her.

'We'll have to stay here,' she warned her. 'Or we might ruin the trail.'

'If we follow it now, then we might be able to see where they've gone,' Clementine said. 'Maybe even catch them leaving.'

Margery thought about it, Clementine had a point. Maybe one of them would take off the cake mix–covered cloak and they would see who it was underneath the mask.

'Okay,' she said finally, her curiosity getting the better of her. Clementine helped her stand upright and together they picked their way along the corridor, following the smashed-up powder as they went. The further they followed, the cooler the trail became, but it was soon clear where it was taking them. They stood outside the door, gaping at it in disbelief. Number forty-six, the same number that had been scrawled on the reception door. Stranger than that, worse still, was that classroom forty-six had been Mr Weaver's own maths classroom.

Clementine reached out with tentative fingers and pressed the tips of them to the door. It swung open, creaking on its hinges and slowly revealing the classroom inside. Margery held her breath expecting all sorts of horrors to be revealed, that any second now they would have to run again. She closed her eyes and was trans-ported back to the cliff top in the summer, she forced herself to exhale. The classroom was empty, boringly mundane as always, except for the powder leading to the open window and covering the windowsill in streaks.

Clementine marched forwards, putting her hands on the frame and leaning out as far as she could without plummeting through to the outside.

'The rain washed it all away,' she said, her voice rising in distress as she looked out over the playground. Margery heard the door open across the hall from the classroom they were in and turned to find the police and Mr Barrow coming towards her.

—

'This is bad,' Mr Barrow said, his head in his hands at his desk. 'Very, very bad.'

'Yes,' Officer Symon replied, he looked nervous. Much more nervous than Margery had ever seen, his hands held the notebook open, but he had barely written anything.

'Can you tell me what on earth is wrong with your police force?' Mr Barrow spat, his anger arriving suddenly, at high speed, like a train clattering through the station unexpectedly. Officer Symon recoiled under the headmaster's fury, hiding behind the notebook.

'No, really!' Mr Barrow continued. 'Why have you left my school at risk again?'

'We made an arrest, so we didn't... we needed to—' Officer Symon began. Mr Barrow didn't let him finish.

'I am dealing with governors and parents who are out for blood, quite rightfully too, and you can't even get a proper security watch in place?' Mr Barrow glared at them both. 'Sort it out!'

Margery and Clementine didn't say anything. They didn't need to. There was a good chance that if all this carried on then the school would indeed be shut down until it was all sorted out. Margery didn't want to think about what that would mean. Selfishly, she wondered where they would work. The next nearest school was all the way in Ittonvale and they had their own full kitchen team already. She and Clementine would be forced into retirement and the other dinner ladies would have to get new jobs. Even if the kitchen reopened eventually and they could retire and then return, it would never be the same. Anyway, she wasn't ready to retire. Wasn't ready to have lots of time to think about what had happened over the summer holidays and the life fading from Thomas's face.

'Are you okay, Margery?' Mr Barrow had turned from the chastised police officer and was eyeing her, a concerned look on his brow. 'You're looking quite pale.'

'I'm fine,' she squeaked, taking her hand off her aching leg. 'Just a bit shocked.'

She was saved from any further explanation by the return of Officer Thomas, who had been securing the scene with the rest of Dewstow's small police team and the bigger team who had arrived unexpectedly from Itton-vale. Sergeant's orders, apparently. Officer Thomas hadn't even pretended to look happy on their arrival, instead, he had shooed Margery, Clementine and the headmaster away so he could introduce them to the new crime scene in classroom forty-six. Mr Barrow had not taken this ushering well, and he had fallen into a solemn mood that Margery and Clementine had not known how to fix.

'They spray-painted over the security cameras,' Officer Thomas explained, almost apologetically as he entered the room. 'Your man in the office had already gone home.'

'Gary,' Mr Barrow sighed. 'What have you found out? Any DNA, or whatever you're trying to find? For God's sake, you must have got something?'

Officer Thomas suddenly looked very tired. Margery wondered if he was counting down the days to his retirement. Mr Barrow looked as though he wished he had had his rant when Officer Thomas had been there too.

'We've got some material from the cloaks and both Mrs Butcher-Bakers' descriptions match the CCTV from the previous incident here,' he said. 'And well, I'd be interested to see your school uniform spec, if you have it.'

Mr Barrow looked puzzled for a moment but then jumped up from his faux-leather chair, the cufflinks on his shirt sleeves glinting in the light, and rushed to his cupboard. 'Of course.' He rummaged inside for a minute and returned with a red folder.

'Here,' he said, handing a sheet of paper to Officer Thomas. 'This year's and last year's price sheet. The parents send the money in during the summer and then we buy in bulk ready for September.'

Officer Thomas took it and considered it. 'Do you have a sample of any of this uniform, by any chance?'

'Why?' Clementine asked from where they had remained seated in the plush visitor's chairs. 'What is it?'

'The footprints you so cleverly managed to acquire,' Officer Thomas explained, 'all seem to me to be from the same type of shoe. I'm wondering what type of shoe.'

'We noticed that,' Clementine said.

'What if it's a school-issue shoe?' Margery suggested, she had been thinking it over since they had followed the footprints.

'Yes, it could well be,' Officer Thomas said, considering the page again.

'From the PE department!' Clementine cried.

'Certainly, could be,' Officer Thomas said softly.

'What about the masks?' Clementine asked him. 'Did you find out where they were from?'

Officer Thomas shook his head. 'The shop on the high street hasn't sold any for months, though they could have bought them online, for all we know.'

The thought hit Margery suddenly as the memory of the conversation came rushing back.

'Rose said that Mr Knight was complaining about his supplies going missing a few days ago,' she said, everyone turned to look at her in confusion. 'The art teacher.'

'She did!' Clementine gasped. 'You don't think?'

'I do! I think the masks were taken from his room. Could you ask him about it, Mr Barrow?'

'He'll have already left for the half-term break,' Mr Barrow said, picking up his mobile phone, 'but I'll give him a ring and find out.'

'How many people are involved in this?' Margery said, suddenly realising with horror that Mr Evans may have had a lot of helpers, all of the students. Would students really help a teacher kill another teacher? It seemed too horrible to be true.

'It's the twenty-seventh today,' Clementine reminded Margery, 'and Mr Weaver's classroom was number forty-six.'

'Just like the numbers on the wall,' Margery grimaced. 'Forty-six, twenty-seven, ten. Classroom forty-seven, the twenty-seventh of October.'

Chapter Thirteen

Margery had never been so grateful for a half-term break. She assumed that as soon as they were away from the school for a few days everything would be much better, but she was wrong. The dread welled up in her, and she couldn't get it to stop. She couldn't for the life of her work out why she felt that way either. She supposed it might be that although Mr Evans was still being questioned, nothing had been proven yet and there were still terrible things happening. If anything, their mere presence in the investigation was making everything worse. They had not caught the strangers wandering the hallways. They had let them escape, believing that the police would be able to easily catch them. And to cap it all off, her leg was not doing well since she had overexerted it.

Margery sometimes regretted ever agreeing to any of it, Officer Thomas's retirement be damned. She was sure Clementine felt the same, though they didn't speak of it. They didn't need to. They sat at the kitchen table on Saturday evening and poured over the facts when they would usually watch the television in the living room. Had the strangers simply decided that school-issue plimsols would go with their already matching costumes? If the strangers were indeed students, whose students were they and what were they doing? Were they Mr Evans' PE students, doing something for Mr Evans in Mr Weaver's classroom? Trying to get back his gambling money? Mr Weaver hadn't kept anything of the sort in his room though; the police would have found it by now. Why would Mr Evans have killed him anyway? Surely it wasn't just because of the money. Margery couldn't get her head around it. She kept picturing the initials in Mr Evans's notebook. LW, Liam Weaver.

Eventually, they decided to enjoy the break instead of worrying. On Sunday morning, after an enormous amount of bumbling around finding shoes and coats, they finally left the house and drove the car into Dewstow town centre, parking in the little car park at the top of the steep high street. They were still early, many shops wouldn't even have opened yet, but they liked to be up and about before the hustle and bustle could begin.

Rising house prices in Ittonvale had forced a lot of the locals to settle in Dewstow and both foot and car traffic had tripled in the last few years, but Dewstow was a lovely town, all be told. Margery didn't regret that they chose to buy a house here all those years ago, and she didn't begrudge anyone else who wanted to live here either – the more the merrier – but it did mean arriving a bit earlier to find a parking space. The town was close enough to Ittonvale to have a bit of life in it, but near enough to the countryside and its unspoiled views to feel like they lived rurally, even if that was not quite the case. Aside from the traffic the only other problem with it, Margery thought, was that the entire place was built on a maddeningly steep hill, and you always seemed to need to walk up it to get anywhere, regardless of where you started your journey. Summerview Secondary sat at the very top on the very nice Summerview housing estate, where Margery and Clementine couldn't have afforded a house in a million years. Running down to the bottom of the hill was the high street, with its double row of quaint shops and cafes, which Margery and Clementine had spent many a lovely hour in, and the riverbank, which swirled around the town like a protective arch.

'Remind me to get Dawn something at the florist to thank her for getting us sympathy flowers when Mr Weaver died,' Margery said, as she put the pay and display ticket on the car windscreen.

Clementine looked appalled. 'You can't buy flowers for flowers, Margery, where does it end?' she said, shaking her head. 'We'll end up in a never-ending cycle of gift-giving. No, we'll just try and keep Crinkles from digging up her flower bed again. That'll be present enough. And make her another cake with the apples she keeps dumping on us.'

'I'm so sick of apples,' Margery groaned. 'I think I might become an apple if I eat another one.'

'I just don't think there's any more recipes to make,' Clementine said sadly. 'I've looked through every Delia Smith book we own, and we've done them all. Do you think Dawn would notice if we just chucked them in the food waste?'

'Maybe we can get another recipe book in the charity shop,' Margery suggested. 'Come on.'

They left the car park and began to walk arm in arm down the high street, enjoying the fresh autumn breeze and the golden leaves strewn everywhere. Something felt off today though. Margery couldn't tell what it was, but she could sense it in the air. A crowd was gathered down at the very bottom of the long street, and before she had time to so much as wonder aloud why they were there, a police car pulled up. If Margery squinted, she was sure she could see Officer Thomas getting out of one side and Officer Symon the other.

'What on earth?' Clementine said, in a bemused voice. Margery shook her head, looking on at the scene.

Clementine let go of her arm and they began to march down toward the cacophonous crowd. As they walked, Margery wondered if they should be heading in the opposite direction, back to the car, away from whatever was happening, but she found herself drawn to the noise anyway. As they arrived closer, they saw what the trouble was. The strange symbol that had been written on the tree and in front of Mr Weaver's body hidden in the leaves, and at the school and at the pub, was written here too. In the town centre, on the glass frontage of all the shops, the same spray-painted lettering. Streaks of green paint ran down from the 'V' shape with a cross through it, like an upside-down letter 'A', dripping with blood. Exactly as it had been everywhere else. There was another string of numbers stencilled below it that read, 2, 3, 3, 1, 1, 0. They stared at it, a heavy feeling settling in Margery's stomach, dread at the symbol, dread at the numbers. Mrs Mugg-lethwaite noticed them and peeled herself away from the crowd.

'Hello, ladies,' she said, as well made-up as ever in her huge faux-fur winter coat, her sunglasses perched on her head. 'Nightmare, isn't it? Look at the state of the shop windows!'

Margery watched as Mr Fitzgerald, the owner of the antique store, scrubbed at the writing on the glass with a sponge and soapy water, his dog Jason on his lead next to him supervising. Mr Fitzgerald's long arms flailed about like spider legs as he balanced precariously on the stepladder and tried to wash the windows with the sponge.

All the other shopkeepers were doing the same, Margery felt terrible for them. All this mess to clear up, when times were hard enough for business owners on the high street nowadays. She looked over to Clementine who had gone very pale.

'Oh God,' Clementine whispered. 'What does it mean? Is it another date?'

'I don't know.' Mrs Mugglethwaite folded her arms, seemingly oblivious to their shock. 'But it's not on. Hoodlums, I bet. I'd put money on it being a group of children from the school.'

'How would anyone do that without being noticed?' Margery wondered aloud, interrupting Clementine's muttering. 'Surely there must be CCTV?'

'Mr Fitzgerald said he has CCTV,' Mrs Mugglethwaite pointed to the ancient camera hanging above the antique shop's front. 'He's going to give it to the police. He said it wasn't good footage though. In that case, he needs to buy a better camera.'

Margery sighed while Clementine nodded in agreement. She wished the whole town would invest in better recording systems; the school could certainly have used a much clearer one last Christmas. As it was, they had only solved Mrs Large's murder by the skin of their teeth. She watched the police officers interviewing people and wondered how much worse it could all get. The answer arrived quickly as the same group of Year Elevens that had been plaguing them with their TikTok accounts and podcast demands appeared. Margery had completely forgotten that they'd agreed to do the podcast, she hoped that they might have forgotten too.

'Hello, miss!' Number One waved at them, but didn't come over. Margery breathed a sigh of relief as they all began recording the scene on their phones instead.

Margery and Clementine watched the commotion in the street begin to fade while the police finished interviewing people. Mr Fitzgerald staggered over, Jason in his arms.

'Did you see those numbers, ladies?' he asked them both. 'Ever so strange, isn't it?'

'It is,' Margery agreed as Clementine nodded so vigorously that her fringe nodded too. 'We think they're dates, so that must mean Halloween. You don't think that twenty-three could be another classroom?'

Mr Fitzgerald looked back to the faded numbers in alarm. 'I did hear about what happened to you at the school the other evening. Terrible shame no one was caught. The next governors' meeting has been moved forward, completely thrown my weekend out but what can you do?'

'Do you think the school will stay open?' Margery asked, having forgotten Mr Fitzgerald's thumb was in many pies – both on the town council and the board of governors.

'I really couldn't tell you,' Mr Fitzgerald said, his face falling.

Chapter Fourteen

Clementine had dragged Margery to the doctor's surgery first thing on Monday morning. The doctor had insisted she return to the walking stick to support her leg. Unfortunately for Margery, as Clementine had accompanied her to the appointment, she hadn't found a way to get out of taking the advice.

Clementine drove them to the farm. When Gloria had called to invite them that morning, they had decided it was just the thing to blow the cobwebs away, or at the very least entertain them for long enough to forget the last few weeks. That was the hope anyway, but Margery was struggling. The doctor had also ordered Margery to have a break from driving. She had reluctantly given Clementine the keys and off they had driven to meet Ceri-Ann and Gloria. Margery had hoped that driving would be enough of a distraction to replace the argument that they had been having since they left the doctor's surgery, but Clementine didn't have any plans to let it go.

'I'm only saying,' Clementine began again for the third time that morning, 'some counselling might be a good idea. I asked for some recommendations on the Dewstow Facebook community page and there's this one that sounds—'

'No, I don't need counselling,' Margery snapped instinctively, regretting her outburst as soon as it was over. 'I'm fine, Clem.'

'Not just for you,' Clementine explained, 'I think I could probably use some too. It was terrifying watching you fall and then when you were in hospital... Well, I thought you were going to die.'

'But I didn't,' Margery said. She turned away from Clementine and looked out of the window at the world going past, folding her arms tightly across her chest. They weren't far from Dewstow, only a ten-minute drive, but it was like stepping foot into the countryside.

'But you nearly did,' Clementine mumbled. Margery decided not to say anything more about it as they arrived at their destination. The leaves crackled under their feet as they wandered across the makeshift car park. Itton farm was packed. Margery hadn't known what she'd expected, but it was teeming with children and parents. She felt a bit silly for a moment for not having brought a child until she saw Ceri-Ann and Gloria waving her over. Gloria's children waved excitedly, and Margery waved back enthusiastically with the arm not leaning heavily on the walking stick.

'Mrs Butcher-Baker! There are pumpkins!' The youngest of the children screeched before they both ran off to join the screaming hordes of other children in the play area.

'Bloody hell,' Ceri-Ann said, looking around wide-eyed at the carnage. 'If I'd known this was my future, I would have been more careful with contraception. You all right, Margery? Clem?' She eyed Margery's walking stick for a second but didn't comment on it, instead giving them both a smile.

'All good, thank you,' Margery smiled back at Ceri-Ann, who always somehow managed to make her feel better with her youthful aura. 'Are you having a nice half-term?'

'Be better once we get some mulled cider!' Ceri-Ann said, then her face fell. 'Oh no, I can't have that, can I?'

'You can have a nice glass of apple juice,' Gloria suggested instead, taking Ceri-Ann by the arm. 'Come on. Let's go in.'

They continued chatting as they made their way through to the farm, where fields littered with pumpkins and haybales came into view.

'Christ,' Gloria said, looking around the bustling fields of people trampling all over the pumpkin patches. 'The website said hedge maze, that's just a few twigs.'

'I don't like the look of that scarecrow,' Margery agreed. 'It looks like it might fall down any minute.'

'I think Elle might fall down any minute,' Gloria said, pointing over to where Miss Macdonald was standing, across the other side of the pumpkin patch. It was obvious to Margery's eyes that she had had a glass or four of something mulled. Though, in all honesty, most of the English department in attendance looked two drinks away from having to be escorted from the site, which was not unusual in itself, though not normally this early of an afternoon. 'I'll go and get us something. Is coffee all right?'

Gloria and Ceri-Ann wandered off to the van that was selling hot drinks, leaving Margery and Clementine to take a seat on the nearest free haybales.

'Gosh, this is quite American, isn't it?' Clementine gestured at the photo opportunity set up with the professional photographer. 'Very posh for Ittonvale.'

'Yes,' Margery agreed. 'Remember when we came here for that wedding? It was just mud.'

The day had been very wet. As they had sat down for the wedding breakfast, a river of mud had poured through into the marque as the father of the bride began his speech. Clementine smiled, but it was wiped away as her GPS key fob began to scream.

'For heaven's sake!' Clementine groaned, pulling her key chain out of her bag and glaring at the offending keyring. 'It's impossible to even forget not to lose my keys with this thing around.'

'You know, I think we've probably spent just as much in batteries for it as we were in new keys.' Margery smiled in relief at the distraction. 'What's wrong with it now?'

'Just the battery again.' Clementine rummaged in her back for the spare pack of batteries. 'These are supposed to be the best batteries Tesco do!'

'Crikey,' a loud voice came from behind them as Clementine tried to wrestle the back off the key fob while it screamed. 'Elle looks worse for wear, doesn't she?'

Dr Roberts stood to the side of them, holding a steaming paper cup of coffee and smirking a little at Miss Macdonald. Margery hadn't even heard her stroll over to them in all the commotion. Margery felt a sudden well of sympathy for the poor woman as she watched her stagger, helped along by Mr Coxley and Mrs George, who were sloshing their own cardboard takeaway cups of cider as they supported her. In comparison, Dr Roberts looked like she might be able to win a best-dressed contest, in her pristine jeans, tall boots and woollen poncho combination. Her hair was tucked away in a perfect brunette plait that could rival even Gloria's.

'I expect I'll end up having to take some of them home.' Dr Roberts shook her head. 'I'm not sure how many I'll be able to squish into my car though. Maybe I'll just go and hide somewhere so they don't see me!'

Margery and Clementine both chuckled, Margery imagining Dr Roberts, in her smart clothes, ducking down behind a mud-covered haybale.

'Sorry,' Dr Roberts said, her face wincing into an apologetic smile, 'I didn't mean anything by that. I just get a bit sick of all the school get-togethers out of work, sometimes there's not even a second to catch your breath.'

Margery could commiserate with that, even if she didn't quite agree with the sentiment. She quite enjoyed their little team's holiday get-togethers.

'Who are you here with?' Clementine asked, finally managing to force the new battery into the key fob and close it again with a click.

'My husband and children are over there somewhere.' Dr Roberts gave a dismissive wave of her hand across at the field. 'We had a photo taken and now I'm at a bit of a loose end really. I can't even eat any of the sugary crap they're selling if I don't want to have a hyper.'

'Well, I suppose the farm's a bit of a break after what happened to Mr Weaver,' Margery said, watching Mrs Mugglethwaite pushing her dog across the field in its pram.

'Yes, and worrying about whether the school will reopen after half term,' Dr Roberts said, with a sigh. She looked as concerned as Mr Barrow had the other day. 'I'll be amazed if we all keep our jobs after. I can't imagine Ofsted will let this all go on for much longer. I read about you being chased, in the paper,' she said in explanation. 'You really didn't see who they were?'

Margery and Clementine both shook their heads. Margery sighed, thinking of how it was just their luck that the paper had managed to catch wind of their failure and print it twice as fast as they would normally manage to. They sat and watched Miss Macdonald being plonked down on a haybale by Mr Coxley who tripped over it and ended up on the ground too.

'You'd think the school would sort out their CCTV, once and for all.' Dr Roberts sucked her teeth. The sound made Margery wince. 'Though I suppose they don't really need to bother now, the horse has bolted, hasn't it? They ought to be preventing any more deaths.'

Margery couldn't help but agree with her. It would really help the schoolboard to put a plan in place to prevent any further deaths occurring. Three in as few years was too many. Even Clementine nodded in agreement with Dr Roberts, who she had never really liked since the third time Dr Roberts had insisted she'd forgotten her debit card and needed another free lunch. Margery suddenly remembered seeing Dr Roberts in the school hall the day before Mr Weaver died.

'Did you see what Mr Evans and Mr Weaver were arguing about?' Margery asked her, watching Dr Roberts' face fall at the mention of Mr Weaver. 'The day before he died?'

Dr Roberts leaned closer and lowered her voice to a conspiratorial whisper. 'Liam loved to gamble; he always has done, of course. I've known him since uni, but I think it's got much, much worse in the last few years. Liv and Liam, well, they were about to get divorced, they'd put the house up for sale.' She looked around to see if anyone was listening to their conversation before continuing, 'I'm sure that's why Mark has been arrested, his little gambling ring. You mark my words.'

She smiled a little at her own joke, Margery grimaced back. Mr Evans' arrest was public knowledge, of course, but the police had somehow managed to keep the reason out of the local press. Dr Roberts couldn't have known how close she was to the truth.

'Well, I suppose it could be,' Margery said, unsure what else to say. 'You say you went to university with Liam, were you close?'

'Quite close.' Dr Roberts had lowered her voice. Realising she was whispering, she straightened up, her voice rising as she did so. 'We shared a flat with friends during our third year. Horrible what happened. He didn't deserve to go out like that, bless him.'

Margery and Clementine nodded in agreement. It was certainly a horrible thing.

'If I were the police,' Dr Roberts continued, ignoring Margery and Clementine's discomfort. 'I'd be looking into Liam's life insurance policy, I bet anything he had one, and the papers certainly seem to think he was murdered, don't they?'

'You can't possibly mean that,' Clementine said in outrage. 'You can't think Mrs Weaver killed her husband? Just for money?'

Margery wondered what she would tell them next, but Gloria and Ceri-Ann had finally made their way back from the van, their arms laden with coffees and iced biscuits shaped like pumpkins. Dr Roberts smiled in acknowledgement and then excused herself to go and find her husband. Margery and Clementine watched her go in bemusement.

Officer Thomas met them at home. He always looked out of place sitting in their living room, and so did Symon. They hadn't found any more clues to help with finding the masked strangers, but they had confirmed with Mr Knight that some of the missing items from his art room were indeed white masks, green spray paint, among other bits and bobs. That hadn't settled her mind at all. In fact, it had made everything even more worrisome.

'Well, what are you going to do about it?' Margery asked. 'Surely twenty-three must be another classroom.'

Officer Thomas looked unsettled for a moment. 'Yes, we're putting a full watch on for Halloween. Dewstow and Ittonvale's full police force will be there. I think we've got a good chance of catching them this time.'

'Why are they meeting again?' Margery mused out loud. It was so soon after they had nearly been caught, what could the masked strangers be up to next? She could hardly bear to think about it.

'When will we be getting our bulletproof vests?' Clementine asked as she brought in the tea things. 'Only I'll probably need a size large after all the Halloween sweets. Rose had a toffee apple-making station and a popcorn dispenser last year.'

'Everyone else was too scared to eat because she'd turned her entire first floor into a haunted house,' Margery said, chuckling at the memory of the dinner lady team bowling themselves back down the stairs screaming while Clementine had continued to help herself to the spooky sweets table. 'I'm amazed it's all still going ahead this year.'

'It'll be a lot smaller this time,' Officer Thomas said sadly. 'The party is going to stop immediately at ten and

Mr Barrow has arranged to take people home in the school's new minibus. It's the only way it could go ahead, given what's happened.'

Margery was surprised Rose had managed to keep her party plans at all. The only way Margery could think that she had, was that she had bribed the entire PTA, who were all invited, who had in turn pressured the Dewstow police force. Officer Thomas continued, pulling her back out of her thoughts.

'We have some news, well not exactly news,' he said, tutting to himself. 'But it does open things up on the case a little bit.'

'What?' Clementine passed him a cup of tea; he took it gratefully.

'We searched Miss Macdonald's desk today, on a bit of a whim,' he explained, sipping from the cup, his moustache brushing the top of it as he did so. 'And we checked the CCTV footage again, for the fourth time now.'

'What did you find in her desk?' Clementine asked.

'Something she shouldn't have had,' Officer Thomas said triumphantly. 'Some confidential teacher files.'

'Dr Roberts'?' Margery blurted out before she could stop herself, remembering Mr Barrow had asked them to find the very file in confidence.

'What makes you say that?' Officer Thomas eyed her suspiciously.

'They've had it in for each other forever,' Clementine spluttered in feeble explanation. Officer Thomas looked mollified for a moment.

'We're double-checking her alibi now, but as we're not sure how or when exactly he died, it's proving rather tricky.'

'What was it?' Margery asked.

'She was apparently waiting outside the leisure centre for her friend to pick her up.' Officer Thomas scoffed. 'But she won't tell us the name of her friend. Or where she was the night before and that bit's in a CCTV black spot so there's no proof either way yet.'

'Dr Roberts told us today that she thinks he was killed for the insurance money.' Margery twisted the napkin on her lap as if wringing water from a tea towel.

Officer Thomas raised an eyebrow. Officer Symon looked between them all, the cup of tea in his hand forgotten, his mouth wide open.

'Well, she's absolutely incorrect there,' Officer Thomas said, his brow furrowed. 'Mr Weaver didn't have any insurance.'

'No insurance!' Margery said in surprise, thinking of Liv having to pay for that huge house alone. 'What on earth will she do?'

Life insurance seemed like something you just set up a monthly direct debit for and then forgot about. It seemed shocking he wouldn't have it. 'So you've already investigated it?'

'We have.' Officer Thomas nodded, grimly. 'I don't know what she'll do, but she will probably get his death-in-service payment from the school depending on how this case ends.' He sat back and stroked his moustache. 'We know you've spoken to Mrs Weaver, and you've already told us her alibi.'

'Yes,' Margery said. 'Maybe Dr Roberts was just being a gossip, it seems odd though, she never seemed the type to get involved with gossip. It did seem a bit out of character.

'I think Miss Macdonald having her staff file is a new lead we can focus on,' Officer Thomas said. 'Are you up for a bit more reconnaissance work?'

'With our new recording equipment?' Clementine asked gleefully.

Officer Thomas smiled in the way you might if you were humouring a child and shook his head.

Chapter Fifteen

Friday's Halloween party seemed like the best place to start. Rose's house was usually as pristine as a new-build show home and today was no different, even with Halloween decorations littering the front garden. They wandered up the drive and Clementine reached across to ring the doorbell, which gave off a horrible shriek as she did so. The party was already in full swing, judging by the booming bass and squeals of laughter emanating through the open living room window. Margery tried to resist the urge to peer over the hedge and look inside. The plan was simple enough: all they had to do was pay attention to what Miss Macdonald was up to and see if they could get her to confess anything. If she was as drunk as she had been the day before, it might be easier than they thought.

'This party gets worse every year,' Clementine said, her lip curling while they stared at the garish decor. 'She must have so many tacky decorations now, where does she keep them all? It's a wonder her attic isn't already full just with Christmas stuff, that tree she had last year was so big it looked like it was a gift from the people of Norway. She probably needed an attic of decorations for that alone— Oh, hello, Rose!'

Rose had opened the door. Margery had to take a full step back to avoid being swept from the doorstep by her enormous pink dress, nearly flinging them back.

'Christ, it's Glinda the bloody good witch,' Clementine breathed. 'How many hours did you get the drama club to spend making that monstrosity?'

'They took as much time as they needed to make it, Mrs Butcher-Baker!' Rose glared at her. 'We can reuse it for this year's play anyway, we're doing the *Wizard of Oz* as the summer concert. Get in the house, the rest of your rabble are here already.'

They followed her inside, taking their coats off as they did so and hanging them up before following Rose through the darkened hallway covered in plastic spiders and cobwebs. The fog machine in the corner of the hall billowed out thick smoke, and they passed the raucous living room with the speaker system on full blast and disco lights flashing manically. Rose had to duck to avoid the tall crown she wore hitting the doorframe as they went inside the quiet kitchen. The rest of the Education Centre Nourishment Consultant team were already there, and stood awkwardly picking at the buffet laid out on the huge marble-topped counter in the middle of the enormous room. They could still hear the other side of the party going on, Rose had spared no expense on the speaker system, but it was much calmer. Rose left immediately to return to the living room, 'The Monster Mash' blaring out until the door swung closed behind her.

'Hello, mate! Love your costumes!' Ceri-Ann said, waving one of the pompoms of her cheerleader outfit at them from her seat on one of the stools, Symon standing behind her dressed as an American football player. He gave them a shy smile and a wave, looking very young outside of his work uniform.

'Oh, thank you.' Margery smiled back at them both, adjusting her hat. Ceri-Ann's youthful happiness was infectious. 'We're salt and pepper shakers.' She pointed to Clementine's white t-shirt and then to her own grey front, which she had sewn the letter P to.

'I guessed that,' Ceri-Ann said. She looked up at Symon, who smiled and put his arm around her.

'Sharon and Karen have come as the twins from *The Shining*,' Gloria smirked, looking resplendent in the ballgown she was wearing, holding a paper plate of crisps in one hand and a plastic glass of something bubbly in the other.

'Have they?' Margery asked in surprise, looking over to Sharon and Karen who were indeed wearing the same dress.

'No.' Gloria laughed, the paper plate wobbling precariously. 'But they might as well have done.'

Clementine, who had been looking around the room and the groups of people dancing and drinking, grasped Margery's arm.

'There's Miss Macdonald,' she hissed, pointing across the room.

Margery turned to where she was pointing. Miss Macdonald was leaning against one of the rows of kitchen counters, holding a glass of wine and talking to Dr Roberts, who had put on a lab coat for the occasion. Margery tried to discern what they could be talking about, wishing she had mastered the art of lip-reading. It would remain a mystery unless they could get closer. Dr Roberts didn't look as though she was partaking in the conversation much at all. In fact, she was stony-faced as Miss Macdonald gesticulated at her with her hands as she babbled. Elle was barely dressed for Halloween, Margery noticed in surprise. Last year she had won one of Rose's ridiculous prizes for her costume, so it seemed strange that she would come but not bother doing much more than putting on a cape. Maybe losing Mr Weaver had been the last straw.

She wondered how they would get any information out of her. They needed to find out why she had taken Dr Roberts's file. It was strange that she would take it and then chat away to Dr Roberts so brazenly at a staff party. Maybe there would be a chance later to confront Miss Macdonald – the police certainly hadn't given them any tips on what they should be doing. Gloria took a ladle of punch from the great steaming bowl of dry ice and green liquid from the centre of the kitchen island and poured Margery and Clementine both a glass. Margery received it gratefully and took a sip, wincing at the strength of the alcohol as she sat down on the stool next to Ceri-Ann.

'Have you seen Mrs Blossom?' Ceri-Ann smirked.

Margery shook her head. She hadn't seen Rose's arch nemesis and Ittonvale School's drama teacher since the summer. They must have been repairing their friendship if she was here and Rose had been babysitting Ada recently.

'She's dressed as Cruella de Vil,' Ceri-Ann laughed. 'She's dressed Ada up like a Dalmatian.'

They both laughed. Margery took another slow sip of punch, the taste becoming more tolerable with each sip. Even if they couldn't get anything out of Miss Macdonald, they may as well enjoy themselves. It had been far too long since there had been a celebration. The worry that the school might close waded to the forefront once again, but she drowned it with another gulp. Mr Barrow pottered in and out, filling up bowls of crisps and handing out bottles of beer. Gloria told them that Rose had tried to get him to be the Tin Man to match her Glinda the Good Witch outfit, but he had instead gone as the Demon Headmaster, wearing his usual day-to-day suit and tie. Seren seemed to have a rare night off from being Rose's lacky; she and Gary were dressed as police officers for the evening and dancing over by the door.

Another group of guests entered the kitchen, and the gathering became as raucous as the parties usually did. Margery wondered how on earth Rose was going to get everyone out of her house at ten o'clock on the dot. It was not going to be an easy task. In the revelry, Margery realised that they had lost sight of Miss Macdonald. She could see Dr Roberts smoking a cigarette out of the conservatory doors that led into the garden and laughing with Mrs Wiggins, but Elle had well and truly disappeared. No matter, Margery thought to herself. They would catch up with her at some point, she was sure of it.

Margery looked around the room and took it all in as Clementine asked Ceri-Ann if her outfit was supposed to be a teenage pregnancy and Ceri-Ann guffawed with laughter at her cheek. There were certainly a lot of people here tonight, maybe even more than there had been last year. With great surprise, Margery realised the woman chatting with Dr Roberts and Mrs Wiggins was none other than Liv Weaver. She'd dyed her hair blue with one of those wash-in dye packs the teenagers at the school were always getting sent home for using and she was wearing a witch's hat and black flowing dress. Margery wondered how long it would have taken her to be able to leave the house if Clementine had died. Probably never. Gloria and Seren would have to drag her from her home, kicking and screaming. She certainly wouldn't be at a party less than two weeks after her husband had been found murdered. But then, she looked around at the party continuing and took another sip of punch and thought, that just for tonight, it was best to leave each to their own.

The night wore on quickly and soon enough the constant blaring of music had stopped in the other room and they were all being summoned to the living room for the costume prize and apple bobbing and all sorts of other unnecessary and needlessly unsanitary games. Likely an effort to wind the party down. Margery stole a look at the time on the kitchen microwave and saw that it had just gone nine.

'Trust Rose to throw a party and organise it the same way as a school event,' Gloria said as they tried to get a good space at the back of the room nearest Rose's dining table, the crush of other people constricting them. 'We'll be lining up to go back to Maths class if we're not careful.'

'Do you not remember when she made Mr Barrow's best man reread his speech at their wedding because he got one of the words muddled up?' Clementine said, holding her glass up by her chest to avoid spilling it as the crowd pushed forward into the dim room, lit only by fairy lights in the shape of skeletons and battery-powered tea lights.

'No, but I remember that we all had a score sheet to fill in for the best bit of the day.' Margery groaned at the memory. She was beginning to enjoy herself now, surrounded by colleagues and friends: Clementine and Gloria joking around without any of the stress of the kitchen; not having to worry if she'd remembered to order potatoes or if they'd defrosted the prebreaded pollock fillets for Friday lunchtime, and the alcohol blurring the edges of the past few weeks making things more tolerable for once.

'Right!' Rose yelled excitedly. She was balanced precariously on her own coffee table, a piece of card in her hands and beaming from ear to ear. 'It's time to announce the best costume!' Mr Barrow held her steadily by the skirt so she did not parachute away under the sheer amount of fabric.

'Ada Bones!' Ceri-Ann whooped. Mrs Blossom smiled smugly from her seat on one of the huge sofas brandishing the red cigarette holder like it was a knife. Several people clapped.

'A dog can't win!' Rose said sternly, turning to Mrs Blossom. 'I'm sorry, Rhonda, but that's just not how this—'

There was a horrible scream from somewhere on the first floor, followed by a loud thump and the crowd all turned as one towards the noise, like a wave heading for a beach. All the hair on Margery's head seemed to stand up, then there was silence. Despite the number of people gathered you could have heard a pin drop. Rose looked over at the closed double doors that led into her hallway, the partygoers had all come traipsing in from the kitchen into the dining room and closed the double doors behind them. Everyone waited, though no one seemed sure why, or what they were expecting. Someone giggled, probably thinking that this was part of the evening, but Margery knew Rose well enough by now to know that this was unplanned. She was listening just as intently as the rest of them, her face pale.

'What was that?' Clementine yelled over the murmuring of the group. 'You haven't paid an out-of-work actor to come and do the entirety of *An Inspector Calls*, have you?'

'No,' Rose snapped, 'I was told not to do any perform-ance this year by the police.'

She stepped down from the table and waded through the group till she could throw open the double sitting room doors and peered out into the dark hallway. The smoke machine poured fog into the room, and the fairy lights seemed to flicker as it curled around them. Margery found herself holding her breath in anticipation, though she did not know what of. Mr Barrow stepped in front of her, gently moving her from harm as he went out into the hallway and peered up the stairs. They began to murmur amongst themselves.

Suddenly, footsteps hammered down the stairs at tremendous speed and Mr Barrow was knocked down by the sheer force of the person launching themselves downwards and barrelling past him in a blur. Their face was covered by a hood, their long cape flowing behind them. Mr Barrow lunged back up and grasped for them as they fought with the door, but it was too late. It opened and then slammed violently again; the sound reverberated through the floor. It jolted back out of the door frame and the cool air from outside blew through the open doorway. Margery gasped when the door swung back inside and revealed the symbol, sprayed onto the front door in green paint. Mr Barrow used the wall to steady himself, and in his hand, he held a glove. He had pulled it off the mysterious person and they had slipped out of it as they escaped.

'Karen and Sharon, come with me!' he yelled for his fellow Dewstow running club members and then left the house. Karen and Sharon peeled themselves out of the crowd and rushed after him.

Rose turned to look toward the rest of the group, her eyes wide. Margery pushed forward towards her,

Clementine following, and they reached the hallway as Rose put her foot on the first stair.

'Stand back.' Officer Symon had easily dispersed the crowd and placed his hand gently on Rose's own. She did as he commanded, turning to him.

'Officer, the noise was probably just that person leaving,' she began, but he turned back to look up at the hallway above.

'No point in taking chances,' he said and headed up, leaving them in the dimly lit hallway.

They all waited with bated breath, listening to Symon's footsteps creaking along the landing. Someone turned on the downstairs lights and Margery blinked as they stung her eyes. The fog machine seemed ridiculous now, and so did the Halloween decorations, dangled carefully over Rose's expensive furniture.

'Call an ambulance!' Symon yelled from a room above.

Rose took her phone out of a concealed pocket in the dress with shaking hands. Margery didn't hesitate and rushed upstairs. She reached the top of the stairs and turned onto the large landing, feeling her way along the wall in the darkness until she reached the open door. Light was streaming from it in a strip, leaving long shadows to frame it. The sight was horrifying; Miss Macdonald lay on the guest bedroom floor by the bed, her eyes open but unseeing, bruises already forming on her neck in the unmistakable imprint of fingertips. Officer Symon's fingers wrapped around her wrist looking for a pulse.

His eyes met Margery's and she could see the fear in them.

Chapter Sixteen

'Trouble seems to follow you,' Officer Thomas said, leaning heavily on the kitchen counter, his notepad in hand. A few years ago, this would have been the most upsetting and exciting thing to ever happen to them, now it was barely in the top five. Officer Thomas continued gravely. 'Another attack, another teacher. God, what the hell is happening?'

'Officer Thomas, please do not… Oh, you know what? Swear all you like,' Clementine said. 'I agree, this is madness. I feel like we're all on a bus headed straight for the moon, or hell, or something.'

'It really is.' Margery sat next to her at the kitchen breakfast bar, in the same spots as they had been earlier.

All the joviality had gone from the evening, swept away and replaced by fear. It did seem very unlikely now that Miss Macdonald had killed Mr Weaver as Dr Roberts had suggested, seeing as she had just been attacked by one of the masked strangers. Unless Miss Macdonald had been attacked by a copycat. But how many people would have known the connection between the strangers and their PE plimsols and Mr Evans? The police hadn't yet released that information in the hope that they could use it to catch the group. It didn't help that it was gone three in the morning and the police officers had waited to interview them last. Margery could barely keep her eyes open, they burned with exhaustion. The glove sat on the table in front of them in a plastic evidence bag, waiting to go away for DNA testing. Margery couldn't stop looking at it. It was a plain black leather glove, and it looked incredibly ordinary for something that had been worn while strangling another person.

'Well, it can't have been Mr Evans,' Clementine whispered, 'he's in custody.'

'He's not,' Officer Thomas said, not looking either of them in the eye. 'We had to release him yesterday. No evidence.'

'Are you joking?' Margery said, feeling her mouth drop open in horror. 'So he could have come here tonight.'

'We couldn't keep him in any longer.' Officer Thomas looked as upset as she felt.

'Officer Thomas?' Officer Symon had reappeared in the room.

'What is it, Symon?' Officer Thomas stood up from the chair immediately, his eyes scanning Symon's face for information. Margery found herself leaning forward to listen.

'The inspector wants to talk to you,' Officer Symon said. Officer Thomas raised his eyebrows and followed him out of the room, leaving them to their thoughts. Margery surveyed the half-finished buffet table and the disposable cups littering the kitchen. Through the utility-room door, she could see the party bags still lining the countertops. They sat for a while longer until it was clear that Officer Thomas wouldn't be coming back any time soon. Margery and Clementine turned to each other and exchanged a look that said more than words ever could have.

'Come on,' Clementine said, gesturing towards the living room. 'Let's go and see how Rose got on with her CCTV camera.'

Margery dragged herself from the stool and followed her through to the living room. Rose and Mr Barrow had driven everyone home but now they both sat on their sofa, quietly processing. Even with everything they'd been through, Margery had never seen Mr Barrow so upset, or Rose so shocked. The remnants of the party remained strewn all over the room, the banner advising them to have a happy spooky Halloween had been crushed underfoot as people had desperately tried to leave and now lay crumpled on the floor by the coffee table. Rose had changed out of her dress into a smart tracksuit sort of thing, the headmaster had obviously not seen any need to, sitting in his Halloween costume still. He had returned from the chase empty-handed. Whoever it had been, they had been faster than him and had got away. Rose's face crumpled at the sight of Margery and Clementine entering the room and slumping down opposite them on the other sofa.

'They haven't found out who did it,' Rose whispered dramatically, eyes searching the doorway in case the officers returned suddenly. 'Honestly! I handed them the security footage on a plate, you'd think they'd be able to get something from it, but no!'

'What did the camera show?' Margery asked, considering reaching over and patting Rose's hand in sympathy for a moment but then thinking better of it.

'Nothing!' Rose rested her face on her hands and groaned. 'Well, just the same masks and cloaked people again! There was only one of them this time, they painted that mark on my door and ran off about half an hour before all of that. And the paint went over the doorbell camera, so the police couldn't see anyone leaving the house after that. My poor door! I'll never get that paint colour again. It was a special run—'

The headmaster cut her off, turning to Margery and Clementine. 'The most important thing is how you are both holding up. How are you?'

'Fine,' Margery said quickly, before she could register her emotions, but to her surprise, Clementine began to sob.

'Another person attacked!' she cried, a tear rolling down her cheek as she closed her eyes tightly. 'I just don't understand what's going on, this town must be cursed. We must be cursed!'

'We're not cursed,' Margery said. She tucked Clementine's hair behind her ear soothingly and rubbed her shoulder gently. She was beginning to wonder if Clementine was right though, maybe they were cursed. She certainly seemed to be. 'Just a bit unlucky, maybe. Did your camera not show anything else, Rose?'

Rose looked afraid. The sight of it made Margery gulp. Margery hadn't seen Rose look so frightened since the day she had collapsed in her office, which felt like decades ago now, though it was only a year or two. Mr Barrow looked on gravely.

'No,' Rose whispered. 'But we saw whoever it was leave, didn't we? It's the same people that have been at the school, I'm sure of it.'

They sat in silence for a moment, mulling it all over.

'We think so too,' Margery said, Clementine took her hand. 'What are the police going to do?'

'I don't know,' Rose cried. 'But they're out there now, pulling up my flowerbeds and fingerprinting my car and pavement and God knows what else. I knew we should have got a set of cameras, James, one wasn't enough. If we had another... we should have bought that set in the Black Friday sale last year, maybe it would have helped...'

'I never thought this would happen,' Mr Barrow said glumly, resting his head in his hands.

'No one could have seen this coming,' Margery said. Clementine had stopped crying and was now sitting in pensive silence.

'The symbol,' she said, rubbing her brow. 'What on earth does it mean?'

'Well, whatever it is, nothing good happens once it's been painted on,' Margery sighed. 'Every time we've seen it, they've turned up again after.'

'I've definitely seen it before,' Mr Barrow said. 'But I can't place it and I don't know what they want.'

'Well, what if we try and Google it?' Margery suggested.

'You can't Google a picture, Margery,' Clementine said, but she opened her phone anyway and tapped at the screen. 'The internet simply doesn't work like that, it simply— Oh, hang on. Okay, there are a few results when I type in upside-down A.'

She moved closer to Margery on the sofa so they could both look at the screen and flicked her fingers over it, scrolling down the results.

'It's a maths symbol,' Margery breathed. 'Gosh, I never would have known.'

'Meaning *for all*,' Clementine said out loud, though the confusion in her voice betrayed that she did not know what it meant either. 'For all, hmmm—'

'Of course!' Mr Barrow cried, sitting up straight again, clicking his fingers together. 'That's it!'

'You're telling me we've been hanging around millions of teachers for days and no one's worked that out already?' Clementine jeered. 'Don't you all have degrees?'

'James was an English teacher,' Rose scoffed. 'And if you'd have seen any of my Drama coursework, you'd know that there is no maths about it. Most of my students can barely read.'

'This must be students, though?' Margery asked. 'The police think they were all wearing school plimsols.'

'Well, they've certainly spent an inordinate amount of time hanging around the school spray painting the place,' Rose said. 'And now my house, which makes sense because I'm obviously their favourite teacher.' Clementine snorted at that. Rose rolled her eyes at her. 'It makes sense I'd be singled out.'

'I don't understand why they would target here?' Margery said, scratching her head. 'The graffiti in the town centre said twenty-three. Is this house number twenty-three?'

'This house is called Heddfan, I'll have you all know,' Rose said, scoffing at the idea that her house would be known under a simple number. 'Meaning, peaceful place.'

'Well,' Clementine said, 'that isn't true, is it? You'll have to change it to "Tumultuous Nightmare" or something.'

They fell into gloomy silence, only the sounds of the police walking around upstairs provided any sound. The mantelpiece was still covered in cobwebs, but it looked like Rose had briefly begun to remove them before giving up. A bin bag full of them sat by her feet, spilling out under the coffee table. What a night, Margery thought. The police had spent hours interviewing each party guest. None of whom had had even the slightest inkling of what had happened. Elle was probably the only person who could have answered any real questions about her attacker, and she had been put in the ambulance and whisked away to Ittonvale Hospital. And the symbol was here, and yet the house wasn't number twenty-three, and Officer Thomas had told them when he arrived that there had been no trouble at the school yet.

'Is there anyone unaccounted for?' Margery asked. 'Who didn't the police interview?'

'Everyone, I think,' Mr Barrow said as he loosened his tie. 'We were all here. The only people who haven't left at all are you both.'

'Whoever it was, was already here, no one came through the back door, did they?' Margery tried to remember who was standing nearest to the patio doors in the dining room, but she couldn't remember.

'No, they were locked,' Clementine said, looking over her shoulder at them. 'But I didn't see anyone wearing that costume either, did you?'

They were interrupted by the arrival of Officer Thomas again. His eyebrows were knitted together in concern.

'We've found some more evidence,' he said, gesturing with his hands as he began to pace back and forth. 'The suspect dropped their cape in the alley leading into your back garden, Mrs Smith. We think they entered your house through the conservatory and re-joined the group.'

They all gasped in surprise.

'Are you sure it wasn't Mr Evans?' Margery asked.

Neither Rose nor Mr Barrow blinked at the mention of his name.

Officer Thomas shook his head.

'We've been to check his whereabouts,' Symon answered for him. 'He was at home.'

'There's more,' Officer Thomas said. Margery held her breath. He took out Rose's phone and showed them the video from her doorbell camera, pressing Play. There was barely anything to see, only a tiny part of the camera hadn't been painted over. It was like trying to look through a keyhole when a coat had been hung on the other side of the door.

'Why are you showing us this?' Margery asked.

'Look at the little light,' Officer Thomas explained, pointing to where he meant. There was a light there, and then suddenly darkness again. Margery assumed that was the door opening.

'Okay?' Clementine said, in a bemused voice. 'What was it? The street light?'

'There's no streetlight opposite the house,' Officer Thomas said. 'We just checked.'

'The neighbour then?' Margery suggested. Officer Thomas shook his head.

'They were all here,' Rose cut in, sitting up straight. 'We're quite environmentally conscious around here, don't you dare say anything about my car, Mrs Butcher-Baker!' Clementine threw her hands up in defeat. 'I'm planning on getting the hybrid model as soon as we've had the electric charger fitted on the drive. Anyway, they wouldn't have left a light on in the house if they were only here across the road.'

'So what do you think it was?' Margery asked Officer Thomas.

'I think it was a phone camera with the flash on,' he said triumphantly.

'So someone will have a video or a photo of the person leaving?'

'Exactly!'

'Mr Evans wouldn't know anything about maths.' Clementine shook her head as they sat at the kitchen table, finally home. They had thought about going to bed but decided instead to stay up. Margery wasn't sure she could have slept even if she tried. 'So why would they paint that maths symbol everywhere if they were working with him?'

'It is strange.' Margery rested her head on her hands, her elbows firmly sat on the kitchen table. 'I can't work it out either. I feel like we must be missing something.'

'It's time to back out of the case, Margery,' Clementine said in a firm voice, folding her arms across her chest. 'We said we'd help until something bad happened and this is possibly the worst thing that could have happened.'

'But, Clem—'

'Really, Margery,' Clementine said. 'We can't keep on going with this. It's time to back out, count our chickens, peel our potatoes, er, hatch our eggs. All that sort of thing.'

'But we could really help,' Margery protested. 'If we can just work out who the group in cloaks are then we'll be on to something.'

'I don't think so.' Clementine shook her head. 'We'll end up getting hurt again and I won't have it. The police are supposed to be able to do this alone, all the other police departments do. Why is Dewstow's so crap?' Margery gasped as Clementine swore. 'No, no, no. That's it, we're out.'

'Fine,' Margery said, wondering if Clementine was secretly contemplating the ways she could drag them back into it. She seemed serious this time, but that didn't mean that in a moment she wouldn't change her mind. 'What if they don't work it out though? The group will get away with it! We need to find out who did it.'

'But how, Margery?' Clementine cried and then slapped her hand over her mouth, realising what she had done. 'No, we aren't getting involved. I'm sure Miss Macdonald will be able to tell them what happened when she gets out of the hospital.'

'Or we could go and visit?' Margery suggested.

Clementine gave her a stern look but said nothing.

'They'll analyse the glove and find out who it was soon enough,' Clementine said confidently. 'And the DNA from the needles in the PE changing room will be back too, and I'd imagine it will all match up.'

'Yes, about that,' Margery said. 'Did you see the glove? I was trying to work out if it was likely to be a man or a woman's?'

'Medium size and unisex, he said,' Clementine groaned. 'I overheard Symon and Officer Thomas talking about it.'

'What a mess,' Margery said. The kettle clicked off as it came to a boil finally and she jumped up to make them both a cup of tea.

'I know they said he was at home, but could Mr Evans have got to and from Rose's before they got there?' Margery said. 'Do you think he could have sent the students in his place to hurt Miss Macdonald? Who do you think would be most likely to do something like that?'

Clementine thought about it. 'I can't really picture anyone we know being capable of it.'

'No, I can't either,' Margery said, putting the tea bag in the food waste bin. 'And actually, it couldn't have been a student in the house.'

'Why not?'

'Because whoever was in the house had been there for the whole evening, Rose specifically always bans students from her parties,' Margery explained, remembering the cape Officer Thomas had shown them in the evidence bag. 'And then whoever it was managed to get back inside the house and re-join us all without anyone knowing. Surely if they were part of the masked group, they'd have had some sort of getaway plan?'

'Maybe going back in through the conservatory was their getaway plan,' Clementine said, tapping her fingers on her lips. 'We were all in costume. Lots of people were wearing black capes.'

'Maybe so.' Margery offered her the cup of tea. Clementine took it gratefully and Margery sat down next to her again. 'Maybe they sprayed the symbol on the door themselves to make it look like it had been someone from the masked group, used them as a scapegoat?'

'Gosh, but who would do such a thing?' Clementine said, stirring sugar into the mug from the pot on the table. 'I suppose the story of the people in masks has been splashed all over the papers. What if the person who strangled Miss Macdonald wasn't part of the group?'

'Yes, agreed.' Margery took a sip. 'And why Miss Macdonald?'

'Maybe someone whose husband cheated on them.' Clementine took a sip from her mug. 'Someone who doesn't like Miss Macdonald for that reason.'

'You're not saying?'

'I am,' Clementine said. 'Mrs Weaver.'

'No, I just can't see her doing that,' Margery said, putting her mug back down on the table.

'Well, anyone could go to the shop in the town centre and get one of those masks, couldn't they? Or on the internet or whatever, even. And she was already wearing a black dress, maybe it had a cape, and we just didn't see it,'

Clementine continued; her tea forgotten as she thought about it. 'But the "for all" symbol thing, well I think that might well be students. I certainly can't think of a better explanation. I think all these things are several events all muddled together.'

'Yes... Well I can't understand that either.' Margery dipped a biscuit in her tea absent-mindedly. She dunked one too many times and the digestive crumbled and sank to the bottom of the mug.

'Yes, but not the strangling,' Clementine said. 'I think that was Mrs Weaver. Why else would she be at the party?'

'Well,' Margery said. 'You certainly have a point.'

They went to bed for a few hours and then got up and tried to make something of the rest of the afternoon, but it was no use. Clementine pottered around the garden for a bit, mowing the lawn before they forgot to do it for the next six months. Margery dusted the entire house from top to bottom and ironed all their clothes, including socks and underwear, in a desperate attempt to distract herself, which didn't work.

They had an early dinner and settled in for the night, Clementine pouring herself a glass of wine from the monthly wine subscription box, while Margery tried out a particularly demanding new crochet pattern from a magazine.

'Clem,' Margery said, interrupting the peace of the quiet living room. The only other noise was the ticking of the various carriage clocks littered around the house and the purring of the cats. 'Are you sure we shouldn't stay involved?'

'Quite sure,' Clementine snapped in a voice that betrayed that was exactly what she had been thinking. She swirled the wine around in the glass and turned the page of the *Dewstow Free Press*, which had moved on from Mr Weaver's death and was now worrying about a large pothole that had appeared on Dewstow Hill and burst several car tyres. There was obviously no mention of Miss Macdonald yet, it had barely been a day, but they hadn't printed anything about Mrs Large's murder at Christmas until she had been buried and the case was safely packed away.

'And you're not even a bit worried or intrigued by it?' Margery said, searching Clementine's face for the answer. It would be their second wedding anniversary next year, but they had been together for more than forty years; Margery knew all of Clementine's facial expressions like the back of her hand. There was a long pause and then Clementine sighed deeply.

'Of course I am, Margery!' she said, dropping the newspaper back down on the coffee table in front of their knees, the wine like a tornado in the glass at the speed of her swirling. 'There's a killer on the loose – the police said so! And that symbol still being painted? Is it children messing around, or is it witches? And at Halloween, for crying out loud!'

'I don't think it's witches—'

Clementine interrupted. 'Well, it's too spooky to be anything normal!'

'So, you do want to carry on investigating?'

'Of course I do!' Clementine said, 'But we can't! We can't risk it. I can't risk you. No, we're going to stay here safe in our house and let Officer Moustache and his idiot savant sort it out.'

'I suppose Officer Thomas will try and find out if someone was recording outside now.' Margery shook her head.

'Officer Thomas probably can't even run a bath, let alone a police force. I bet he puts washing-up liquid in there instead of bath salts and uses a scourer instead of a flannel,' Clementine said, before realising that she was supposed to be talking Margery down. 'But I have faith that they'll get it all sorted in the end,' she said with a grimace, as though it was physically painful to say out loud.

Margery considered her response. She certainly could see where Clementine was coming from, they had got into an awful amount of trouble. But still, if they didn't keep trying to help, then what good were they? Before she could muster anything, the letterbox clanged as it opened and then closed again. They froze, staring over at the door to the hallway.

'What now?' Clementine whispered, getting up to have a look.

She opened the door, ruining the cosy atmosphere of the living room as the cool air found its way inside.

'Christ, Margery,' she said, 'you won't believe this. I know I said I wanted to stay at home, but not like this!'

She came back into the living room and handed her a piece of paper.

'What's this?' Margery asked in confusion. She needn't have asked. As she read the page, she learned everything: there was to be a town-wide curfew, starting tonight and lasting until this was over. No one was to be out of their house after eight p.m. without special permission from Dewstow police force. There was to be a town meeting on Sunday and the entire town was invited.

'Christ, they can't do this, can they?' Margery asked. 'Keep us all locked in our houses for weeks before we can even say anything about it?'

'Margery, please do not swear,' Clementine said, but she shook her head as Margery handed her the paper again. 'I think they can, that's the most frightening thing.'

Chapter Seventeen

The Sunday evening rolled around and with it, the town meeting. The rest of the half-term week had not held up to its relaxing promise, and Margery wondered if everyone else was as stressed about returning to school tomorrow. Judging by the sour faces around them, they were dreading it too.

Dewstow town hall was full to the rafters – the entire population of the town was uncomfortably crushed inside. Margery dreaded to think how many health and safety laws they were breaking. Everyone she knew and several hundred that she didn't were stuffed into the hall, and even more were listening to the hastily set up PA speakers that had been put in the car park. Margery and Clementine had arrived early enough to get seats, but now they were trapped in them by the sheer number of town's people lining the rows between chairs. Usually, they would all have been at the school playing fields ready for the usual firework night celebrations, which had been cancelled due to the curfew.

Margery looked around for the people they knew and saw Mrs Mugglethwaite sitting with Seren and Rose, who was becoming more agitated as the wait dragged on. Sharon, Karen and Gloria were all squashed together a few rows in front, they must have arrived together as they usually did in the morning for work. Margery kept wondering if they were even going to be allowed back to the school tomorrow. The rumours flying around the town centre were that the school governors were trying to stop the school from reopening for the rest of the year, fearing rebuttal from Ofsted. The school was surely going to lose its 'Good' rating at the next inspection at this rate. Margery remembered her own imminent environmental health inspection and gulped. Mrs Mugglethwaite said she had heard that Mr Barrow was facing a very hard road if he intended to carry on as normal.

Up on the small stage, Officer Thomas sat with the rest of the force, nervously twiddling his hands together. Mr Barrow sat to the side of them, looking pale and drawn, his brow so creased with worry Margery wondered if it would ever unfold again. Dewstow police's Sergeant Davis was plonked in between Mr Barrow and the police force, looking like he might fall asleep at any moment. He should have retired years ago, Margery thought to herself. She would never have said the nasty words out loud, but he was truly ancient, so many years past his prime that it was almost comical. Officer Thomas gave him a nudge and Sergeant Davis gave a start before he stood, dragging himself out of the chair with a groan and up to the spindly microphone stand in front of the row of chairs.

'Right, yes.' He unfolded a piece of paper from the top pocket of his uniform and cleared his throat. 'We are here to discuss the town curfew and answer any questions you might have.'

He sat back down. Officer Thomas looked bemused and gave him another nudge. Sergeant Davis huffed but refused to look at him, folding his arms with a harrumph. It began to dawn on Margery why the Dewstow Police

Department might be struggling so hard to solve a single case. Eventually Officer Thomas stood instead.

'As we all know, there has been another murder in Dewstow. This is the second in as many years. More than that, another member of the public has been attacked and very nearly strangled to death.' He spoke strongly, the hall quiet enough to hear nothing but people breathing. 'In order to protect the people who live in the areas shown on the map that were included with the curfew order, the town curfew will remain in place for another two weeks. After which we will reassess. Do we have any questions?'

Half the hands in the hall shot up. The first person to stand was the landlord of the Bell and Hope, who asked what on earth they were supposed to do to keep their business going if no one was allowed to drink in it after eight in the evening. The meeting quickly disintegrated after that under the braying of the gathered crowd. Officer Thomas looked like he wanted the ground to swallow him whole on several occasions. Margery decided finally that she needed to ask a question, raising her arm. Officer Thomas turned to her.

'Yes, Mrs Butcher-Baker?'

'Have you found who strangled Miss Macdonald yet?' Margery asked, regretting it as soon as she had spoken. Officer Thomas stared at her. The gathered crowd gasped. The wave of anger she had felt subsided, though she didn't know if it was because she had upset the apple cart or all the apples inside it.

'Yes! What about the safety of the children!' someone called from the back of the hall.

'We are currently following leads, Mrs Butcher-Baker.' Officer Thomas glared at her. Margery pretended she couldn't feel the stare burning into her skin.

'Who?' she asked. 'You haven't made another arrest though, have you? Mr Evans has been let out.'

'We do not currently have anyone in custody,' Officer Thomas admitted, his face reddening. 'But we are following all the leads.'

An awful realisation suddenly flooded Margery's mind. 'That cape that you found at the scene… Miss Macdonald was wearing a cape at the party. The person who ran out of the house wasn't wearing her cape, were they?'

The crowd began to whisper again. Sergeant Davis looked over at Margery with great interest and then back to Officer Thomas, suspiciously, like he knew exactly what had been going on. Officer Thomas sat down. Mr Barrow stood and approached the microphone.

'I know there has been some talk about the safety of the school,' he said, running his hands through his hair anxiously.

Margery sat back down, feeling much too exposed out in the open. She looked at Clementine whose eyes were wide, staring at the stage ahead.

Mr Barrow continued, 'But I can assure you all that we are going to do all we can to prevent any further incidents. Namely upping the security at the school building and grounds.'

Margery couldn't see how that would help when Miss Macdonald had been attacked at a party by either a member of school staff or someone known to a member of school staff. There was hardly any chance that an outsider had been involved, someone would have noticed them entering the house. Up on the stage, the headmaster looked almost grey. The last time they had been invited to an unexpected assembly had been for Mr Barrow to tell them that music teacher Mrs Large had died, and this meeting kept reminding her of it. At least there was no music playing today, which Margery took as a good sign after the announcement of Mrs Large's death. Rose now ran the recorder club as the new music teacher had no interest in it, Margery thought more out of guilt for never being nice enough to Mrs Large than anything else. The hall fell into quiet again as the headmaster cleared his throat.

'We've also made a decision that will affect the return to the school,' he said gravely. 'As you all know, poor Miss Macdonald will not be returning to work tomorrow, but she is recuperating and enjoying all the cards and flowers that have been sent.' He took a deep breath and Margery felt Clementine grab her arm as she braced herself. 'Her attacker hasn't yet been found and we at the school –' He looked behind at the PTA '– want to help the police as much as we can. I'll hand back over to Sergeant Davis now so he can explain further what we have in mind.'

There was a silence as they waited for him to speak again, but he didn't. Instead, the large police sergeant stood, dragging himself up from the chair again, it creaked as his weight left it.

'We are searching for DNA evidence discovered following Miss Macdonald's attack and we need your help to do it,' he said brusquely, resting his hands on the pockets of his dress tunic as he spoke. 'We will be stationed at the main entrance after school tomorrow and every day the rest of next week and we're asking for a DNA sample from each of you, which we will then be cross-examining against the evidence.'

The hall erupted into murmuring. Margery and Clementine exchanged a surprised look. The rest of the dinner lady team watched on open-mouthed.

'The headmaster's lost his bloody mind,' Gloria said from the row in front. Margery opened her mouth to reply but Mr Barrow stood again. 'No murderers are going to volunteer for that, are they?'

'This is all completely voluntary,' he said, waving his hands at the baying crowd. 'Completely voluntary and a consent form will need to be signed by each parental guardian for school pupils. If you wish to support the school and the police, you'll be supplied with a form today to take home and from tomorrow your child can come for testing. A simple saliva swab at the main entrance.'

The row of teachers at the side of the room were whispering among themselves. If the shaking heads and muttering was anything to go by, they agreed with Gloria's sentiment. Margery felt her chest constrict.

'Teachers and support staff over the age of eighteen can volunteer too at the school and a station will be set up in the leisure centre for other townspeople,' Mr Barrow continued. 'Please consider doing so, so we can get to the bottom of all of this and find Miss Macdonald's attacker.'

Chapter Eighteen

Rose managed to find them as the crowds were streaming their way out of the hall, grasping for them, her hands outstretched. Margery suddenly felt exhausted, unwilling to talk to Rose about whatever nonsense she had planned. Rose looked as panicked as the rest of the town did. All Margery wanted to do was go home and forget all about how she had embarrassed herself by asking a question, in a sudden wave of fury for the police not being able to solve any of the horrible things that had happened in their lovely town and for involving them. The police were supposed to defend them, Sergeant Davis looked as though he couldn't care less. And the headmaster had the brazen cheek to ask for DNA samples from students and staff. No murderer was going to willingly pop up to the leisure centre and give their DNA. It was the punchline to a bad joke, as far as Margery was concerned. Clementine was right, Margery admitted for the first time. They shouldn't be involved.

Rose managed to grab hold of the sleeve of Margery's coat, and Margery found herself being spun around to face her. She looked around for Clementine and found that she was already out in the carpark with Gloria.

'What is it, Rose?' she snapped, still bristling from the meeting's revelations. Rose's eyebrows flew up to her hairline in surprise. 'Sorry, I didn't mean to… What do you need, Rose?'

Rose looked around before lowering her voice. 'Have you had any luck vis a vis Seren?' She whispered her name like it was a bad word.

'No,' Margery said. 'To be honest, I'd forgotten all about it with what's gone on. And haven't you heard? We're terrible detectives, aren't we? Mr Evans has been let go and we've got no other suspects, we shouldn't be trying to solve anything at all. I think we'll probably have to sell our Cluedo set.'

'I don't care if you're crap detectives!' Rose scoffed. 'Anyway, you've solved way better murders than this one. You can't get them right every time; a jot of trial and error, that's all there is to it. Do you think I became the esteemed actress I am today without forgetting a few hundred words of a script and being dropped from the Ittonvale Musical Drama Band's production of *Cinderella*? No, of course not!'

Margery paused.

'Well, you're going to have to do something about Seren soon.' Rose harrumphed, ignoring her stunned silence. 'She's refusing to admit anything's missing, but I counted all her socks and she's down to two pairs,' she hissed. 'Two pairs! And she's been going to Slimming World five times a week, you can't tell me she hasn't got Slimmer of the Week at all in the last few months if she's going that much, I haven't seen a single certificate!'

'Fine,' Margery said, more to get Rose to stop than anything else. 'Well... what exactly do you want us to do?'

'Follow her,' Rose whispered. 'Follow her to wherever she's going at night instead of coming straight home with me to watch *Coronation Street*.'

'You sound a bit like you love Seren more than Mr Barrow,' Clementine had snuck up behind Margery, leaving Gloria and the rest of the dinner ladies to it. 'Or has she just stopped doing all your ironing?'

'She may or may not be still doing the ironing,' Rose said, smoothing the sleeves of her blouse, which looked much more rumpled than usual. 'Regardless, it's not normal, is it?'

It wasn't normal for Seren. Margery groaned. 'Fine, where is she now? Surely you can't have lost her in the two minutes we've been out of the hall?'

'She's talking to Karen and Sharon.' Rose gestured across the car park. 'But she said she was going to Slimming World straight after and not to wait up. What on earth is she playing at?'

'Why don't you just ask her?' Clementine said. Margery gestured in agreement. Rose glared at them both and stomped away again. Margery shook her head as she went.

'What should we do?' Margery asked Clementine, pulling her coat up past her ears, avoiding catching the eye of anyone leaving the hall.

'Well, Officer Thomas has just texted me,' Clementine sighed, showing Margery the message on her phone screen. 'We're off the case, the sergeant's rumbled us and he's in a huge amount of trouble.'

'It had to happen sooner or later,' Margery muttered. 'So, we're free agents for the evening then?'

'Didn't even get to wear a wire or a trench coat,' Clementine said sadly. 'Or a phone that can record conversations.'

'You don't need to be undercover to wear a trench coat, Clem.' Margery reminded her. 'And all phones can do that.'

'Of course you do!' Clementine scoffed. 'That's what they're made for. You can't tell me a normal coat would have that many pockets.'

'You wanted us to come off the case anyway!' Margery reminded her. Clementine didn't look aggrieved.

'That was when I thought we'd at least helped a little to solve it,' Clementine said gloomily.

She folded her arms over her chest and looked up at the darkening sky, her face falling. It was threatening rain again and neither of them had remembered an umbrella. Margery sighed to herself, realising there was one way she could cheer Clementine up.

'Come on,' she said reluctantly, 'Rose has given us a new, and much less dangerous spy mission that I think we might actually be able to manage.'

Following Seren didn't prove to be an easy feat. For one thing, the crowds were still dispersing, which made finding Seren quite difficult, though they eventually managed it somehow. Maintaining a comfortable distance then became the next problem, especially as they knew so many of the town's people and kept being dragged into conversation. Dawn Simmonds caught them on their way out of the car park and forced another few carrier bags stuffed full of apples into Clementine's reluctant arms, even as they protested that they didn't know what to do with the ones she had delivered yesterday.

'I feel terrible about this,' Margery said as they trailed behind Seren out of the Town Hall car park, the bag of apples hitting her on her good knee as she struggled with the walking stick. Seren wasn't with Gary, for once, Margery had assumed she might walk home with him, realising then that she hadn't seen him at the town meeting. Maybe he was working tonight, overtime at the school reinstated after the recent events. Underneath the guilt, she was as intrigued as Rose was to discover the reason for Seren's mysterious coming and goings. She and Rose had been attached at the hip for the last year and a half and Margery didn't really know what to make of it. Clementine seemed just as uneasy.

'Me too,' Clementine said, holding both the bags she was holding up. 'What are we supposed to do with another bag of apples?'

'That's not what I meant,' Margery said with a shiver. The cold night breeze becoming too much.

'Yes, I know what you meant,' Clementine said. The weather had finally caught up with the season and it was getting colder at night now, the pavement slippery with rainwater. 'Let's just see where she goes, probably some-where entirely normal, like the library or swimming or something and then we can get home, have a cup of tea and tell Rose she's being paranoid.'

'The library closes at five.' Margery shook her head, the hood of her coat brushing her face as she did so. She had to fully turn her head to look at Clementine with it pulled so far over her head. 'And the only place to go swimming in Dewstow is at the leisure centre attached to the school, she doesn't seem like she's headed up that way.'

'Well, maybe she wants to get a book that the library doesn't have,' Clementine suggested. '*The Necronomicon* or something, from Mr Fitzgerald's oddity shop.'

Margery chuckled. They followed Seren out through the pedestrian exit of the car park and down through the old housing estate that led to the riverbank. Maybe

Seren would wait for a bus, she could be going anywhere, according to Rose. Seren wandered at an easy ambling pace, the fog disguising Margery and Clementine slightly as they followed. They had already decided that if Seren caught them they would come clean.

They continued around past the Bell and Hope, falling into a steady pace behind Seren, careful not to slip on the leaves lining the pavements. The night was dreary at best, Seren's orange anorak the most notable thing on their journey. As they passed the pub, Margery suddenly realised where they were headed.

'This is the way to Caroline's,' she told Clementine, who nodded seriously.

A few minutes later and their suspicions were confirmed. Seren entered the house and closed the front door behind her. Margery and Clementine stood stupidly staring at it for a moment, as though Seren would suddenly reappear and yell, 'Fooled you! That'll teach you for following me!' Instead, the light went on in the hallway.

'Well, I mean it makes a certain kind of sense, doesn't it?' Clementine shrugged. Gary Matthews stepped into the bay window of the living room and dragged the long curtains shut. 'Rose isn't going to like this.'

'No,' Margery said, on the brink of wild maniacal laughter. Seren and Gary had moved in together right under Rose's nose and she was so dramatically wrapped up in herself that she hadn't been able to work it out. Seren did not think that Rose would give her blessing, or she wouldn't be sneaking around between the houses. She turned to Clementine. 'What should we do? Should we knock?'

'Could do, maybe we could offer to tell Rose?' Clementine said. It began to rain again, and Clementine pulled her coat closer to her face. Before Margery could answer a door down the street opened and a figure stepped out of it. Clementine gasped in surprise. It was Miss Macdonald.

She still had the bandages around her neck from the hospital and her face was horribly bruised, but she was alive and well enough to be visiting people. She disappeared up the street, and from the doorway of her house Liv Weaver watched her go, her arms folded, leaning against the wood.

'I don't understand,' Clementine said. 'Her husband had an affair with Miss Macdonald. Liv told us as much.'

'So why would she invite her in?' Margery whispered.

'Hey!' came a yell from behind them. Liv looked up at the noise and noticed them, stepping back into her house and slamming the door. Margery turned and saw Jess had stepped out of the Bell and Hope and was beckoning for them to come over. Margery and Clementine exchanged a look and then they both independently decided to go and see what she wanted.

'I think you've got someone to apologise to,' Jess said, glaring at them both as they approached the pub. 'Come on.'

They followed her down the steps inside and found themselves in the warm bar area again. Tonight, it was nearly as empty as it had been the first time they'd visited. The curfew couldn't have been doing any good for the town's businesses. Mr Evans sat on a bar stool looking grey and tired, nursing a half-empty pint of beer.

'Hello,' Margery squeaked, she hadn't expected him to be here. She didn't know what she had thought when Jess demanded they follow her.

'Hello, Mrs Butcher–Baker,' he said. He didn't seem angry, which made Margery feel worse about it.

'You want to say sorry to him for what you've done,' Jess spat, heading back to her usual spot behind the bar. She put her hands on her hips and looked between them all pointedly. 'Getting an innocent man arrested!'

'We didn't know you were innocent,' Clementine said, 'how could we when you lied about your alibi? And the needles we found—'

'They're for my steroids,' Mr Evans said, picking up the glass in one giant hand and taking a glug.

'Your... what?' Clementine asked.

'My steroids.' Mr Evans put the glass back down and shrugged. 'Not point me lying about it now, my body-building career is over, isn't it?'

'What?' Margery began, but Jess interrupted.

'He had that set of needles for personal use,' she said, folding her arms. For a moment she looked like she might cry, but instead, she pulled herself together, steeling her jaw. 'They couldn't find Liam Weaver's DNA on them because he was using them for himself.'

'Is that true?' Margery turned back to Mr Evans in surprise. He nodded.

'I'm... I was a semi-professional bodybuilder, but not without help,' he said in a small voice. 'I injected steroids to help keep my physique. It's hard getting older, you have to work so much harder at it, I just couldn't keep up.'

'But anabolic steroids aren't illegal for personal use, are they?' Clementine waved her hands as she tried to grasp hold of the situation. 'I thought you could get them on prescription.'

'They are illegal for competitions,' Mr Evans said gravely. 'And I had a big one coming up in a few months.'

'But you still lied about your alibi.' Clementine was red in the face. 'There's nothing to prove what you're saying is true.'

'He was with me.' A tiny man at the back of the pub stood from his seat in the window. Margery hadn't even noticed him in the darkness of the pub. He was older and balding but still looked like he could outrun all of them in a one–hundred–metre sprint. 'I'm his coach. He asked me not to say anything, said it would all come right in the end.'

'See.' Jess gestured to the man.

'Can you prove that?' Clementine asked him, before turning back to Mr Evans 'Where were you the day Mr Weaver died?'

'We were at the betting shop in Ittonvale,' Mr Evans said. 'The police got the CCTV and after they checked the needles they let me go.'

Clementine went white, realising immediately what it meant. Margery sat down on the stool nearest. The crushing guilt was too much, she didn't know if she'd ever be able to pull herself back out from underneath it. After knowing that in their haste to solve a crime an innocent man had been accused. It made her feel sick.

'It's your fault,' Jess barked. Margery felt herself going red as she confronted them. 'The Dinner Lady Detectives! If you can call yourselves that. You've done nothing but fuck everything up for everyone. What if the killer put those needles there to frame him? You didn't have any trouble coming to the pub and accusing me of stuff!'

Margery wanted to disappear under her chair and never come out. She expected Clementine to yell some-thing back, but Clementine had the same dejected look plastered on her face. A wave of shame and guilt rose up inside her ribcage, Jess was right, what on earth had they been playing at? What if Liam Weaver's killer had walked free because they'd been too busy making false accusations?

'You're not police officers!' Jess heckled. 'Why are you acting like you are?'

She finished her rant and finally sat down on her chair behind the bar.

'It's not their fault, Jess,' Mr Evans said kindly. 'I hid the needles up there, and anyone could have found them. I don't know what else is going on though, the police asked me a lot of weird questions. Showed me some weird shape thing...'

'The turned A,' Clementine said. 'Had you seen it before?'

'Never.' Mr Evans shrugged. 'They think the students have got something to do with it, I told them not my students, my students would have painted some swear-words or something.'

'Wait, what did you and Mr Weaver argue about at the harvest festival?' Margery asked him and Mr Evans took another sip of his beer before answering.

'He owed me loads of money from the gambling debts,' he said. 'I know you must know about that, but I didn't kill him for it. Why would I? I'll never get my money back now. Christ, his poor wife. He owed money everywhere; they were going to lose everything. I don't know how she put up with it.'

Neither did Margery.

Chapter Nineteen

Back at work in the canteen the next day, Margery thought it all over, though it was hard to concentrate with all the normal kitchen distractions. As per usual, her plate was loaded so high with things to do it was as though she was at Ittonvale's all-you-can-eat carvery. Today, not even work could snap her out of her thoughts. They hadn't yet seen Rose to try and explain what they had seen of Seren. The talk they'd had with Mr Evans kept whirling around in her head.

The dinner lady team had arrived at the school too early to give their DNA swabs and it had caused a debate before they even began work.

'What have we all got to hide?' Clementine had shrugged. 'Nothing. And if it helps catch the attacker or that group of strangers then that's a good thing.'

'What if one of us did a crime and then forgot?' Sharon had wailed. 'Or we're really closely related to the killer and we've got the same DNA!'

'That's already happened to me once and I was fine!' Clementine had laughed.

Karen wondered if their DNA would be used to make clones and then an argument had broken out about whether they were already all clones and if you'd remember being a clone or not. Margery had needed to step in after Clementine suggested that she'd never seen

Karen or Sharon in the same room as the killer and the room had descended into chaos. After Karen and Sharon had calmed down, it was decided that they would all go and give their samples immediately after they finished work, clones be damned. Though they were all still a bit wary.

Margery had tried to get involved with the latest inane team conversation – the dinner lady team's favourite toothpaste. It had culminated in Clementine telling the story of how she had squeezed a blob of face scrub onto her toothbrush accidentally – 'My teeth would have been full of purifying grains!' – but nothing was quite distracting enough. Now there would be no more mysteries, no more murders to solve. They had to admit to themselves that they were not good enough to be involved. They could have very well have ruined Mr Evans' life with their meddling. Though Mr Barrow had stopped her in the main corridor before work and told her that no matter what had happened Mr Evans would be suspended anyway. To be a suspect in an unsolved murder investigation was one thing, but to add steroid use on school grounds and the illegal gambling ring – which may or may not have led to Mr Weaver's death – was another. He assured her he was glad that they had brought the matter to light, and he didn't blame them for any of it. That didn't seem to alleviate her fears, however, and lunch time was well underway before Margery realised that in all her worrying, she hadn't remembered to switch the panini machine on.

'You'll have to have something else,' Gloria told the Year Seven, not unkindly. 'We've had an electrical problem with it, you see. Why don't you have a nice filling jacket potato or a KitKat Chunky instead?'

'Thanks, Gloria,' Margery said when the line had begun to move away again.

'That's all right.' Gloria looked at her with concern. 'Are you okay?'

'Yes,' Margery said firmly. 'I'm absolutely fine.'

'Sure?' Gloria asked, with an eyebrow raise that told Margery she didn't believe her. 'You just don't seem very with it today.'

'It's just all a bit strange, isn't it?' Margery explained as the line of children began to thin. 'They haven't caught those people in masks. We should have known it wasn't Mr Evans. Even if it had been him who killed Mr Weaver, he isn't a group of people, is he? Like the people outside Rose's on Halloween. Who are they?'

'I agree.' Gloria sighed, folding her arms, and leaning back on the nearest counter, ignoring the children in the queue. 'It's all a bit weird and I don't like the idea of this curfew. I saw the police on the way in, they've started searching students' bags. What if they search our bags and find all the crisps we've stolen from the vending machine?'

Miss Macdonald's attacker was still at large. Nervousness filtered down from staff to the students, the latter were much better-behaved than usual. Usually there was jostling and shoving and children screeching at each other in the lunchtime queue, but today was very different. It was almost as though they had all been scared into submission. They were interrupted by the arrival of the TikTok group, who weaved their way through the canteen all holding a shop-bought sandwich, they were the only students left who were still on normal behaviour.

'What the hell is that?' Gloria stood to attention as they sat at the table nearest and clicked at them with her fingers.

'Hey! You can't eat outside food in here! School dinners or packed lunches only!'

'My mum got us all a meal deal. It's a supermarket packed lunch!' Number One beamed at them from her seat. 'Hey, miss, will you please be on our school podcast now? We did a video to promote it last night and it got loads of likes. Miss Grant says we're probably going to get an A on our media studies coursework.'

'No,' Margery said, at the same time as Clementine said, 'Yes.' She turned to stare at her in dismay, she hadn't even seen her return from washing up in the main kitchen.

'Oh, come on, Margery, we promised them before,' Clementine said, pulling off the washing-up gloves. 'Anyway, it might be fun, we need a bit of amusement, don't we? And it's for, oh what is it called...? Education!'

Margery couldn't do anything but agree. For once, Clementine was entirely right, if nothing else it was certain to be very distracting. She sighed and turned back to the teenagers who had already started on their crisps.

'Fine,' she said through gritted teeth. 'Where do you usually record it?'

'The library!' Number One looked extremely pleased with herself. 'We've got Miss Grant next lesson, so we can ask if she'll help us set up the equipment. How about half three today? The library closes at four.'

'As long as it's okay with Miss Grant.' Margery said. It wouldn't do to upset any other teachers, not after the debacle with Miss Macdonald and Mr Evans.

The English department were no longer on speaking terms with the catering department and that had been before Miss Macdonald's attack. It was making things very complicated indeed. Now they would post their tea and coffee orders underneath the door once the canteen was shut. More than once the form had ended up under a prep table overnight and gone missing, leaving the English department in an even worse mood when they didn't get their biscuits. She hoped they could find a way to patch things up. Maybe if they could then they would be able to find out why Miss Macdonald had Dr Roberts' personnel file and why she had been at Liv Weaver's house. Were the two related? She tried to squash all the thoughts down now they had officially been removed from the case by Officer Thomas. She thought about the text message, and Jess's accusations at the pub afterwards, remembering the details bitterly.

'Okay!' Number One jumped up, meal deal forgotten and rushed out of the canteen, not even waiting for the end of lunch bell before deciding to go and ask Miss Grant.

'Gosh, what are we getting ourselves into?' Margery asked as Gloria chuckled.

There was a shout from the back of the canteen, they whipped their heads around at the sound. It was Ceri-Ann, rushing towards them all in her big outside coat.

'How did it go?' Gloria asked her, not waiting for Ceri-Ann to make it inside the prep area before yelling over to her. Ceri-Ann didn't reply with words, instead, she pulled out a photograph from her coat pocket and handed it over, beaming from ear to ear.

'Oh, Ceri,' Gloria said, smiling down at the scan photo, her eyes filling with tears.

'Let's see.' Clementine barged over and took the photograph from Gloria. 'Oh, that is lovely. Well done, Ceri-Ann, marvellous work.'

'They said everything's all growing and that,' Ceri-Ann beamed, looking proudly at the photo. 'I got Symon to bring me here after the scan, he's got to go back to work monitoring the testing station anyway and I thought you'd all want to see.'

'Did they say what it is?' Gloria asked.

'A boy!' Ceri-Ann said. The dinner ladies all oohed at that.

'Good, Margery and I will need someone to open jars and reach the tall shelves for us when we get older,' Clementine said, 'it's a miracle we've got this far.'

She took the ultrasound and stuck it to the whiteboard with Blu-tack, next to Margery's ordering list.

'Welcome to the family, Clement!' she said, stepping back to admire the photograph again.

—

It didn't take long to pack the kitchen down and turn everything off, even with the interruption of Ceri-Ann, and soon they were all putting their aprons and tabards into the kitchen washing machine and getting ready to go and get their coats. They were interrupted by Dr Roberts who had entered the kitchen through the canteen door and was staring at them wide-eyed.

'Oh hello,' she said, 'I didn't realise you'd all still be here.'

'Of course,' Margery said, looking at the clock. They had run over a little bit, but it wasn't even three o'clock yet. Dr Roberts looked ready for home, her laptop bag swung over one arm and a large yellow, plastic box balanced in the other. Margery recognised it from somewhere, but she couldn't put her finger on it, though the shape was familiar.

'Right, right,' Dr Roberts said, frowning at the sight of them. They all looked at each other in surprise.

'Can we help you?' Margery asked, remembering her manners. 'Do you need an apple or a banana?'

'The food bank hasn't come to collect the out-of-date sandwiches yet.' Gloria smiled, offering her a stale cheese and onion from the trolley she had put aside for collection.

'Oh no, no thank you.' Dr Roberts gave a forced smile in return, it looked strained and the warmth of it didn't quite meet her eyes. 'I'm just going to use your fire escape.'

'Why?' Margery asked. 'It gets very slippy out there, especially in this weather. It's probably best if you don't.'

'Oh, well.' Dr Roberts looked around at all of them, suddenly realising she was outnumbered. She clutched the box closer to her side and gestured to the door again. 'Are you sure I couldn't just—'

'I just don't see why you would want to.' Margery shrugged. 'Why don't you just go out the main entrance so I can lock the kitchen up? I really wouldn't like you to fall on the stairs, honestly, I'm not sure it would be worth the risk even if there was a need for the fire escape!'

She smiled in what she hoped was a kind way at Dr Roberts, but Dr Roberts only grimaced back, blinking rapidly. It was early for a teacher to leave work, Margery thought suddenly. They were all here right up until the final bell rang at three-thirty at the very earliest and much later than that usually. Especially now in the run-up to the Year Eleven mock exams after Christmas. She would have expected Dr Roberts to be rushed off her feet with work to do at this time of year.

'All right,' Dr Roberts said briskly.

She turned on her heel and disappeared back through the canteen as quickly as she had arrived, leaving them all staring after her as the door slammed shut again.

'What just happened?' Margery asked Gloria and Clementine, who were standing nearest to her. They both shook their heads, their eyes narrowed.

'That seems very odd, doesn't it?' Clementine tapped her fingers to her chin. 'Very odd indeed.'

'You don't think she was trying to go out that way, so she didn't have to go past the DNA-swabbing area?' Margery said, the epiphany arriving suddenly.

'Why would she do that?' Gloria asked, crossing her arms. 'Do you think she'd have some objection to it for scientific reasons?'

'Yes, like Karen and Sharon and the cloning.' Clementine snorted. 'No, I think that maybe there is something more nefarious going on.' She looked at Margery with bright eyes for a moment before realising her own vow to stop being involved in any of it. 'Well, I mean… it's probably nothing. Let's all just go home.'

'We've got to go and do that interview with the children.' Margery sighed, regretting agreeing to it already. 'I hope it won't take long.'

Chapter Twenty

They gave their DNA samples, which involved a simple swab and a consent form that Margery tried to read fully but ended up signing anyway after the first hundred words in teeny-tiny writing. Then they rushed upstairs to the library for the dreaded interview. They walked past the desk where Mrs Buch usually handed out bookmarks and over to the back of the room where the outdated computer suite full of big boxy desktops still lived, though Margery doubted anyone still used them. The wallpaper was peeling and the books themselves were dusty and their spines broken. They dodged a pair of Year Sevens eagerly running past them on their way to finish their homework and made it across to where numbers one and two sat, laptop and microphones at the ready.

'Hello, miss!' Number One leapt from her seat as they arrived and rushed around the table, dragging their chairs out for them. They had both changed out of their school uniforms and were dressed casually, in huge sweatshirt tops and big chunky trainers. Margery found it quite comforting; if you squinted hard enough you could pretend it was 1997 again. 'We didn't think you were going to come! Mrs Buch keeps trying to kick us out.' Margery could see Mrs Buch glaring at them all through the nearest shelving unit, she was the sort of person who called the police if a delivery driver was outside of their house for too long.

Margery and Clementine sat down and Margery tried not to let the concern show on her face. It wasn't that she was scared exactly, but the last time she had spoken in public had been their wedding day and she had stammered and stuttered all through her speech. Her nerves were not quelled at all when they all put on their headphones attached to the very professional-looking mixing desk and Number Two flapped about them all, pulling condenser microphones on little stands to and from them as he listened to their general chatter through his own headphones. It was all increasingly nerve-wracking, Margery thought, as she pulled her jumper away from her neck, the wool suddenly feeling tight and itchy. And it was a prime example of where the headmaster spent the school budget. Of course, technology was important, she scoffed to herself, but so was nutritious food full of vitamins from good suppliers.

Number One walked them through 'the plan', as she called it, which was just a series of questions she was going to ask them about the events of the last few years. Then they would have a chat about the new murders.

'No,' Margery said, 'both Mr Weaver's killer and Miss Macdonald's attacker are still at large, it would be grotesque. And that's without considering that it would be risking an active investigation.'

'I agree,' Clementine nodded. 'It would be disrespectful to the dead.'

She took Margery's hand and squeezed it. Number One looked perturbed for a minute, but then agreed reluctantly, her face falling as her scoop was ruined.

Number Two started the laptop's recording program and then they launched straight into it.

'Don't worry,' Number One said, her eyes bright with excitement. 'I've got a theme tune too, we recorded my nan singing and it sounded creepy, so we put some piano under it. We put it on after when we edit.'

'All right then,' Margery said, hoping her face didn't reveal that she hadn't understood a word of that.

'Welcome to "Well That's Scary!" with me, Amelia Hill,' Number One said.

'And me! Oliver Moore,' Number Two said.

Margery and Clementine exchanged a look and Margery vowed to write the names down later if she could still remember them.

'And on today's show, we're going to be talking to...' They both began to drum on the desk in front of them. 'The Dinner Lady Detectives!'

'They've solved loads of crimes at school and now they're here to tell us how!' Oliver said. 'So, without further ado, welcome to the podcast!'

'Hello,' Clementine said weakly.

'Miss,' Amelia said, and Margery wondered for a moment if they didn't know Margery and Clementine's names either. 'Can you tell us about the Kitchen Freezer Murder, or KFM for short? We've spoken about it on our TikTok before...'

'At "Well, That's Scary!"' Oliver said, in his best radio voice.

'And on our blog,' Amelia said in hers.

'W-w-w dot well that's scary dot com!' Oliver singsonged. Margery could feel the confusion written on her face.

'But we'd love to hear the story from you in person!' Amelia smiled between them. 'When did you find out that your kitchen manager had died?'

'Oh, it was just a normal day! I'd spent it organising our under-sink storage in the kitchen and we were just settling in for the evening after an exciting tea of buttered crumpets,' Clementine began, completely in her element, telling a long story to a captive audience. 'Then our very good friend and colleague Seren came to tell us all about it…'

'Thanks, miss,' Amelia said as they all got up to leave. Oliver began packing the equipment away in bags ready to take back to the media studies room.

'Not a problem.' Clementine smiled at her. 'Anytime! We've had a great time, haven't we, Margery?'

'Yes,' Margery croaked. In truth she had not had the greatest of times, barely speaking unless Amelia or Oliver had asked her a direct question. And every time she had done so, her voice had constricted. The two students would have some editing work cut out for them going to make the podcast listenable.

'Will your parents give permission to give DNA samples?' she asked out of curiosity as they tucked the chairs back under the library table. Mrs Buch was standing nearby waiting for them to leave so she could lock up, her red indignant face peering out from behind her desk. It was late again.

'Yeah,' Amelia and Oliver both said together, and then began laughing at the look on the other's face.

'I'm not doing it though,' Oliver said and then squeaked. If Margery hadn't known any better, she would have been sure that Amelia had stamped on his foot.

'I hope they get something useful out of it,' Clementine said with a sigh. 'All those strangers in masks. The school needs to sort it out.'

Amelia's face fell, Oliver went red, and they exchanged a look that might have gone unnoticed if Margery had not been paying attention.

'What?' she asked. 'Is there something you're not telling us?'

'No,' they said in unison again. Though this time they didn't find it so funny.

'We'd better go, we'll miss the bus,' Amelia said, grabbing her bag quickly.

'Yeah, and I've got to return the mixing desk and microphones.' Oliver grabbed for his own things, neither of them would look Margery and Clementine in the eye.

'I'll help you,' Amelia began to grab bags and cases and together they quickly marched away.

'Wait!' Margery called. 'You forgot your book!' It was no good, the students had already left. Mrs Buch jangled her keys loudly again from the library door.

'Come on,' Clementine said, grabbing Amelia's school-issue Maths book in one hand and Margery's hand in the other. 'They can't have got far.'

By the time they had escaped the library and Mrs Buch's annoyed glares, they realised that of course two people a third of their age would be able to escape in time, even laden down with equipment.

'Well, that's annoying.' Clementine said, looking at the notepad. The library door locked behind them ominously and Margery turned just in time to see Mrs Buch scuttling away from them down the corridor.

They went back to the changing room to get their own big winter coats. Gloria had long gone of course, along with Seren, Karen and Sharon. In the chaos of the day, they had completely forgotten to ask Seren about her house. Well, Rose would just have to wait for the mystery to be solved, especially as she wasn't going to like the answer to her questions anyway. She pulled her coat on, zipped it up to her chin and pulled her handbag over her shoulder before she turned to Clementine to try and convince her of what she had in mind, leaning on her walking stick. The conversation with Dr Roberts had begun to niggle away at the back of Margery's mind. Dr Roberts had never asked to leave through their fire escape before. And she'd have struggled to get into the kitchen without them knowing. If Dr Roberts wasn't going to go and give her DNA, she thought, then they would just have to see what she was hiding. Margery cleared her throat as Clementine struggled with the laces on her boots.

'Look, Clem, I really want to find out a bit more about Dr Roberts...' she began, testing the waters with her little toe. Clementine murmured as she tied the lace to show she was listening. 'She's only been at the school for a few years, we don't know much about her...' Margery thought carefully about what she could say next to pique Clementine's interest. 'I just keep thinking... well... we didn't see her leave after the Halloween party, did we?'

'No,' Clementine said, 'but we didn't see Karen and Sharon, or Mrs Winkle sneak out either, did we? Granted, Mrs Winkle is only about three foot, so she is quite hard to see...'

'Well…' Margery said, reaching out with her hands to try and articulate her thoughts and then not knowing what to say next.

'We saw Miss Macdonald leave Mrs Weaver's house yesterday though, didn't we?' Clementine reminded her. 'What was she doing there? I'm sure that's more interesting than Dr Roberts.'

'Maybe she went to apologise?' Margery suggested. 'Pay her respects?'

'Giving condolences?' Clementine said as she scratched her head. 'Bit late, but maybe she wanted to wait for the crowd to thin a bit. The funeral is next week now they've done the autopsy. Maybe she went to apologise for the affair. That seems weird too though.'

Margery wracked her brain, but she couldn't think of a single thing that would intrigue Clementine enough to change her mind.

'What was she holding in the box?' Margery finally said. 'The box under her arm?'

'What box? Oh…' Clementine tilted her head to the side and paused. 'Gosh, I don't know. But you can't think a box had something to do with this.'

'Well, I'm going to have a look at her classroom,' Margery said finally. 'I can't stand not knowing. Imagine if she did have something to do with it and we didn't do anything.'

'You can't be serious! We've told the police we aren't going to help any… Officer Thomas said they wouldn't hesitate to arrest us! Why Dr Roberts? You can't go poking at things for a hunch.'

'I know what we said,' Margery said in as firm a voice as she could muster. 'But you've dragged me into numerous things over the years…'

'Like what?' Clementine gaped at her indignantly.

'Like when you said we should see if we could find out how Caroline died, and we got locked in the freezer,' Margery said.

'That could have happened to anyone...' Clementine gasped in outrage.

'Or when we broke into Ittonvale School with Rose and nearly got arrested,' Margery pointed out.

'Admittedly that was a bit of a mistake...' Clementine spluttered.

'And I still remember that day in 2016 when we were nearly pecked to death by a seagull because you wanted to have a better look at its nest.' Margery held up her hand to silence Clementine. 'We've done all those mad things on your say-so and now that I want to do something you say it's too dangerous.'

'It *is* too dangerous,' Clementine said softly. 'You know how I feel about it all after the summer holiday. What if you get hurt? The police won't be around to help us now.'

'I'm fine!' Margery cried, slumping down on the bench behind her, her bag falling over her shoulder and clattering onto it with a thump. The walking stick fell to the floor and rolled under the bench. 'I'm absolutely fine!'

'I don't think you are, Margery.' Clementine played with the sleeves of her own coat, avoiding looking her in the eye. 'I think you're trying to avoid dealing with the trauma on the cliff by running around solving murders. This case is way too big for us this time.'

'No, it isn't!' Margery snapped.

'Yes, it is!' Clementine laughed. 'It's crazy, we should have never let them drag us into it. This is the last thing you need after everything that's happened.'

'I'm fine!' Margery yelled again, feeling anger well up inside her. Clementine didn't even recoil, she looked up at her calmly.

'What if you just took some more time off, got your head around it all—'

'I can't,' Margery said. 'What about the kitchen and the EHO inspection?'

'We'd all survive,' Clementine said. 'Deep down, you know we would.'

Margery took a deep breath. Clementine was right, the voice of reason in the darkness for once. But she didn't know how to go on otherwise. Clementine sat down next to her on the bench.

'What should we do now?' Margery said, looking over to Clementine, who reached for her hand and held it tightly in her own.

Clementine looked like she was considering things, mulling it all over in her head. Margery ran her fingers over the wrinkles on the back of Clementine's hand and across her wedding band, remembering the day she had put it on her finger.

'For what it's worth, I think you might be right about Dr Roberts.' Clementine gave her hand a squeeze. 'And I'm sorry about all the other times I dragged you into something. It's not so much fun being the one who doesn't want to get involved, I never realised!'

Margery chuckled. 'A taste of your own medicine, I suppose!'

'Look, let's tell the police about it and see what they say,' Clementine said.

'Okay,' Margery sighed. 'But what about Officer Thomas? He told us to leave it.'

Clementine groaned and pulled Margery up from the bench. 'Come on then.'

'Really?' Margery smiled at her as Clementine threw her hands in the air.

'We must be losing our minds.' Clementine groaned. 'But let's do it.'

Chapter Twenty-One

Dr Roberts' classroom wasn't locked as the PE changing room had been. In fact, they managed to simply wander up the stairs to the second floor and straight into the room. Margery had always disliked this bit of the school. The science labs were cold and dark, and they hadn't dared turn on the long strip lights that ran across the room in case they were seen from the outside as the science lab had no curtains. Instead, Clementine turned her phone torch on, the narrow beam projecting an orange glow across the room, bouncing off the schoolwork on the walls. Margery closed the door, fingers accidentally brushing against Dr Roberts' white lab coat hanging on the back of it as she did so, and she was glad that they had the foresight to wear the plastic gloves they usually used in the kitchen to prepare raw meat. The door creaked as it shut and then the room was completely silent.

'Where should we start?' Clementine whispered, looking around the room, the beam from the phone torch leaping wildly. 'What are we looking for?'

'I'm not sure really,' Margery said, scratching her head. 'You begin over there,' she gestured at the other side of the room. 'I'll check her desk.'

Clementine nodded and made her way to the cupboards on the far side of the lab, wooden stools scraping on the floor as she squeezed past the rows of them lined against the tables. Margery approached the desk, which had nothing unusual about it at first sight. She looked the digital whiteboard over first but could see nothing of interest, so she began to open the desk drawers and look inside, everything made harder by the lack of dexterity in her gloved fingers.

There was not much to look at in the first two, just the normal sort of thing a teacher might keep in their desk; pens, pencils, a stapler, half a sandwich that was going stale, a letter in an unmarked envelope. *A letter in an unmarked envelope!* Margery thought to herself. She leaned her walking stick against the desk and then took it out of the drawer and quickly opened it with both hands. The envelope's seal had been broken a while before, judging by how worn it was, but the paper inside was still pristine. The letter was written in green ink, the kind from a fountain pen or similar. The handwriting was familiar, but she couldn't place it.

> *a new chance arrives*
>
> *at the spot in the wood*
>
> *money will free you*
>
> *Yours,*
>
> $\forall$

Margery read it three times. What a strange note. The symbol stared back at her in the colour she now associated with all the strangers in cloaks: green. She wondered why they kept using that colour.

'Margery!' Clementine half hissed, half cried out into the silent classroom. 'Look at this.'

Margery whipped her head around to the noise, just in time to see Clementine wheel the full-size skeleton out of the walk-in cupboard at the side of the room. She put the letter back in the envelope and slid it into her bag before she moved to chastise Clementine.

'Put that back,' she hissed as Clementine rolled it towards her. 'We don't need it.'

'It scared me!' Clementine whispered back, like that would absolve her of any new actions involving the skeleton. 'It was just in this—'

They were interrupted by the door handle turning and in the split second after they turned to stare at each other in wide-eyed horror. Clementine grabbed her by the sleeve and dragged her into the cupboard, pulling the skeleton on wheels with them. Margery stumbled, nearly falling, until she managed to steady herself, realising with horror that she had left her walking stick leaning against the desk. The cupboard was very dark, and Margery could barely see a thing as Clementine struggled to turn the light off on her phone, the glow beaming madly over the walls.

They waited and waited. Margery felt the room begin to constrict around her under the black of the darkness, her chest heavy as dread settled into it. Even Clementine's fingers against her own couldn't help. Despite her better judgement, she reached forward and opened the door a tiny crack, just enough so they could peer out into the classroom. The lights had been turned back on and it was almost blinding as a sliver of it reached the inside of the cupboard. The shelves were full of textbooks and scientific equipment she wouldn't know how to use. At the back of the room was a ladder, she noticed dimly. And there was a toolbox on the floor underneath it.

She peeked through into the classroom and saw Dr Roberts sitting behind her desk, tapping away at her laptop casually until the sound of Netflix starting up began and she leaned back in her chair. If she had noticed Margery's walking stick perched to the side of her desk, she had not paid it any attention. Margery breathed a sigh of relief. Dr Roberts took an apple from her bag and bit into it. Margery began to wonder how long they would be there. How long would Dr Roberts watch television for? Was she still trying to avoid leaving through the main entrance? There were too many unknowns and variables and questions.

Maybe Dr Roberts thought that if she waited long enough then there would be no police. Margery wondered why she hadn't tried another fire escape or back entrance, but maybe Dr Roberts had had just as much trouble as she had trying to leave through their fire escape. They all had cameras outside now, thanks to all the horrible incidents over the past few years.

Clementine had begun her own plan. She had managed to turn off the torch but now the room was lit by the soft glow of her phone as she wrote a text message. Margery leaned over to see what she was typing. *SOS*, it said, *stuck in the science lab. Help distract Dr R!* Clementine paused to think for a moment and then added, *We know where Seren goes, help us or we won't tell you!* It took her a very long time to tap out the whole message and Margery began to wring her hands together in worry. Clementine pursed her lips in thought and then finally added, *Kind regards, Mrs Clementine Butcher-Baker.* She considered it again, tapping the fingers of her free hand on her chin, and then deleted the word *Kind* and replaced it with the word *No.* Margery snatched the phone from her and pressed

Send before Clementine could add another time-wasting epitaph.

The message whizzed away, and they stood as still as they could manage. Margery distracted herself by trying to think of the note, and why she knew the writing. They had certainly seen the symbol before, and they knew it had something to do with the Maths department. Had Mr Weaver written the note? Was he the culprit behind the 'for all' symbol they had come to find everywhere? If he had been, Margery noted sourly, someone had taken his place once he was dead. She realised with a sudden clarity that she knew exactly where she had seen the handwriting before.

'Clem,' she whispered quietly into the darkness. 'I found a poem like the ones we saw in Mr Weaver's office.'

Clementine oohed at that, and Margery wished she could have taken the piece of paper out of the bag and shown her it. Instead, she leaned back against the wall and waited for whatever fate had in store for them both if Rose would come to their rescue. For all they knew she might have left work and gone home already.

If Miss Macdonald had written those poems, why would she write an identical one for Dr Roberts? Though there had been no name addressed on the poem she had just found. Only the symbol, as stark as always, filling the page at the bottom. Margery lowered herself to the floor, careful not to catch her leg as she did so, it was still painful. Standing without her walking stick wasn't helping at all.

There was a knock of the classroom door, though it was barely audible over the show Dr Roberts was watching. Margery peered through the gap again just in time to see her get up and open it. Rose was waiting on the other side of the door, and she didn't waste any time before she was swooping into the room without an invitation, pottering in on her tall heels and surveying the place with her usual stern eyes.

'Well, you've certainly made this room your own,' she said, wandering to the poster of the periodic table stuck to the wall by the whiteboard. Dr Roberts looked on from her chair, her arms folded. If she was nervous about the deputy head's presence, not a single drop of it showed. Rose noticed Margery's walking stick immediately, Margery saw her eyes flit to it and then look away again just as quickly.

'Can I help you with something?' Dr Roberts' eyes were steely, she looked ready for a fight.

Rose sized her up, giving her a cool once-over. Margery worried for a moment that Rose wouldn't be able to come up with a reason to distract Dr Roberts long enough for them to escape and they would be stuck here for another few hours while she watched the laptop, or worse, caught hiding in her cupboard. What if she decided to get the next day's class ready while she was up here and needed to get out the Bunsen burners sitting behind them on the shelf? She needn't have worried. Years of drama training had prepared Summerview School's Head of Drama for such an eventuality. In fact, Margery thought, it almost sounded like Rose was enjoying herself.

'I need you to come to my office and sign some paperwork,' Rose said, in the matter-of-fact manner of someone who spends all their time telling people what to do. 'It seems when you started here we didn't get an up-to-date emergency contact or health questionnaire. I'm afraid what with all that's gone on recently we need to amend that right away.'

'Really?' Dr Roberts scoffed. 'What a thing to admit to a member of the health and safety team. I'm sure they'll have a field day at our next meeting.'

Rose didn't say anything, just crossed her arms and gave her a cold stare. Dr Roberts still didn't look entirely convinced but she sighed and then stood, gesturing for Rose to lead the way anyway. They left, the door slamming behind them. Margery and Clementine waited a moment before they scuttled out of the cupboard, looking at each other in relief.

'That was a close call,' Clementine whispered as they crossed the room to the classroom door. Margery eagerly grasped for her walking stick, glad to be reunited. 'How long do you think we should wait before we leave?'

'I'm not sure.' Margery leaned again the door and listened. She couldn't hear anything, but that didn't mean that if they bounded straight out of the classroom and into the corridor they wouldn't accidentally catch up to Rose and Dr Roberts. Clementine was looking under Dr Roberts' desk with interest.

'Look at this,' she said, lifting up the yellow box Dr Roberts had been holding when she had tried to use their fire escape. She turned it over, showing off the biohazard symbol plastered to the side and Margery realised why she had recognised it. It was a sharps box. The very same type her mother used to have for her insulin injection needles. Clementine shook the box and the lone rattle of the object inside caused them to look at each other.

'Can you open it?' Margery asked, hunching over to have a better look.

Clementine shook her head, trying to lift the plastic lid, which was stuck fast. 'It's one of those lockable ones.'

'She's diabetic though, isn't she?' Margery said, thinking back to the conversation they had had with her at Ittonvale Farm when she had mentioned sugar causing a potential hyper. 'That must be why she has it.'

'Why is there only one thing inside though?' Clementine said, shaking the box again to prove her point. 'Why would she try and take it out of the building with her?'

'Gosh.' Margery scratched her head. 'Mr Weaver's puncture wound, you don't think? No, that's silly, Clem. Maybe she's run out of sharps boxes at home? Or this is her work one? She must check her sugar levels during the workday.'

'We should still get the police to come and have a look.' Clementine put the box back and stood again, brushing the dust off her trousers. 'They can test whatever's inside it with all the other DNA, can't they? If it's her DNA then that's fine.'

'That seems like a massive overstep of boundaries,' Margery said, her voice rising in pitch. She had wanted to poke around, but not like this. 'What if we're wrong? What if it's another Mr Evans situation?'

Clementine's eyes widened, and she put it down while she looked around for a solution. 'Well, maybe we can hide it somewhere in here or take it with us?'

'No,' Margery shook her head. 'She'll know it's missing. Wouldn't you? And we can't take medical equipment away with us, what if she needs it?'

'There's got to be a way,' Clementine said, reaching to pick it up again.

'She could come back at any moment,' Margery said, wringing her hands together. 'We're wasting time just standing here. And if she comes back and sees it's gone then all hell will break loose.'

Clementine looked truly conflicted for a moment, but then relief washed over her face. 'My keys.'

'What?'

Clementine pulled her keys from her handbag and took off the GPS fob. 'Do you have any glue, Margery?'

Margery stared at her. 'No. Of course I don't.'

'Not even a bit of tape?'

'No, why?'

'If she takes it home,' Clementine explained, 'then the fob will go home with her. But if she takes it somewhere else...'

'Oh,' Margery said, understanding at once. 'Then we can tell the police.'

'Exactly!'

'There must be something in here, surely it's part of teaching college to be prepared to glue all sorts.' Margery rummaged through Dr Roberts' desk, finding an old roll of Sellotape and holding it up triumphantly. 'Quick, tape it on!'

Clementine taped the fob to the bottom of the sharps bin, they put everything back where it had been and rushed out of the classroom. Nervously, they crept down the corridor and down the stairs, not daring to speak until they were near the police checkpoint in the main entrance.

'That was too close!' Margery said. 'That was good thinking though, Clem, with the key fob and Rose.'

'Thank goodness she's an insane workaholic,' Clementine said. 'I knew she'd still be here, especially now Seren isn't around to wait on her hand and foot.'

'Did you find anything else apart from the skeleton when you were looking inside the cupboard?' Margery asked. 'Aside from that sharps bin, of course.'

'No,' Clementine admitted. 'I did try and get the toolbox in the cupboard open, but it was locked.'

'I saw that too,' Margery said. 'I wonder if there's anything inside it. I don't see why there would be, but always best to check all the angles, I suppose.'

'What about that poem you mentioned?' Clementine asked as they paused before the entrance to the vestibule. The corridor was almost deserted now, the police having managed to work their way through the line. 'You seemed to be quite engrossed in it.'

Margery took the letter out of her bag and showed her. Clementine raised her eyebrows.

'Well,' she said. 'It's just like the one we think Miss Macdonald wrote, from Mr Weaver's photo frame.'

'Yes!' Margery exclaimed. She rummaged through her bag and found the heart-shaped piece of paper they had discovered before, the one that had started the trouble with Miss Macdonald in the first place.

'We saw her side of the conversation then, didn't we?' Clementine said, rubbing her chin in thought and comparing the two pieces of paper. 'That's different handwriting altogether. What's to say Mr Weaver didn't write her back in the same way? And then decided to send the same type of message to Dr Roberts?'

'But why?' Margery said, she couldn't see the significance. 'You don't think Miss Macdonald sent that to her?'

'No. I think Mr Weaver wrote it to conceal his identity,' Clementine said, pointing at the poem. 'The symbol is a maths symbol. So, maybe he was using it as a signature. Dr Roberts is clever, she must have known what it meant, and look, this bit in the note; our spot in the wood, money will free you. Money for his gambling debts, I'd bet.'

'He was blackmailing her,' Margery thought out loud. 'Gosh.'

'I think so.' Clementine nodded.

'But how was he blackmailing her?' Margery looked at the note again. 'What for? It doesn't say.'

'I doubt this is the only message she got.' Clementine shrugged. 'I'd imagine she knew exactly who they were and where they wanted to meet her by this point. I wonder what he had on her though.'

'So do I,' Margery said. 'Do you think his wife was involved?'

'No, idea,' Clementine said, any worries she had earlier seemed to have vanished. 'But I think it's about time we found out. Here, give me that, I'll put it in the book to keep it safe till we get home.'

Margery passed her the note as Clementine took the student's Maths book out of her bag and opened it. A slip of cardboard fell out and twirled its way down to the carpet below. Margery picked it up.

'Oh,' she said as she was confronted by the symbol they had spent so much time examining. 'Clem!'

'What is it?' she asked. Margery flipped it over and read the writing in green felt tip pen on the back.

'It's an invitation,' Margery said. Clementine locked eyes with her and they stared at each other in surprise.

Chapter Twenty-Two

It wasn't hard to read the writing. In fact, it was much easier than trying to read huge letters written in green spray paint. Whoever had written the invitation had given up being inconspicuous. If the murderer was getting cleverer about it, what hope did they have of solving the case? Margery felt a bit sick. She wanted to find Amelia and ask where she had got it from. Surely she hadn't been given the invitation? After the first time they had accidentally been at a meeting of the strangers they knew that the numbers were a date and time. To the untrained eye the invitation would look like any other, the kind the students sent around on WhatsApp now instead of printing them out. Whoever the strangers were, they were meeting in the school drama studio at eight in the evening tomorrow, just as the curfew would begin. They hadn't bothered to even conceal that particular piece of information. It was written boldly underneath the numbers. Judging by Amelia and Oliver's reactions to their gentle questioning, the students did have something to do with it all, as they had thought they might. But how did they keep getting into the building? Margery couldn't make hide nor hair of it all. Her first thought had been that they needed to tell the police. Clementine had other ideas, pulling a sour face at the mere mention of it.

'Right,' Clementine said, helping herself to a slice of apple pie. 'Here's my mad plan…'

'I'm listening,' Margery said. She poured herself another cup of tea from the pot on their kitchen table and turned to Clementine eagerly.

'We won't tell the police.'

'What?'

'We'll tell the headmaster instead,' Clementine said. 'Let him tell the police if he wants to, but it'll give us a chance to see who these people are without damaging the reputation of the school any more. You saw the governors' faces at that town meeting, none of this is good for Summerview School.'

'I heard that they were both on thin ice after the wedding anyway,' Margery said, thinking back to the governors' judgement of the headmaster's extramarital affair with his deputy. 'But you don't think the board of governors would do anything extreme?'

'Like threaten to shut the school down if there was one more issue?' Clementine recalled. Margery winced as she remembered the fear in the headmaster's eyes the last few times they had spoken to him.

'Hmmm, that doesn't sound good, does it?'

Margery agreed. She began to cut the apple on her plate into slices, topping it with a spoon of peanut butter.

'No, so the next step, if that happens, is replacing the headmaster, I'd put money on it.' Clementine sighed, biting into the piece of pie that was rapidly going cold on her fork. 'What if we tell the police, they don't manage to catch whoever the strangers are and then the paper publishes it? We can't have that; we'll look awful. We can't be wrong this time.'

'Right,' Margery said. She wasn't sure that this was a good idea, but she didn't have any of her own and she agreed with Clementine that nothing else could go wrong at the school or with their reputation. She picked up the invitation from the middle of the table and looked the symbol again. Tomorrow didn't seem very far away, Margery thought nervously.

'Mr Barrow will never go along with it,' Margery warned Clementine. 'In fact, he'll definitely try and talk us out of it.'

'Do you really think so?'

'I really do. I think he'd try and sort it himself and something else would go wrong.' Margery tutted. 'Gosh, what can we do? How will we even hide in the drama studio?'

'That little cupboard with the mixing desk in?' Clementine suggested. 'Like Rose did at Christmas?'

Margery smiled at the memory of Rose being caught in the cupboard, yelling into a microphone. 'No,' she said, shaking her head. 'If we were checking no one had followed us, that would be the first place we'd look, wouldn't it?'

Clementine sighed and slumped back in defeat. 'Yes, probably.'

'Well, probably just won't cut it,' Margery said sadly.

'You know,' Clementine said. 'There might be another way, but it's terrifically mad and stupid, even for us!'

'I'm listening.' Margery leaned in closer.

'We'll have to go out.' Clementine stood, wiping her hands free of crumbs; they scattered on the kitchen table. She looked up at the kitchen clock on the wall. 'And hope the shops are still open. The big supermarket will be, I'll drive.'

'Are you sure?' Margery asked her.

'About the driving?' Clementine frowned. 'Of course. I've worked roundabouts out and everything, haven't I?'

Margery smiled despite her serious mood. If the roundabout seemed too confusing, Clementine just came off at the first exit and let the satnav redirect her. One day they had gone around the same roundabout six times before they reached the right exit. Clementine continued, 'And then we can go and see what Liv Weaver was doing meeting Miss Macdonald.'

'That's not what I meant,' Margery said, but Clementine had already rushed off to put the pieces of her mad plan together. Margery looked up at the kitchen clock and realised that it was almost half past five, whatever they were planning would have to be done quickly to avoid the curfew.

–

They had made it to the supermarket and bought what they needed for the next evening, using the self-scan checkouts to try and be less incriminating, but even so Margery had felt like a criminal. When they had finished shopping, they made their way down to Liv Weaver's house again, parking up in the Bell and Hope car park and walking over to the house.

Neither of them was particularly sure what they were going to ask her, or why they were going. Margery wasn't even sure it was really a good idea, but on the other hand, they were on a roll with the impulsive meddling and might as well careen down every avenue while they were at it, before Officer Thomas found out what they were doing and slammed the brakes on it all. They reached

Liv Weaver's house and rang the doorbell, hearing the booming ding go off through the house and echo around the walls. There was no answer. They rang again and were met with the same, but the hallway lights were on. Clementine lifted the letterbox flap and looked inside, tutting as she closed it again.

'Hmmm.' Clementine looked at her watch. 'It's half six, maybe she's still at work?'

'I'm sure she said she works at home,' Margery reminded her. 'Maybe she's gone to the shop or something?'

The front door to their right opened and Seren stepped out. She turned to close the door and then noticed Margery and Clementine. Her eyes were huge with surprise, and she froze in the doorway with her key in the air, halfway to the deadlock.

'Hello,' Margery called, giving Seren a wave. She knew from experience to try not to spook her because if they did then she'd rush out of the house and up the street and then the next day at work she'd blank any questions about it. 'Are you doing up your house?'

Seren looked to Margery as though she were questioning how much to tell them, turning her house key around in her fingers.

'Yes,' she said, though she avoided looking them directly in the eye, instead looking at the front door again. The wood was freshly painted, Margery could see by the streaks of old paint that were still visible underneath.

'Let's have a look then!' Clementine stomped over the wet pavement. Margery tried to hide her smile as Seren hastily fumbled with her keys again.

'Oh no, I don't think...' she began, but Clementine was already standing next to her, eagerly waiting to see inside. When Seren realised they were not going away, she unlocked the yale lock, pushing the door open again. They entered, Seren followed and closed the door behind them and began to take off her boots, putting her bag for life down on the top of the little table in the hallway.

Margery hadn't been sure what she was expecting when they had realised what Seren and Gary were probably doing, but it was nothing like she'd imagined. It was much lovelier. When the tall, long terrace had been Caroline's it had been dusty and dank. Somehow Seren and Gary had made it look wonderfully bright in the hallway, the staircase repainted with a brand-new runner running down it. The embossed wallpaper had been stripped off and the walls no longer housed Caroline's strange charity-shop purchases and odd newspaper cuttings, but photos of Gary and Seren and their friends and families on a sage-green background. It was somehow much more intimate with the personal photographs. There was even a photo of the dinner lady team at last year's Christmas dinner; Margery remembered Mr Barrow taking the photo of them after he had come to thank them for a job well done.

The living room was a picture-perfect expression of maximalist interior design, but it was lovely and effortlessly cosy, the smell of paint still hanging in the air. Seren gestured for them to sit down on one of the squishy burnt-orange sofas. Margery thought that they might be Caroline's old ones, but reupholstered – they were the same shape. The coffee table was the same too. It was nice to see that Seren hadn't removed every trace of the house's former owner, just made things her own. Maybe she had kept some of the remnants of Caroline so she could remember how she got here.

'Cup of tea?' Seren asked. Margery and Clementine nodded, relaxing back on the settee that faced the television on the stand in the corner.

'When are you going to tell Rose you've moved in here?' Clementine asked Seren before she could disappear into the kitchen. 'She's convinced you're being abducted every day.'

'She does know! Well, I tried to tell her anyway.' Seren sighed, rubbing her brow. 'I did try and explain a few weeks ago but she just doesn't want to hear it. She kept pretending she'd misheard me. Let me get the tea stuff and I'll tell you all about it.'

She left them in the living room and Margery admired the little bar area in the corner, all set up for guests with a selection of lovely flavoured gins and matching gin glasses.

'Wow,' Clementine said to Margery as they gazed around, and once Seren was out of earshot. 'Let's ask if we can move in.'

Margery laughed. 'We'd ruin it with all our things. Where would you put your collection of interesting bells?'

'With my Argos catalogue collection, of course.' Clementine smiled back. 'On top of that bookcase with all Gary's James Bond books. We'll be really quiet, they won't even realise we're here!'

Seren arrived back in the living room with a tray of steaming mugs and put it down on the coffee table between them.

'Thank you.' Margery smiled at her.

'No problem,' Seren said, plopping herself down on the sofa and taking a cup of tea from the tray. 'Why were you outside? Have you been to the autumn trail on the riverbank?'

'We wanted to speak to Mrs Weaver,' Margery said finally, after a long pause where she had debated whether to lie or not and then could see no reason to. 'We thought she'd be in, but she didn't answer.'

'She's home, I think.' Seren stirred the last of six sugars into her mug. 'I just helped Gary take a load of stuff out into the garden, we're going to have a bonfire,' she explained at the sight of Margery and Clementine's questioning faces. 'Her lights are on. You can see straight into her house because the fence came down in that storm a few weeks ago. We've been arguing over whose boundary it is. The deed says it's a party wall. You see, home ownership, ha!' Seren smiled toothily again, it lit up her face with her happiness.

'Are you sure?' Clementine asked, scratching her head.

Margery wondered why Liv Weaver hadn't opened the door. Surely she would have, just to see who it was, even if it was just the post being delivered? Even if she'd only gone into the hallway and peered through the front-door window. Wouldn't one of her house cameras tell her who it was? Maybe that was the problem, maybe she had seen Margery and Clementine standing outside and decided that answering the door was more trouble than it was worth.

'Yeah, you can see right into the house.' Seren nodded, putting the mug back on the table and standing. 'Come and have a look.'

They stood and followed her out through the dark hallway and into the kitchen. Seren unlocked the back door, and they stepped outside into the garden. The garden was much neater, the bonfire of garden waste piled up ready to burn. Margery poked with her walking stick at a rock that had come from the path running down to the shed and ended up on the grass.

'It's on our left side,' Seren said, gesturing to the fence, which was still there but was lying down in next-door's garden where the wind had blown it. 'Which we thought meant it was their side of the fence, but when we went to ask, Mr Weaver said he wasn't sure that was correct and then I couldn't find the deed from when Seth sold it to me, so I had to pay three pounds on the HMRC website to download it and I couldn't find my bank card so I had to ask Gary to pay...'

Seren continued to chatter about the details of her garden boundary and Margery walked closer to the fallen fence to have a better look. There was music playing from next door, the house was all lit up from the back, perhaps Mrs Weaver hadn't been able to hear them knocking over it. Margery looked up and realised that Seren had been right about Mrs Weaver being at home. Liv was in her kitchen, which you could see straight into, thanks to the huge floor-to-ceiling windows of the extension she had been so proud of, with its burn risk taps, but she wasn't alone. Margery found herself blinking to make sure her brain wasn't inventing the scene in front of them, and she was glad that they were hidden out here in the dark garden.

'Look!' she hissed at Clementine and Seren, they both stepped forward to where she was standing and looked where she was pointing with her walking stick. 'She lied to us!'

'Oh!' Seren cried in surprise, her mouth dropping open. 'What?'

Clementine laughed out loud and then covered her mouth.

'Did you know about this, Seren?' Clementine asked, unable to keep the smile from her voice, though Margery could barely see her face in the dark garden. 'Why didn't you tell us!'

'Of course I didn't,' Seren said. 'I'm no good at keeping secrets, you know that! I'd have to tell everyone!'

A teacher's wife couldn't have an affair with another teacher without anyone knowing at all. Liv Weaver was either picking up where her husband had left off, or, much more likely, she had lied to them. It was obvious now that it was Liv who had been having the affair as Margery watched her kiss Miss Macdonald in the Weaver's kitchen while they cooked dinner together.

'Do you think there'll be enough of us to do a Dewstow gay pride event next year now?' Clementine nudged Margery.

Margery suddenly felt much too much like a voyeur to stand there any longer.

'Come on,' she said, her voice determined. 'Let's go and have a chat with them.'

'What?' Clementine said, trying to grab her hands. Margery was already making her way across the border of a broken fence and stomping into Liv's garden, any worries she had falling to the wayside, her walking stick snagging on the wet mud of the lawn.

'What's happening?' Seren called. 'Are you coming back to finish your tea?'

'Yes, this won't take a minute, Seren!' Margery called back, but she wasn't so sure that was true.

Chapter Twenty-Three

Seren went back into her house as they continued up to the Weaver household's extended kitchen doors. Margery tried the door handle first. The lock was stuck fast, but Liv and Elle looked up in surprise at the noise. Margery waved at them through the window with her free arm. Clementine finally arrived behind her, huffing and puffing and waved too. Liv's face – calm and serene before Margery had knocked – now twisted into something else entirely. Elle Macdonald still looked surprised, staring at them.

'What do you want?' Liv demanded to know. 'How did you get into my garden?'

'That doesn't matter,' Margery found herself saying, she didn't know what had come over her. 'What matters is that you lied to us. You told us your husband was having an affair, when clearly...' She gestured with a hand towards Miss Macdonald. 'You were.'

'I didn't tell you anything of the sort,' Liv said, but she seemed to know that the game had been lost. She took a deep breath and swung the kitchen door open fully with force. 'Just... just get in here,' she said. 'Stop screeching about it outside my house.'

Margery and Clementine did as they were told, entering the lovely new kitchen and joining Elle Macdonald awkwardly at the long table, which was set up for dinner. Behind them in the main kitchen both ovens were on, and the stove was bubbling with steaming pans.

'What are you making?' Clementine asked excitedly. 'Two ovens! It's better than being at work. Maybe we can make all the school dinners here and then ship it all up for lunch!'

Liv ignored her, instead sitting down at the table next to Elle and topping up her wine glass from the bottle in the centre. 'Shepherd's pie,' she said bitterly. 'Vegan mince.'

'How are you feeling?' Margery asked Elle before she could stop herself. Elle gave her a weak smile. Her throat was still badly bruised; Margery hated to think what it would have looked like just after the attack had happened. Even now, the marks where her attacker's fingers had been were prominent, the bruises turning yellow and green around the purple indents.

'I'm doing much better, thank you, Margery,' she said, biting her lip.

Margery watched as Elle began to wring her hands together without seeming to know she was doing it, until Liv reached out and stilled her fingers with her own. Elle did look better though, Margery thought. Her hair was washed. Though Liv took up the wine glass and gulped from it, Elle's glass only contained water from the pitcher next to it.

'For God's sake, sit down,' Liv bellowed at them both; they had remained hovering awkwardly over the kitchen table. 'Let us explain ourselves before you go off shrieking into the night about homewreckers and affairs.'

They took seats at the table opposite Liv and Elle; Margery tried to decide what they should ask first. Liam and Liv had never seemed particularly unhappy and yet here she was, weeks after his death with a new suitor. How long were you supposed to wait after your partner died? How much of your life were they allowed to keep, even after they had gone?

'Liam wasn't the saint everyone at the school seems to think he was,' Liv began, not letting her guard down for even a second. 'He loved to gamble, I didn't realise how much at first, and by the time I had any idea of the extent of it, the wedding was all booked and paid for. And the honeymoon… in Las Vegas.'

She laughed bitterly, and Margery thought back to Liv's miserable face in the wedding photograph on his desk.

'We've been married three years and, in that time, he's gambled away his savings, then my savings and then put himself in thousands of pounds in credit card debt, every single day for the past year I've had people coming to the door asking us for money. That's really why he put the cameras in all over the house.'

'Liam's initials were all over Mr Evans' diary,' Margery said. 'He obviously owed him a lot of money too.'

Liv nodded, she picked up her glass and took a sip.

'Did you see who attacked you, Elle?' Clementine asked as they sat awkwardly looking at each other. Elle shook her head.

'No, it all happened so quickly.' She winced. 'One minute I was leaving the bathroom and the next I was being pushed into a bedroom and being strangled.'

'Gosh,' Margery said. 'I'm so sorry.'

'That's okay,' Elle said. 'I kind of feel like I brought it on myself.'

'What do you mean?' Margery asked.

Liv had frozen, wine glass halfway to her lips, her mouth dropped open. She reanimated as quickly as she had stilled, grasping for Elle's hand again.

'Don't,' she said, 'don't say any more.'

'I'm sick of lying about it.' Elle shrugged her hand away. 'I need to tell someone.'

'You can't,' Liv hissed back. 'You'll get in trouble, and I can't… you can't do that.'

'I'm going to tell them,' Elle said, her voice firm. 'I'm sick of hiding when I don't think I did anything wrong.'

Liv got up from the table with a heavy sigh and stormed over to the other side of the kitchen, under the pretence of checking on the food. She slammed the oven door shut again much too heavily and Margery watched her grasp the kitchen knife and begin chopping herbs so forcefully that the chopping board rattled against the counter. Bits of parsley escaped and found their way to the floor.

'Where should I start?' Elle put her hands over her eyes for a moment.

'The beginning, maybe?' Clementine suggested kindly.

'Yes, but which part of it?' Elle folded her arms across her chest and sat back in her chair.

'Can we help?' Margery asked, reaching into her bag and pulling out the piece of heart-shaped paper she had been carrying around for weeks. 'We found some notes in Mr Weaver's classroom and we thought that—'

'That I wrote them?' Elle said, taking the poem from Margery's fingers with her own. 'I did, yeah.'

'What's that?' Liv said, gesturing with her head to the paper.

'It's one of the poems I wrote you.' Elle held it up so she could see. Liv dropped the knife onto the chopping board with a clatter. 'You found it in Liam's classroom?'

'Yes,' Margery said. Liv had gone almost purple, her hands gripping the kitchen counter. 'There were lots of them.'

'He stole them,' Liv spat, 'that's how he found out. I was stupid, I should have known he'd go through my things. That's how he knew what they looked like so he could write them.'

'Yeah,' Elle said with a sigh. 'He couldn't have blackmailed me without seeing them. Those notes he gave me were a mockery of my poems. Didn't think he had it in him.'

'What notes?' Margery asked, at the same time as Clementine said, 'He was blackmailing you?'

'Yes, for weeks now. He's asking me to leave him money in the woods.'

'What?' Margery couldn't help but exclaim. She had been sure he had been blackmailing Dr Roberts.

'He sent me all these poems,' Elle said, her voice very small like she couldn't believe any of it had happened.

'We found one of them in Dr Roberts' office!' Clementine said, eyes widening.

'I gave it to her, so she'd help me,' Elle explained. 'He said he'd tell everyone I was sleeping with his wife if I didn't give him money.'

'For his gambling debt?' Margery asked. Liv hadn't moved, her knuckles white as her hands gripped the counter tightly.

'Yeah,' Elle sighed. 'Dr Roberts went to uni with him, I thought she might be able to get a handle on the situation, make him back off. Which was awkward to try and explain without telling her the exact situation. I said he'd taken a dislike to me, and he was desperate. Which I guess is partly true! Anyway...' She rubbed her eyes again, as though it would help draw the memories from her brain. 'I don't know if Christina believed me or not, but she said she'd speak to him and get back to me.'

'Did she?' Margery asked in curiosity.

'She did,' Elle said, 'she said he still wanted his money, he'd told her I owed him it! As if.'

'Why did you have her personnel file?' Clementine asked.

'Well, I needed it to get her phone number at first.' Elle sighed. 'I couldn't risk having that conversation with her on school grounds, what if Liam had seen us? And then I could never find a way to put it back, I was lucky I didn't get seen taking it.'

'Why do you say "at first"?' Margery asked.

'Well, I had a bit of a mad moment and decided the obvious thing to do was to look through Christina's file. That way I could, I don't know, get some dirt on her and blackmail her for the money. Maybe a disciplinary record I could use that she wouldn't want to be public knowledge.'

'And did you?'

'No, of course not!' Elle laughed. 'She's squeaky clean. Her CV reads like a headteacher's dream – loads of teaching and real-life work experience. She worked as a phlebotomist to pay her way through uni and then had an entire lab career before she even stepped foot in a classroom. Got her doctorate at a really good university and then changed careers, you see?'

Margery supposed she did, though she wondered if Dr Roberts sometimes found the more mundane aspects of daily teaching unfulfilling after her glittering array of jobs from her life before. Summerview School was not known for being well-funded. If Dr Roberts had wanted an easier life, she could have gone to work at Ittonvale Comprehensive with their fully equipped lab, full of brand-new equipment, and shiny new sixth-form department. Margery was sure the Bunsen burners at

Summerview were older than both she and Clementine put together.

Liv had stopped listening and was now crashing around the kitchen with crockery and sloping food onto plates haphazardly. Margery almost jumped out of her skin when Liv slammed a plate down in front of her and another in front of Clementine, the pile of mash still steaming invitingly.

'Vegetarian, I'm afraid,' Liv said sharply, as if warning them from saying a word, and then she went back to get her and Elle's plates.

'That's quite fine with us,' Margery said, watching Elle watching Liv in concern. 'Thank you very much.'

Margery wondered for a moment if Elle would stop talking now, stop telling them whatever she had that she wanted to get off her chest. She didn't. She picked up her fork when Liv brought her the plate and thanked her, but the fork hovered to the side of the food as she cleared her throat again. Margery took a bite while they waited and then another and another, until Elle was ready to continue.

'So, I gave him all the money I had in my savings account, and then I ran out,' she said, matter-of-fact. Margery and Clementine nodded and the temperature at the table suddenly plunged down to an Artic snow drift. Liv slammed her fork down onto the table, though she had barely eaten anything, and poured herself another glass of wine.

'How did you know where to? "Our spot in the woods" isn't very specific,' Clementine said.

'Not our spot meaning mine and his,' Elle explained, 'our spot as in his and Liv's.'

Liv had gone white, even the wine in the glass in front of her forgotten. 'It was where he proposed to me.'

'Where?' Clementine whispered.

'The Devil's Yew,' Liv said, dropping her knife down to join the fork. They clanged together on the smooth metal surface of the dining table.

'Under the first poem it said to leave him five hundred pounds inside the hole in the Devil's Yew,' Elle explained. 'Which I did until I ran out of money.'

'What did you do then?' Margery asked. Liv sat back and folded her arms.

'I told Liv what had been going on,' Elle said, looking at Liv and biting her lip. 'The day Liam died.'

Liv finally spoke. 'I confronted him, on that video I showed you. That was what we were arguing about.'

'You showed him one of the poems?' Margery said. Liv got up, the chair squealing as it slid over the stone floor, and opened one of the drawers in the kitchen island. She found what she was looking for and brought it back over, sliding it across the table so Margery and Clementine could look at it.

I have lost it all

you must really help me out

pay me what is owed

Yours,

∀

'We had a big fight, as you know,' Liv continued, though her voice dropped to a conspiratorial whisper. 'And I tried to throw him out, even though that wasn't our deal…'

'What was your deal?' Clementine asked.

'We were going to live together until we'd sold the house and take half the equity each, divorce and start new lives.' Liv sat back down next to Elle, who took her hand. 'I thought Liam was on board with that, it was his idea, but then blackmail… it was strange because it wasn't like him.'

'The poems or the blackmail?' Margery wondered out loud.

'Either,' Liv said, her mouth turning upward in bemusement. 'God, I feel bad about it now, I didn't let him get a word in edgeways.'

'So what happened then?' Margery asked Liv, but Elle spoke instead.

'He text me, it must have been after he left here,' Elle said. 'Telling me to meet him by the tree, where I'd left the money, so he could explain. I went to meet him there, but… well, it was strange. When I first arrived, I couldn't see him, I thought he was really late. I nearly decided to go home, it wasn't like him, and I was sick of playing games. But I found him lying at the bottom of the tree.'

'Because he'd been stabbed?' Clementine murmured.

'Yes,' Elle whispered, 'but I didn't know that then. I just thought he was being strange, and I was nervous enough about meeting him and I didn't have any money for him. I was scared about what he'd do.'

'Tell them what happened,' Liv said quietly.

'I told him I didn't have any money and that I loved his wife, and he could tell whatever to whoever he wanted because I wasn't going to leave her.' Elle's eyes were wide and frightened like she was reliving the moment again in her head. 'And he tried to get up.'

She was breathing very quickly, and her fingers grasped the fork very tightly, though the food had been long forgotten. 'But he couldn't stand and when I helped him up he collapsed.'

'He collapsed?' Clementine asked in disbelief.

'Yes, right there in the woods,' Elle said. 'He was making a weird noise and clutching his chest and then he was dead, I watched the whole thing, but it was like I was frozen.' Without warning, she put her free hand over her face and began to sob. Liv stood and put her arms around her shoulders.

'It wasn't your fault,' Liv soothed. 'The autopsy showed he had an embolism, you couldn't have done that, it wasn't your fault.'

'But I left him there!' Elle wailed, before managing to calm herself. She turned back to Margery and Clementine with red eyes. 'I rang Liv and she said to leave him there and come here so I just left. I ran away. What if he could have been saved?'

Liv had obviously decided that the jig was up and had wandered over to the kitchen counter and she returned a second later with her iPad. She tapped at it for a moment before turning it to show them.

'This is why you wouldn't show the police,' Margery said as they watched Elle enter the house on the CCTV cameras. 'Because they'd have taken the whole lot away and eventually seen Elle arriving after you'd fought with him.'

Liv didn't deign to reply, but she nodded. The silence swirled around them again, cold and intrusive. Margery found herself hoping that the police would find a DNA match for the glove soon, somebody had to be responsible for this.

'For what it's worth,' Clementine said, 'you really didn't kill him.'

'So, who did?' Elle asked. Clementine couldn't answer that, and neither could Margery.

The rest of the impromptu meal dragged on and there seemed nothing left to be said. Clementine checked her phone and Margery watched over her shoulder as she brought up the GPS fob's location. It was still at the school, exactly where they had left it.

Chapter Twenty-Four

They spent all day becoming more and more nervous about that evening's plan and watching the clock tick the minutes away. Margery's head hurt with all the new information she had tried to stuff into it. She couldn't believe Elle had just left him there, it would certainly not have been her first thought if she had been in their shoes. Though she decided that she couldn't see herself being in a situation like that. Who had killed Liam Weaver, if not Elle and Liv?

The autopsy had revealed a puncture wound, the sort from a needle, and a blood clot causing an embolism, which Liv and Elle swore they had known nothing about until the autopsy had returned and Elle had realised she was in the clear. Margery's mind flitted back to the sharps box in Dr Roberts' classroom. Clementine had checked again when they had got to work and the phone app still showed the box safely stored in the school, the little symbol flashing comfortingly over the building.

Lunchtime dragged awfully, though Margery was sure that it was a good thing. It was nearly over, but there were still a few stragglers left to serve and returning visitors after pudding. Clementine's plan for the evening was so saturated with plot holes that she could have used it as a colander. Still, she wasn't going to back down and neither was Margery. They had come too far and got too involved to let it go now. She was so wrapped up in her thoughts about the evening ahead that she didn't notice Rose enter the canteen and come storming over to the counter, from where Seren was gingerly serving portions of trifle from a gastronome tray, until it was too late. Seren seemed to feel Rose's arrival before she saw her, dropping the spoon into the tray, sprinkles, cream and custard splattering all over the inside of the display fridge.

'Rose,' Seren said, flinching at the sight of Rose, glowering at her from over the counter. 'What can we get for you?'

'Nothing,' Rose whistled through clenched teeth. She turned to glare at Margery and Clementine too. 'How long has this been going on?'

She held up the piece of paper she was holding, swishing it into the air with a flourish. Margery grimaced at the sight of it. It was a printout of Seren's house title deed.

'Your solicitor sent this to the house. Why would you need this when you live with me?'

Margery expected Seren to wilt under the sheer force of Rose's anger, but she didn't. In fact, her facial features suddenly slanted upwards from where they had been slouched in surprise and a steely expression took its place. The queuing students took a step back in preparation for what was to come.

'I don't live with you, Rose,' Seren said, picking up the spoon and beginning to ladle the trifle into bowls once more, the custard and cream flying everywhere under the force of her anger. 'I've told you so many times. I love you, you're my best friend, but I have my own life. I want to live with Gary.'

The last words were punctuated by cream spraying from the spoon all over the inside of the display fridge. Rose just gaped at Seren. For a horrible moment Margery thought that maybe she was so shocked she might collapse on the floor. She opened and closed her mouth again, like a fish drowning in air.

'How dare you!' Rose finally choked out. 'What about me?' She pointed a perfectly manicured index finger at Seren. 'What about us? Who's going to help me work the Sky box?'

'Your husband!' Seren shrieked. 'I can't always be there to turn the TV on for you, Rose.'

'Well, I'm sure *Gary* will appreciate all your help.' Rose said his name with so much sarcasm Margery briefly wondered if it was really a name at all. 'While he's lording it up in your house.'

'We're engaged!' Seren spat. Rose gasped, and so did the rest of the dinner lady team.

'Seren!' Clementine squawked, throwing her hands up. 'Engaged!'

'Oh, mate, that's so nice!' Ceri-Ann beamed at her. Seren turned around and stared at them like she was just realising they were still there. She smiled a small half smile back and then turned to Rose, who was leaning against the display counter, clutching her chest, her mouth opening and closing but no sound coming out.

'Engaged,' she spluttered. Seren nodded. 'But why didn't you tell me?'

'Because I knew you'd act like this.' Seren gestured at Rose's dramatic posture, her arm flopped over the counter fridge limply. Rose dragged herself upright again, smoothing the creases from her starched blouse.

'Seren,' Rose said. 'I didn't know.'

'Well, now you do,' Seren said, all her anger and bravado gone. 'I haven't even worn my ring in case you saw and got upset.'

'Why would I get upset? I think that's lovely news,' Rose said. 'God, I'm sorry. You must think I'm awful.'

'No, I don't.' Seren shook her head, her shoulders slumped. 'Of course I don't. I should have talked to you about it all and then we wouldn't be here yelling at each other over the kitchen counter.'

'Well, I'm sorry,' Rose said. Margery had never seen her look so sincere. 'I really am, I've been a fool. Of course you would want to move in with your fiancé. I think I've just relied on you too much.'

'I was hoping that you'd, well...' Seren smiled at her. 'Would you be my maid of honour?'

Rose looked like she might burst into tears, flapping her hands in front of her face. 'Of course! Of course, I will.'

Margery watched the tension break, the wave receding back down the beach, and the room breathed a collective sigh of relief.

'When is it?' Rose asked, not waiting for Seren to answer. 'We haven't got much time to plan. You'll need a dress, of course, and then there's the hair and make-up to think about. Where is the venue? No matter, you'll need food regardless. So few venues in this area could hold a candle to this lovely array...' She waved a well-jewelled hand towards the sad-looking trifle and the hot plate with its empty trays that the team hadn't managed to bring into the pot-wash area yet.

Rose turned to Margery. 'Mrs Butcher-Baker, you'll need to begin preparations at once. We'll need a lot of ice if you're going to do a full sculpture of Gary as well as

Seren. I'll be in touch to discuss vol-au-vent fillings and the cake! We need to work out how many tiers we'll need. Are there many vegans coming, Seren? No, don't answer that yet, let me go away and make some nice spreadsheets for all of this.' Seren nodded, but she was frozen to the spot like a deer in headlights. Rose continued, 'I must say, it would have been much easier if Gary had asked you before the summer and then we could have had a joint wedding, wouldn't that have been lovely?'

She turned on her designer heels and swept out of the building, leaving the dinner lady team to look on in dismay on Seren's behalf.

'Were you hoping to plan any of your own wedding, Seren?' Clementine chuckled while the last of the queue began to thin out in Rose's wake.

'A bit,' Seren squeaked, but her eyes were brighter than they had been.

'Looks like you can just pop your feet up, mate,' Ceri-Ann laughed. 'Just give Rose your measurements and I'm sure she'll get you a dress.'

'She'll probably have hers adjusted to fit you,' Sharon joined in the teasing.

They all laughed at the thought of Seren wearing the huge off-the-shoulder gown Rose had married Mr Barrow in. The train had been so long that when they had bundled her inside the wedding car you couldn't see her head over the great swathes of tulle.

'Where's the ring?' Sharon asked. Seren reached into the neckline of her polo shirt and drew the simple but elegant diamond ring out on the chain she was wearing. They all oohed and fawned over it while it glinted in the light. Seren blushed proudly.

'Margery!' Margery heard Gloria's voice calling for her from across the canteen and she looked over just in time to see Karen and Gloria pushing the tea trolley through the canteen's double doors. Margery and Clementine usually did the tea runs but they hadn't since Margery's leg had become bad again. Karen waved over at them as Gloria manoeuvred it around the tables carefully so as not to catch the wheels on the carpet or hit any of the students.

'The trolley is screaming at us!' Karen yelled over to them. 'It won't stop.'

Gloria continued to heft the trolley towards them, and Margery realised that Karen was right. Alongside the usual clattering of crockery caused by the wobbly wheel, the trolley was emitting a high-pitched wailing, which Margery thought she might recognise but couldn't immediately place.

'It's the bloody key fob!' Gloria moaned in annoyance. 'Again!'

'Ooh yes, it is,' Clementine said, proudly. Gloria wheeled the trolley into the kitchen, kneeling down to see where the awful wailing was coming from. 'It just needs its batteries changed.'

They were right, Gloria pulled the fob out from where it had been taped to the underside of the trolley. The realisation dawned on Margery at the same time as the colour drained from Clementine's face, unease setting in. There was something grotesque about the sight of it laying there in Gloria's hands, so inconspicuous that only Clementine and herself would know what its arrival meant.

'Oh,' Clementine said, stepping forward to take it from Gloria, 'but it was on Dr Robert's sharps box! How is it here?'

The GPS tracker had not told them the fob had left the school, because it hadn't. Dr Roberts must have found it and stuck it to their trolley instead. How did she know it was theirs? Her blood ran cold as she remembered it going off when they were at the pumpkin patch. Dr Roberts must have seen Clementine fumbling around with it. Her walking stick, she remembered in horror; she had left her walking stick out in the classroom while they had hidden. Surely Dr Roberts hadn't known they were there at the time? Surely she would have said something. The other dinner ladies looked between them in concern at their shocked faces. Clementine could tell what she must be thinking from her expression.

'She's a type-one diabetic, Margery,' Clementine said. 'She probably didn't like us touching her things and decided to play a joke on us.'

'Who are you talking about?' Gloria asked. 'What's happened with this fob? You both look like you've seen a ghost.'

'Yeah, like you've been doing a séance in a haunted house,' Ceri-Ann said. 'Who's diabetic?'

'Dr Roberts,' Clementine explained. 'We stuck the fob to the sharps box she has in her classroom.'

'Why would you do that?' Gloria asked, her hands still on the handles of the tea trolley.

Karen and Sharon had begun to take things off it to clean them, but now they stood and watched the conversation in silence, the tea mugs hanging from their fingers by the handles. The afternoon sun poured through the kitchen windows and reflected off the biscuit crumbs on the trolley, making them glint like shards of glass.

'Because of the way Mr Weaver was killed,' Margery said, her hands shifting against each other, the movement betraying her worry. 'He was stabbed by a needle, and he died not long after from an embolism.'

'Are you sure Dr Roberts had a sharps box?' Gloria scratched her head. 'Why would she need one?'

'She's diabetic,' Clementine said, for the second time.

'Yeah, but she's got one of those pumps.' Gloria motioned at her own side. 'She only has to change it every couple of days. It's like a needle thing and she can monitor her glucose and it gives her insulin.'

'Maybe she keeps some spare needles and syringes here?' Ceri-Ann suggested. Margery flinched, she had forgotten how exposed they were having this conversation in the middle of the open kitchen.

'That makes sense,' Margery said. 'Maybe that's it.'

Clementine didn't look convinced. 'Does anyone know if there's a fridge in the science block?'

'No, I don't think so,' Margery said, thinking back to the maintenance documents the headmaster always sent her copies of that inexplicably included every fridge in the building. 'Hmmm. She couldn't keep her insulin at room temperature, could she?'

'No, it needs to be refrigerated,' Clementine said. 'And wouldn't you keep the things needed to inject it close by?'

'Rose will know if there is one,' Seren said. 'They keep records of any student medication, maybe the teachers have something similar? I know that there's a fridge in the nurse's room.'

'Okay,' Margery said, trying to think. 'All right, well, can you ask her? Now that you've made up?'

Seren nodded grimly.

Chapter Twenty-Five

The revelation of the GPS fob had completely thrown Margery off. She had almost forgotten about Clementine's plan to return to the school and catch whoever had been invited with the invite they had found from the students. Now they were creeping through the dark school corridors, and the worries poured back in. Clementine's grand scheme had turned out to be not much more than a badly sketched idea. The cape she wore was incredibly long, a trip hazard that would never have passed a risk assessment. For another thing, they weren't even sure what they were going to do once the strangers arrived. It had said drama studio on the note, but that meant very little. It was just a piece of card after all, as worthless as the leaflets advertising Dawn Simmonds' choir that were pushed through their front door almost weekly. They had decided after a hurried conversation that they shouldn't even tell the headmaster. Reasoning that it would be better to ask for forgiveness than permission.

For all the talk of the police watch, it had not been difficult to get into the school building after hours. It was as easy as leaving the canteen kitchen window ajar so they could clamber through it and then creep through the building in the dark. It would probably be much harder to get away from the school and back home without being caught, and they had left the car on the drive, planning to walk back. Dawn Simmonds had come out of her house to chastise them for being so late back home the evening before, nearly waking the entire street up with her rant about murderers and the curfew.

'What time is it?' Clementine hissed next to her ear. They were hiding in the alcove under the stairs next to the door of the drama studio, Margery on one side of the door and Clementine on the other. It was a much tighter space than either of them had realised before they squashed their way in. Though they had managed to get under here quite easily, it was not a pleasant experience in any way imaginable. Margery could feel the burn in her legs from crouching for so long.

'Just gone seven,' Margery whispered back, turning her head to look at Clementine, their masks clashing together as she did so. Clementine groaned in annoyance, trying to stretch her arms around and gain more space. 'Stop it, Clem! We'll fall out and it'll be just our luck that's when the strangers turn up. Do you want to get murdered before we find out what they're doing here?'

'Well, it'd be better than having pins and needles, Margery!' Clementine hissed back.

'Clem.' Margery suddenly felt panic well up inside her. 'We aren't wearing the right shoes.'

'What?' Clementine forgot all about whispering. Margery could feel her trying to turn to look at her.

'The shoes, Clem!' Margery squeaked. 'They all have plimsols on and we've...'

Clementine gasped and stared down into the darkness at their own comfortable but white trainers that they had bought in the January sale at the beginning of the year. Margery prepared herself for the argument about whose stupid idea this was anyway, but they didn't have time to even begin. From down the hallway Margery saw the lights of several torches, the beams batting about as the caped figures rushed down it towards them. The strangers.

They paused at the staircase as though looking for something and Margery held her breath; Clementine's grip on her arm tightened. The leader of the group gestured for them to follow, and they did, their cloaks whipping along behind them. Clementine slipped out from the alcove and Margery followed. Her legs turning to jelly as she stumbled out from under the stairs and stepped carefully into the march behind the other caped, masked strangers, trying to keep her cloak as low as possible so her white shoes would not show. They should have told the headmaster, she thought desperately as she followed. He could have loaned them a pair of plimsols each from the lost property box to make it less obvious.

The drama studio door creaked as the ringleader pushed it open and they all entered quietly, their feet softly stepping over the carpeted floor. From the side of them, one of the shorter strangers flipped the lights on. Margery blinked as the room was flooded in light from the beams running across the ceiling.

'Turn them off!' The ringleader's voice rang out. Margery felt numb with terror. This had not been a good idea. Maybe there was some way to escape before anyone had noticed. Too late, she thought as the ringleader gestured at her. 'You! Turn them off! Amelia, get the candles!'

Margery stopped and stared at the figure, realising that she recognised the voice but couldn't quite place it. Amelia. Number One, Margery reminded herself, put her backpack on the floor and scrambled inside it, pulling out a box of table candles. The sort that Margery and Clementine kept under the kitchen sink with their torch in case of a power cut. Margery ignored the voice in her head that said to run, and turned back to the wall, flicking the light switch off. Anything to keep anyone from seeing their shoes. Another stranger had made for the chairs stacked up at the side of the stage and now they were all picking them up and arranging a circle in the middle of the hall. Margery could feel her breath against the mask, clouding her face and her thoughts. Which one of the cloaked strangers was Clementine? She couldn't tell. The thought caused her to clench her hands into tight fists.

'Anyone see us?' the nearest to Margery asked, turning to the others as another handed her a chair. Resigned to her fate, she took her own place in the circle. Whatever happened now, it was too late to back out, she decided. They would just have to try and act however the strangers acted and get through it.

'No,' another replied. 'But I'll lock the door behind us.'

How did they get the key to the drama studio? Margery's thoughts raced. The only people who would have a copy were teachers and security staff. Amelia had dragged a little fold-out table from the mixing-desk cupboard, Margery thanked the gods above that they hadn't decided to hide there now, she wished she could see Clementine's face to see if she had noticed too. She felt truly alone for the first time in a very long time. She stared down at the bottom of the capes the strangers wore, but she couldn't see Clementine's white trainers at all under the long fabric.

'Get the blinds.' The nearest figure gestured to the person on their left. 'We can't risk anyone seeing us from the outside.'

They all leapt into action, securing the room as Amelia set up the candles and lit them with a zippo lighter. For what? Margery asked herself. What horrible thing were they planning, not some demonic sacrifice like Clementine kept suggesting? It sounded so silly in her own head, but they knew so little about them that her mind began to jump to the most frightening conclusions. They had trapped themselves in the room with them. The fear returned, a chill went down Margery's spine. Blinds closed and door locked, the strangers began to sit in the circle. Margery held her breath and then, though every inch of her wanted to run, climb out a window and escape. Instead, she joined them.

'Let's begin,' the voice said, 'with what we finished last week.'

There was a lot of rustling as everyone in attendance opened their rucksacks. Margery found herself gripping the chair with her nails at what horrible thing might be revealed, but instead each, in turn, pulled out a sheath of papers and a pencil case. One took a pencil sharpener out, another a gel pen. It was not quite the scene of murder weapons and crucifixes Clementine had envisioned last night when they had been discussing the problems that might unfurl.

'Everyone got their past papers?' the voice asked, the rest of the group murmured. 'If you're going to beat Itton-vale then we've got to get on it. Right, paper two.'

Margery looked around at them all, realising that Clementine must be sat directly opposite her, the only other person without a piece of paper on their lap. The only other person whipping their masked face back and forth as though trying to work out what was going on.

No one else had noticed yet, so engrossed in whatever the pages contained. The ringleaders' voice continued.

'Right, so first we've got a few nice easy linear equations to solve. First problem: 6x plus 5 equals 2x plus 15. It's got an unknown value on each side. How do we work out what x is?'

'I subtract 2x on both sides of the equation first,' the voice belonged to another teenage girl, Margery was sure of it. 'Then that means you've got 4x plus 5 equals fifteen. Then you can take away 5 on both sides and that gives you 4x equals 10.'

'Yes, that's correct, Charlotte,' the voice said. 'So what does that make it?'

'Four doesn't go into 10 perfectly so it gives you a fraction,' another young voice piped up. 'Which means x equals 10 over 4, divide that to get 5 over 2, x equals 2 point 5.'

Margery could have laughed out loud. They had gathered here, at eight o'clock at night, to do maths, it boggled the mind. It was only her surprise that stopped her from accidentally revealing herself with a bark of laughter.

'That's exactly right,' the voice said. 'Now, what do we do now we've isolated the xs?'

'I'm sorry, but can we not take off these masks? It's boiling in here,' another voice said. There was a murmur of agreement amongst the group and Margery felt her eyes widen.

The one with the booming voice paused as though considering, though it was very hard to tell under the expressionless masks.

'Oh, go on then,' he said jovially. 'I suppose we're all fucked if we get caught here anyway, might as well!'

They all began removing the hoods of their cloaks. One by one they removed their masks until it was only Margery and Clementine wearing them in the circle. Amelia was there, and Oliver, then there was the boy called Ahmed, another girl called Ella Martin from Year Ten, and another seven or eight students that she couldn't immediately place.

Margery had a split second to decide what to do, but she remained where she was, frozen with indecision. On one hand, these were students, but on the other they were students who were sneaking around the school after hours wearing Halloween costumes.

'Are you not going to take off your mask?' the owner of the voice asked them, looking between them in surprise. A red-haired young man with a freckled face, Margery recognised him as Will Millar. A rather timid Year Eleven who always had an egg mayonnaise sandwich with spring onions and a bag of cheese and onion Walkers crisps at lunchtime. The dinner ladies often wondered how badly his breath would smell in afternoon classes after the lunch hour and debated whether he was oblivious to it, or if he did it on purpose.

'No,' Clementine said through the mask, touching the front of it with her fingertips to hold it on. 'I'm going to just keep it on, it's lovely and smooth.'

There was a pause as all the students turned to stare at each of them in turn in suspicion. Will glared at Clementine with narrowed eyes, realising there were more people there than should have been. The papers lay forgotten on the students' laps. They sat for a moment longer and then Margery jumped as she heard Clementine's GPS alarm begin to ring from inside the pocket of her cape.

'Mrs Butcher-Baker?' Amelia asked. 'Is that you?'

'No,' Clementine said, fumbling through her pockets for the key fob.

'Take off your mask,' Will said sternly.

'No.' Clementine said, the mask swaying as she shook her head. 'I've told you, I've got to keep it on. I forgot to, er... I forgot to, um, contour my face before we came here.'

'Take it off.' Will stood and strode over to Clementine, reaching for her mask.

Clementine pulled the mask from her face before he could manhandle her any further. 'Oh, you know what? Fine! Gosh, for a group of people who love maths enough to go sneaking about *learning* after hours...' She said the word learning as if it were a grave insult. 'You'd think you'd be better at counting and realise there were extra of you!'

The game was up. There was a collective roar of surprise from the group of students. Margery took her mask off, and they all turned to boggle at her too.

'Hello,' Margery said weakly. The group of students stared at them, wide-eyed from the circle of chairs. Oliver scrambled to pull his mask back on. Clementine rolled her eyes at him.

'What?' Amelia said, her face contorted in confusion. 'Why are you here?'

'Why are you here?' Margery said pointing at her. 'How on earth did you get the key? You didn't kill...'

'We didn't have anything to do with Miss Macdonald!' Will said, flushing a deep shade of red.

'Oh really?' Clementine scoffed. 'Prove it!'

'We can't,' Amelia said. 'We can't tell the police where we were because we were here at Halloween.'

'Yes, sneaking around.' Clementine pointed at them all in turn. A few of them looked sheepish, but Amelia glared at them.

'We aren't sneaking around!' She rolled her eyes, gesturing to the paper on her lap. 'We're practising.'

'What on earth are you practising?' Margery asked, gesturing at the capes they were all still wearing.

'Yes,' Clementine said, motioning at the flickering candles, dripping wax all over the table. 'Witchcraft on school property!'

Amelia rolled her eyes so dramatically that they spun like two well-polished marbles. 'We're not doing witchcraft, we're doing maths.'

'One and the same,' Clementine snorted. Margery couldn't help but smile, even in the severity of the situation.

'We are, miss.' Amelia showed them the paper they had been doing. 'It's for the end–of–year mathematics competition. We're going up against Ittonvale next week. Last year we lost by six points.' The entire group looked aghast, the memory of their defeat still fresh and raw. And now that they had mentioned it, Margery did remember Mr Weaver asking if he could put a sign–up sheet in the canteen.

'So, you're practising?' Margery asked. 'But why not practise during the day?'

'Mr Barrow banned all groups after the past few weeks,' Amelia explained. 'We had no choice.'

'You mean he banned all groups because there was a murder and then you were all wandering around dressed up like the grim reaper,' said Clementine, gesturing to their capes again.

'The group in the town centre wasn't us!' Amelia shrieked as though it was an offence to be compared to them. 'And it wasn't us who chased you either. That was Media Studies group B, they've been stealing our logo because they think it looks *scary*.'

'S-sorry. Who?' Margery shook her head in confusion. 'Who's Media Studies group B?'

'The Media Studies class, of course,' Amelia said, the rest of the students nodded. 'They were making a short film series for TikTok, but it all got out of hand.'

'But the logo is yours?'

'The turned A?' Amelia said. 'Yeah, it was Mr Weaver's idea for our Mathletics group, because it was "for all" and the group was for all, er, as long as you can do maths.'

'They've been using the turned A,' Margery tried to clarify, 'but you've been wearing the same cloaks and masks?'

'They gave us that idea,' Amelia said. 'So, yeah.'

'But you've still been spray painting it around the school,' Clementine pointed out. Amelia looked annoyed.

'That was Oliver's idea.' She glared at the boy. 'He said if we painted when we were supposed to meet and where on the wall, then we could all see it but if anyone had their phone confiscated a teacher wouldn't find out.'

Margery sat back in the chair and folded her arms, thinking. She still had questions to ask. 'How have you been getting into the school at night?'

'My mum is one of the cleaners here,' Amelia admitted reluctantly. As soon as she said it, Margery realised that she did look rather like Louise.

'Of course,' Margery said. 'Does she know you're here?'

'No,' Amelia said shiftily. 'I borrow her keys sometimes.'

'Borrow!' Clementine scoffed. '*Steal*, you mean.'

'But couldn't you practise somewhere else?' Margery shook her head. 'Like at home, or the library? During the daytime!'

'We didn't want any spies from Ittonvale overhearing,' Will said, sitting up straight. 'And the curfew means it's basically impossible to arrange to go to someone's house. My parents are well freaked out about the murder.'

'Mine too,' Oliver piped up.

'And mine!' Amelia said. 'So, it made sense to sneak out of our houses and meet here, miss. Please don't tell the headmaster on us.'

Margery looked around the circle at their pleading faces and found herself unable to be angry or even annoyed at any of them.

'You really didn't chase us through the hall?' Margery asked.

'No,' Oliver said, sitting up straight for the first time. 'My girlfriend is in Media Studies group B and I told her when we were meeting and then they all turned up. We didn't know they were here till they all came running into Mr Weaver's room and told us we had to escape out of the window with them.'

'Did group B paint the turned A on Rose's front door at Halloween?' Margery asked. 'It wasn't there when we arrived at the party.'

'No,' Amelia shook her head, looking nervous again. 'It was already painted on there, we were all out trick or treating.'

'So, you saw the turned A but neither group painted it?' Margery said, trying to think who else could have painted it. 'What did you do when you saw it?'

'Group B decided to record it for their film,' Amelia shrugged.

'If the Media Studies group were filming the door,' Clementine said, 'does that mean they have footage of who left the house after strangling Miss Macdonald? The police think someone was filming on their phone.'

The look on Amelia's face told them that they did.

Chapter Twenty-Six

'So, it was just students?' Gloria whispered. 'Good Lord.'

They were holed up in Margery's dry store office while the rest of the staff cracked on with the lunchtime prep, getting the tea trolley ready for its afternoon journey to the English department's homework club.

'I know,' Margery said. She gathered the fancy tea bags while Gloria balanced on the stepping stool to bring down the good biscuits from their secret hiding place – away from Clementine – on the top shelf of the storage unit. 'The worst bit is that we don't really know what to do now. Obviously what Miss Macdonald did was wrong, she shouldn't have left him there, but I think she just panicked, there was no malice in it. The students supposedly have some footage of the night at Rose's.'

'It doesn't prove who killed Mr Weaver,' Gloria said, handing down the box. Margery took it.

'No, it doesn't,' Margery said, opening the box and decorating the tray with biscuits in the perfect concentric circles she had refined over years of practise.

'Did they say who they filmed?' Gloria asked, she had climbed down from the step ladder and was leaning against the shelving unit. Margery put the empty biscuit box on the top of the chest freezer and folded her arms, wishing for a moment that she could close her eyes and teleport herself far, far away from here. Anywhere would do.

'No, I don't think Amelia knew what they had,' Margery explained, 'just that they have it.'

'Gosh,' Gloria said, blinking at her with wide eyes.

'I know,' Margery said, again feeling stupid.

There was a sharp rap on the open dry store door and the intimidating figure of Rose Smith stood in the doorframe, towering over them both on her heels and holding a cardboard cup of coffee. Margery found herself thinking that Rose could probably have reached the secret biscuits without the step stool.

'Get that cup off her, Margery!' Margery heard Clementine yell from the corridor before she saw her arrive behind Rose. 'She hasn't paid for it, just waltzed behind the counter and made herself one!'

Rose clutched the cup so tightly the knuckles of her hand went white. She looked between them, then seemed to decide that she could say what she needed to in front of Gloria as well.

'I'll pay for it when I've said what I need to say,' she admonished Clementine, who had joined them in the room. 'You wanted to know about the schools' medical list?'

'Yes,' Margery said. 'Is Dr Roberts on it?'

'She is,' Rose said, taking a sip of coffee while looking Clementine directly in the eye. 'I know that's probably not what you were expecting to hear, but she has a spare vial of insulin that she keeps in the science lab fridge.'

'Just in case her pump runs out,' Margery said. It was just as they had thought when they had stuck the GPS tracker to the sharps box.

'Exactly,' Rose nodded.

'So, it's perfectly plausible she has a sharps box,' Clementine said.

'I suppose so,' Rose said before she took another sip of coffee. 'Well...'

'Well, what?' Margery asked.

'The school has its own sharps box in the nurse's office,' Rose said. 'And all record of medicine is supposed to be kept for health and safety reasons, regardless of position. Even I've got to record my medication for the records.'

'I have to declare my asthma inhaler,' Clementine shrugged.

'Yes,' Rose said, 'so for safety reasons if she's used that insulin then she should have made a record of it, but when I checked the science lab fridge, it wasn't in there and nothing's been added to the communal sharps box. No record of it anyway.'

'And her sharps box has gone,' Margery said. Rose took a sip of coffee while they all thought about it.

—

The mathematics team had been on to something, Margery thought as they knocked on the classroom door. It had been heard enough to slip away, leaving the rest of the dinner lady team to tidy up, which she felt guilty about. She felt like she was constantly shirking her duties everywhere at the moment, though she didn't see what else they could do. They had to follow the lead.

Amelia welcomed them in. Miss Grant was gone already, which wasn't a surprise. She was usually one of the first teachers to leave, Margery often saw her strolling across the playground at three o'clock on the dot, laptop bag over her shoulder.

'This is Megan,' Amelia explained, taking them over to another blonde teenage girl who was also dressed as though she could have been an extra on the set of a 1996 episode of *Friends*. 'She's the head of group B's project.'

'We've just been checking through the film,' Megan said excitedly. 'Amelia's been helping us edit! We're doing a found-footage type thing!'

'Right,' Margery said, deciding not to waste time asking what that meant. 'Has Miss Grant not wondered why you've been running about in Halloween masks and capes?'

'She doesn't know,' Megan shrugged. 'She thinks we're working on something else. This is our end-of-year project, but we wanted to shoot it now while its autumn, easy set dressing.' She gestured for Margery and Clementine to sit down next to her and they all took a seat around the table on which a laptop and an iPad sat.

'Is it on the big phone, then?' Clementine jabbed a finger towards the tablet as Megan unlocked the screen and began to flick through TikTok.

'There's loads of behind-the-scenes stuff too, I'll show you once we've watched this.' Megan said. 'It's looking great, isn't it, Mills? Well, some of it is. I had to put a few filters on it and stuff.'

Amelia grinned in agreement and then leaned over and pressed play on the screen. The film began.

'What on earth is this?' Margery asked, horrified as spooky shots of the woods flickered past their eyes, interspaced with scenes of what she was hoping were was blood and gore. There were more videos than Margery could count, Megan flicked through them with ease.

'It's our spooky TikTok account, miss!' Megan grinned. 'It's well good, isn't it?'

'It's certainly something,' Clementine said, her eyebrows raised so high on her forehead that they had disappeared under her fringe. Megan didn't seem to notice. 'What's the story supposed to be?'

'We wanted it to be a mixture of newer horror and classic horror, like *Smile* mixed with *The Craft*.'

'*The Craft* isn't that old, we went and saw it at the cinema!' Clementine said in uproar. Margery was sure she heard Amelia snigger quietly.

'You're both in it!' Megan said, clicking on a video that showed Margery and Clementine running away down the corridor in terror. Margery found herself gripping the handle of her walking stick very tightly as they watched.

'How are you going to fit that into the story?' Clementine scoffed, jabbing her finger at the screen. 'We didn't even have any lines to read.'

'We were going to ask you to be in it properly, but we haven't had a chance,' Megan said, grinning at them both.

She skipped through the reel of videos, right back to the beginning, to the very first video, and tapped on it.

'That's where Mr Weaver died,' Clementine said grimly as they watched the screen.

'Yeah,' Megan nodded, her eyes wide, 'we painted the A on it like two days before, well creepy that he died there.'

'Why did you paint it there at all?' Margery asked.

'The Devil's Yew is properly scary,' Megan said with a shrug in explanation. 'It's what the whole film is based around.'

They watched as the strangers appeared on screen and the real story began. Each video was only a few minutes long, but they all seemed to drag. The script, if you could call it that, was awful. Margery couldn't tell if it was supposed to be a comedy, a horror, or some sort of satire – the acting was dire. They really should have dragged some of Rose's drama students in to help. The editing was well done and interesting, but still, it would win no awards at Cannes. Just as she was beginning to wonder how much of it they would have to sit through. Megan lunged with her hand to the screen of the iPad and paused the video.

'Look,' she said, tapping the computer screen, 'look there! This is the video you need to see!'

Margery and Clementine looked to where she was pointing.

'The door?' Margery began, she was a bit confused about what they were supposed to be looking at until she realised that the purposefully grainy footage was of Rose's house at Halloween, the turned A had already been painted over the door in red paint.

'Watch it,' Amelia said knowingly. She started the film again and sure enough the door opened, and a figure left the building, their face almost concealed, until they pulled the hooded cape from their face and tore it off.

'Dr Roberts,' Margery gasped.

'Oh my!' Clementine gesticulated at the screen. 'It was her! She really tried to kill Miss Macdonald. Gosh, I can't believe it's true.'

'Do you think she painted the turned A herself?' Margery asked the students. 'You really didn't paint it on the door?'

'No,' Megan scoffed, 'we only use green paint because it's the spookiest colour.'

They watched the screen as Dr Roberts threw the cape and mask off as she rushed around the side of the house, opening Rose's fence door and going back into the garden. Presumably to get back into the house through the conservatory. A moment later Mr Barrow stepped out and rushed into the street, looking left and right before deciding on a direction and sprinting away down the road.

'You should have given this straight to the police,' Margery scolded Megan, who dropped her head in shame.

'I know,' she said. 'But I didn't know how to without getting into trouble.'

Margery sighed. 'The whole town is still under curfew because of you!'

'Yes, we had to do our big shop straight after work!' Clementine accused. 'We usually do it at five in the morning on Saturday, but we weren't allowed out till seven!'

'Has anyone else seen this, Megan?' Margery asked the girl, who shook her head.

'No,' she said. 'The account is private because we were going to do a big reveal, but then Mr Weaver died and Miss Macdonald got attacked and it didn't seem very good to post it anymore.'

'I have to agree there,' Margery said.

'I'm sorry though,' Megan said sadly. 'Do you think this film will help?'

'I think it will help very much,' Margery said. 'Can we have it? We'll tell the police we have it on the under-standing that you won't be in trouble. I'm sure Officer Thomas will be very pleased that he finally has some evidence.'

'Do you think this is enough to convict her though?' Clementine said, her voice wavering. 'It doesn't prove she killed Mr Weaver any more than a missing sharps box does.'

'It can't hurt,' Margery said. Clementine didn't look convinced.

'I'll upload it to our shared drive and send it to you,' Megan beamed, unconcerned with their disagreement. 'What's your email?'

'I don't have an email,' Margery said. Both Amelia and Megan looked at her like she had just announced that from now on she would only be wearing plastic carrier bags for hats.

'I've got email,' Clementine said smugly. 'But don't send it to me because I can't remember the password.'

'I'll put it on a USB stick for you,' Megan finally said, after she and Amelia had stared at them for what Margery had felt was an age.

Chapter Twenty-Seven

They waited in Dr Roberts' classroom nervously. Margery couldn't stop twiddling her fingers around and around. Clementine kept pulling at the sleeves of her cardigan, the threads becoming more and more frayed. If someone could kill another person, Margery reasoned, they would have no problem doing it again to keep it covered up. Waiting in the classroom as the autumn sun rose low in the sky, Margery hoped all their meddling hadn't been in vain.

The doorknob rattled as it was turned from outside and Margery held her breath. Beside her, she felt Clementine freeze, and could hear her sharp intake of breath as well. This was it. Margery could barely believe they were here, it hadn't seemed likely a few days ago. The door opened and Dr Roberts entered the classroom laden with bags and took a few steps before she realised that they were there. If she was surprised to see them, it didn't show at all.

'Oh, hello,' she said. 'I thought I might be seeing you soon.'

'Did you?' Margery asked in surprise. Dr Roberts gave her a small cold smile.

'Yes, of course. You bugged my sharps box.' She smirked at them both. 'Not very well. What were you doing in my room the other day? Was that all you came to do?'

'You did see my walking stick.' Margery grimaced as she leaned on it.

'I did,' Dr Roberts said. She put her laptop bag on the desk, and the big tote bag she was carrying under it and then she took her coat off, sauntering over to the cupboard they had been hidden in two days before, opening the door and hanging it up on the hook on the inside. It was as they had left it on Tuesday afternoon, the skeleton hanging limply on the wheeled stand at the back. 'Neither of you are very subtle, I knew what you'd done as soon as I saw your little keyring thing.'

She shook her hand towards Clementine, who opened her mouth to say something and then slammed it shut again when she realised there was nothing to say in return. Dr Roberts crossed back through the room, tidying chairs as she did so until she reached her desk again. She took her laptop from her bag and began to set it up for today's first lesson.

'You're lucky I don't have a form class to take the register for,' she muttered. 'You'd be in the way then. Why are you here?'

'We're here to ask you a few questions,' Clementine said sharply, but she didn't move an inch and Dr Roberts barely looked up from the laptop, plugging it into the cable for the digital whiteboard and turning that on too.

'We know you attacked Miss Macdonald,' Margery said. Dr Roberts' head snapped up to stare at her, fingers staying behind on the laptop keyboard.

'Nonsense,' she said, turning away again and busying herself with the tote bag she had under her desk, which was full of her classes marking.

'We have video proof,' Clementine told her. Dr Roberts swallowed and dropped the pile of books onto her desk with a thump.

'Do you?' Dr Roberts finally looked at them, picking at one of the textbooks with her fingers.

'We do,' Clementine said. 'That's what we want to ask you the questions about.'

Dr Roberts moved to the front of the desk and leaned against it. 'Well, detectives...' She smirked again. 'Why don't you tell me what you think happened? Come on, it's time for your little drawing-room reveal, let's have it then.'

Margery hadn't been expecting that and she knew that Clementine hadn't either. She had expected Dr Roberts to deny it all, get angry, maybe try and throw them out of her classroom. Instead, she folded her arms defensively across her chest and waited for them to continue.

'Okay,' Clementine gave Margery a surprised look before stepping forward. 'Well...'

'We really don't have all day,' Dr Roberts said, pulling the sleeve of her blouse up to look at her watch. 'My first class starts in half an hour.'

'Fine,' Clementine said, scratching her head.

'I'll start.' Margery said, stepping forward to stand next to Clementine and resting both hands on the walking stick. 'We think you strangled Elle Macdonald.'

'Why?' Dr Roberts asked, the question was not a denial. It was a challenge more than anything else.

'Well.' Margery inhaled deeply while she put the thoughts together into words. 'We know she asked you for help because you knew Liam Weaver from university, and he was blackmailing her.'

'That's true,' Dr Roberts admitted, sitting back on the desk and using her arms to support herself. 'But why would I strangle her?'

'We think…' Margery turned to Clementine, who nodded for her to continue. 'We think you tried to kill Elle to get her out of the way.'

Dr Roberts sighed and sat up again, tapping her fingers on the desk. 'That's…' She grimaced. 'That's partly what happened, I suppose, but not the whole reason.'

'You thought that she knew you had killed Liam Weaver,' Clementine said. 'Which was a waste of your time because she didn't realise that at all. In fact, you'd have probably got away with it if it wasn't for one thing…'

'And what's that?' Dr Roberts smirked again. 'Dewstow's terrible police force and two old dinner ladies who keep accidentally solving murders?'

'Well, yes.'

Clementine continued, 'You would have gotten away with it if you'd known that Elle thought that she'd killed him.'

'Ahh,' Dr Roberts said, moving to start setting up her classroom again. Taking the workbooks and beginning to put them out on the desks. 'You're saying if I hadn't tried to kill her then no one would know? She came to me at that party, ladies, blabbering about how she needed to confess that she'd left him for dead. I just assumed she would put it all together and realise what I'd done because she knew we were meeting. I don't want to blow my own horn, ladies, but I just assumed that she was as intelligent as I am.'

'I think she was too shocked to even consider how he had died,' Margery told her. 'She thought she'd killed him. But we know it was you.'

'There's no proof that I killed Liam though, is there?' Dr Roberts continued. 'If there was then neither of you would be here. You had Mark Evans arrested quickly enough, didn't you? On the tiniest amount of evidence, and even then, it wasn't even evidence in the end!'

'Why not just confess?' Margery asked, watching as Dr Roberts finished slapping the books down on the desks and then returned to her own desk, pulling up the lesson plan on the laptop where it projected behind her on the screen.

'I didn't even know what I'd done. Obviously, I knew I'd stabbed him.' Dr Roberts sat in her chair. 'But I didn't realise I'd killed him until the autopsy came back.'

'The embolism?' Clementine said, shaking her head. 'You used to be a phlebotomist, you can't tell me you aren't good at finding veins! The phlebotomist at our GP surgery is amazing at it, it's like magic. She took about fifty litres of my blood last time I had to have a test.'

'I was good at my job,' Dr Roberts admitted. 'But I really didn't. In fact, I just wasn't expecting him to react like that at all and he caught me off guard.'

'What happened?' Margery asked. Dr Roberts gave her a look that told her she'd been waiting for them to finally ask the question.

'After all that, you're not even going to have a guess?' Dr Roberts said with a dismissive shake of her head.

'Okay,' Margery said, thinking again. If this was how Dr Roberts wanted to go about it, then they had no choice but to play along. 'I think that you were here, and your insulin pump stopped working.'

Dr Roberts cocked an eyebrow, 'Go on.'

'And then...' Margery tried to think. She moved over to the desk and examined the area behind it, with the little box fridge that Rose had told them about. She hadn't noticed it the first time they'd come. They had been too busy searching the desk and finding the note Liam had used to blackmail Elle. It wasn't on any of the school paperwork either, perhaps Dr Roberts had bought it herself. 'I think you did your sugars after the harvest festival and realised that it wasn't working.'

'And then you did your insulin the old-fashioned way.' Clementine stepped around the other side of the desk, she'd noticed what Margery had said and had picked up on her train of thought. 'With a needle, like the ones you probably keep...' She reached into the front of Dr Roberts's laptop bag and pulled out a smaller hard case. She unzipped and opened it; for a moment Margery thought it would reveal an expensive pair of designer sunglasses or something else of the sort. Instead, Clementine turned to reveal the set of microfine syringes and the separate sealed packs of needles that screwed into the top of them. Clementine smiled at the discovery.

'It took me a while to realise,' Clementine said, 'because I just assumed you'd have an injection pen and I thought, "How would she inject air into his vein with a pen?". My mother had one, you see, she really liked it, found it much easier to do. But you use—'

'Separate syringes.' Dr Roberts nodded, her face didn't reveal any emotion. In fact, she seemed far too calm. 'Yes. I attach the needle and then fill the syringe from the insulin I keep in the fridge if I need it. Not that the pump is ever supposed to stop working! But if it does, I just prefer it and, you know, you've got to put insulin in the reusable pens anyway. Then what did I do next? Go on, tell me.' There was a nasty hint of amusement in her voice that Margery found distressing.

'You injected yourself like you needed to,' Clementine said, closing the case again and putting it down on the desk behind them. 'And you usually report that you've done that on the school register with the nurse.'

'You never forget because safety is important to you,' Margery suddenly remembered. Dr Roberts snapped her head around to eye her. 'You're on the health and safety team after all.'

'How did you…?' Dr Roberts said, before remembering that Margery and Clementine would have heard her say that to Rose. 'Well, yes, I am, go on.'

'But before you had a chance to do any of that, Liam Weaver arrived to talk to you as you had arranged.' Clementine had begun to pace the small space in front of the desk, tapping her fingers to her mouth. 'And you argued.'

'About Elle,' Margery suggested, knowing she was right by the surprise written on Dr Roberts' face. 'And it became physical.'

Dr Roberts waved a hand for her to continue.

'The used needle was on your desk.' Margery gestured to it. 'So you picked it up and pulled the plunger back to fill it with air.'

'This is just a hunch,' Clementine said. 'But I think you told him if he didn't leave you alone, you'd stab him with it and he didn't take you seriously.'

Dr Roberts gave a bark of laughter that made Margery jump. 'Something like that.'

'Why did you argue?' Margery asked. 'It can't just have been about Elle.'

'It wasn't about Elle at all,' Dr Roberts admitted. 'I wanted my money back. Elle came to ask me to get him to stop blackmailing her, but obviously that was never going to happen because blackmailing her was my idea in the first place.'

Margery felt her jaw drop. 'You mean to say...?'

'Yes!' Dr Roberts laughed. 'Liam owed me money. A lot of money.'

Her too, Margery thought. 'He came to tell me about his wife's affair when he found out about it, oh, months ago now, and so I thought, the easiest way to get the money back would be if I were to blackmail Elle pretending to be Liam. To get the money back that he'd borrowed to supposedly pay off Mark, obviously that money went straight to the bookies.' She scoffed. 'Liam always was an idiot, even at school. Well, I suppose now he's dead and I'll never get it back, so maybe I'm the idiot really.'

'So the poems he sent her, they weren't from him?' Clementine began to say.

'You don't think Liam could have written those haikus?' Dr Roberts laughed. 'I wrote them and put his silly little maths club signature on them and gave them to her.'

'All that time you were blackmailing her!' Margery gasped. 'She came to you for help! She was desperate.'

Dr Roberts didn't look sorry in the slightest, holding her hands up. 'Well, it's all's well that ends well, isn't it? Elle gets his wife; I get away with murder. Everyone's happy.'

'Except the dead man,' Clementine snorted. 'So, he arrived here after he'd found out what you'd done and then...'

'He shouldn't have threatened me!' Dr Roberts said, folding her arms over her chest and leaning back in the chair. 'He had it coming. He didn't even stop after I stabbed him with the needle, I had to hit him with a textbook, nearly broke his nose!'

'Did he hurt you?' Margery found herself asking.

'No,' Dr Roberts said sadly. 'But I didn't know if he was going to. It's always better to act pre-emptively, ladies, you should keep that in mind going forwards.'

There was silence for a moment as they all returned to their own thoughts. Margery realised that the confession hadn't shocked her. Somehow, she had come to expect it. She had always used to assume that everyone around her was decent and good until they proved her wrong. Time and time again she had been proved wrong. Maybe that was her downfall – seeing the best in people who had nothing good left in them. Liv had shown them the video of her arguing with Liam, he must have rushed straight back to the school to confront Dr Roberts. And she had killed him.

'Right, ladies, you'd better get off,' Dr Roberts said. 'Like I said, I've got class. And who's doing the breakfast club bananas and Weetabix and all those bits and bobs you chuck out at the kids?'

'Gloria's doing the breakfast club,' Margery said weakly at the same time as Clementine cried, 'You'll never get away with this!'

'I will,' Dr Roberts said coolly. She stood and moved to the classroom door, ready to usher them out. 'Of course I will. There's no evidence.'

'The sharps box you had,' Clementine began.

'I'm not that stupid.' Dr Roberts said. 'Do you think I'd keep the murder weapon in an actual sharps box?'

'The DNA from the glove!' Clementine said, gesturing into the air as if she could summon it. 'The DNA testing.'

'I'm not going to give them my DNA,' Dr Roberts scoffed, putting her hand on the door handle and beginning to turn it.

'You wouldn't keep it in the sharps box, you needed that for a genuine reason,' Margery said, realisation arriving like an unexpected bus. Dr Roberts and Clementine stopped their argument and turned to look at her. 'That would be too obvious if the police ever did come calling. No, you would keep it somewhere else and you wouldn't take it out of the school while there was so much police attention. You'd keep it somewhere safe until this all blew over.'

'The toolbox!' Clementine said, pointing at Dr Roberts with a gotcha sort of motion.

'Yes!' Margery cried.

Dr Roberts lunged for the cupboard door as soon as they did and the three of them began to fight with the door handle. Dr Roberts shouting and swearing and Margery and Clementine desperately trying to open it. Margery fell back, her walking stick lost in the tussle, and caught herself on a desk.

'Stop!' A booming voice came from behind them. 'It's over, Dr Roberts!'

Officer Thomas burst into the classroom, followed by Officer Symon racing behind him and what looked like Dewstow and Ittonvale's entire forces put together. He grasped Dr Roberts by the wrists and handcuffed her before she could realise what was happening.

'Doctor Christine Roberts,' he said, as the steel snapped shut around her wrists. 'You are under arrest for the murder of Liam Weaver. You do not have to say anything but it may harm your defence if you do not mention when questioned something that you later rely on in Court. Anything you do say may be given in evidence.'

'This won't stand in court! You've got no evidence!'

'That toolbox will have the needle, the glove will have your DNA and it'll all be over,' Clementine said. 'How stupid are you to leave your glove at a crime scene anyway?'

Dr Roberts protested but was overwhelmed and dragged away. The headmaster stepped out from behind the police officers and nodded to Margery and Clementine, who began to take off the recording equipment the police had given them first thing that morning that had been hidden under their cardigans.

Chapter Twenty-Eight

'Well, that could have gone horribly wrong, couldn't it?' Mr Barrow mused, shaking his head at them in disbelief from behind his desk, which they were sat in front of once more.

They had been in here way too many times for Margery's liking. She was sick of the room now, sick of sitting in the ugly, uncomfortable visitors' chairs after another dangerous thing had happened. This time it had been their choice, she didn't know if that made it even worse.

'It really could have,' Margery agreed, once again they had got lucky.

It was only Dr Roberts' certainty that they were too stupid to get her arrested that had stopped anything worse from happening. In a way, she felt like Dr Roberts was testing them to see how much she had got away with. She had completely underestimated them, just as Officer Thomas suspected she would, and she was going to pay the price for it. Officer Thomas and his team had already left with her and now they were sat in the headmaster's office for a sort of bizarre debriefing.

'Well, I just wanted to thank you both for saving the school, again!' Mr Barrow said, smiling tiredly at them. His smile had been so rare lately that it took Margery by surprise for a moment.

'Will all the trouble with the governors go away now?' Clementine asked with a grimace. Mr Barrow's face dropped again.

'I don't know,' he said. 'There's been talk of an audit and an Ofsted inspection, but nothing's come from it yet.' He seemed to realise that he'd said too much and put the smile back on, though it was very forced this time. 'Forget about that, you've just saved the school, again! I can't ever thank you enough, I'll make sure they mention it in this term's newsletter.'

'No problem at all,' Clementine said jovially. 'Well, I suppose it was a bit of a problem, but we got there in the end.'

There was a rap at the door and Mr Barrow sprang up as Dewstow's sergeant beckoned for him to follow. He closed the door behind him with a soft click and Margery took Clementine's hand.

'I think you were right,' she whispered as soon as she was sure he was out of earshot. Her thoughts had been simmering gently the entire time they had been sat in the office and she had to get them out before she lost her nerve. Dr Roberts lunging towards them with fury in her eyes had made her realise just how much she wasn't over the summer.

'Of course I am,' Clementine said, smiling before cocking an eyebrow at her in confusion. 'About what?'

'I think I need help,' Margery said, Clementine aahed in understanding. 'I don't think I'm really over what happened in the summer yet and I know you don't blame me…' Clementine opened her mouth to protest, but Margery cut her off. 'But I still blame myself for what happened.'

'You shouldn't!' Clementine said, clutching Margery's hand tightly. 'It wasn't your fault at all. None of it was.'

'I know that,' Margery said. 'But for some reason a bit of my brain doesn't.'

Clementine hummed beside her, her brow furrowing. Margery knew she was trying to think of a solution.

'What if we both see that counsellor? Get some help?' Margery said, staring at her feet. 'I don't think I can carry on like this.'

'I'd love that,' Clementine said, looking over at her, a rare serious look on her face. 'You know I would. All I want is for you to feel better again.'

'All right,' Margery finally agreed, feeling a weight lift from her shoulders that she hadn't realised was there. They sat for a moment longer, enjoying the peace before Mr Barrow came back.

-

It was nearly half eleven by the time they had given their statements to the police. Mr Barrow offered them the rest of the day off, but it seemed like the right thing to do was to go back to the kitchen and help serve lunch. Margery was looking forward to having a cup of tea after lunch had finished and explaining all that had happened to the team. As soon as they entered the room, she knew they wouldn't have a chance to. Something was off about the canteen. It just didn't feel quite right, but she couldn't put her finger on what it was. They walked through anyway, with no fear after the horrors of the morning, pulled on their hairnets from the box of new ones on the wall and stepped through the door into the kitchen as they had done a thousand times before.

Ceri-Ann was putting out the last of the lunch trays, all still covered in their silver tin foil to stop the food from going dry under the powerful heat lights of the serving station. She turned at the sound of running water from the hand wash sink and noticed them. She hissed over to them and then made a series of dramatic gestures like she was trying to demonstrate a very difficult clue in a game of charades, all flailing arms and wide eyes. Behind her at the back of the kitchen, Sharon and Karen were busily washing up at a speed that Margery had never seen either of them achieve in the entire time they had worked at Summerview. Seren was frantically labelling the pre-packaged sandwiches she had been making, piling them all up on the trolley ready to go into the service fridge.

'Are you all right, Ceri?' Margery began to ask when Ceri-Ann's flapping didn't stop, but she fell silent as she noticed the door opening down the long corridor that contained the walk-in freezer and her office. A woman in a white food hygiene inspector coat with the clipboard emerged from the dry store, with Gloria following behind in her shadow.

Margery's heart sank as the woman peered at the cleaning rota and allergen sheet in their holders lined along the corridor wall, Gloria waiting patiently behind her. She hadn't been there to remind them to fill in the paperwork that morning; a wave of fear washed through her. Before she had time to decide what to do, the woman sensed that she was being watched and looked over to where they were standing, giving them both a small smile. Margery decided that it was best to get it over with, stepping forward to greet her.

'Hello,' the inspector said, her cheery voice taking Margery by surprise. 'Which one of you is Margery?'

'Me,' Margery managed to squeak out. 'I'm ever so sorry, we were held up by—'

'Gosh, yes, I heard all about it!' The inspector gasped, holding her clipboard to her chest dramatically. 'Don't worry, it's not a problem at all, your sous chef took me around.' Gloria smiled at her sheepishly. 'I was just signing off on your final score.'

She scribbled something to the sheet attached to the clipboard, took the paper off and handed it to Margery, who took it gingerly. She forced herself to look at it, glancing at it quickly so as to soften the blow of the bad score she was sure was scrawled there and wondering how on earth she was going to explain her failures to the headmaster. Instead, she squinted at it and then did a double-take, her mouth falling open in surprise.

'Five?' she gasped, almost not believing what was written in front of her and its accompanying note that read two simple words, *high standard*. 'You scored us the highest mark?'

'Of course,' the inspector said, shrugging as she waved towards the main kitchen. 'You run a fantastically tight ship here, Mrs Butcher-Baker. Very well done. All your systems are good, your HACCP and COSHH paperwork are up to date and the kitchen's spotless, I can't fault it at all. Your staff know your processes well too, I'm very happy to give you a five.' She chuckled. 'I only wish I could give more a five, you ought to see the kitchen in the Bell and Hope, they barely got a three last visit.' She blushed as she realised what she had just done. 'Gosh, I really shouldn't have said that! Sorry, I'm quite new to this.'

Margery stared at the certificate again in shock as Clementine clapped her on the back. Over in the corner

Ceri-Ann was grinning madly, even Sharon and Karen were smiling as they got the serving utensils out ready for lunchtime.

'You'll get your new sticker in the post to replace the old one. Very good work.' The inspector smiled again. 'I suspect I won't need to see you again for a while, congratulations all.'

'Shall I show you out?' Gloria gestured to the door. The inspector followed her out of the canteen and Margery waited for her to go with bated breath. She couldn't take her eyes off the piece of paper in her hand. She kept glancing at the score expecting the letters to suddenly rearrange themselves, for the number to transfigure into a two or a three. She should have known it would all work out all right, it was proof that she hadn't had anything to worry about really. All their hard work in the year since Caroline had left the helm was paying off. The team didn't need Margery to succeed, they were all perfectly capable in their own way. Margery smiled to herself, Clementine was going to be insufferable about being right as usual. This time though, Margery would let her enjoy the moment.

The canteen doors reopened, and Gloria rushed back in with a grin on her face. She joined Ceri-Ann, Seren, Sharon and Karen in descending on Margery and Clementine in a way that would have been completely overwhelming if they didn't know them all so well. Margery leaned into the group hug, happy to be among friends in the apex of their little world again. Far away from anything that could hurt them.

Epilogue

The party had already started by the time Margery and Clementine arrived at the Bell and Hope and though they wouldn't call it raucous, it was in as full swing as it was going to get. It wasn't like them to arrive late to anything, but they had really debated on whether or not to come at all after all the trouble with their accusation of Mr Evans and Jess calling them into the pub to confront them. They needn't have worried. Jess was outside the entrance when they arrived, smoking a cigarette, and said hello to them without a hint of malice. It had been a much calmer few weeks in between everything that had happened and any anger had died down, especially now that Mr Evans was back from suspension and had returned to his classes.

They entered the events room in the old stables and Margery took it all in as Clementine placed their gift bag in the pile on the table next to the door. She smiled at the decorations. The caution tape dangled all about the place, the cake shaped like the beat hat she always saw Officer Thomas wear, and the blue and white balloons floating from the backs of all the chairs. She decided that she wouldn't try anything from the buffet table lined with sad-looking sandwiches and cheese and pineapple on sticks after what the EHO officer had said.

She scanned the room as Clementine made for the bar to get them both a gin and tonic. Ceri-Ann was certainly showing now, she noted, as she watched her laughing at a story Symon was telling her. Both of them looking young outside of their work uniforms and effortlessly happy in each other's company. She didn't really know many other people, if you didn't count Mr Barrow and Rose in the corner. Rose gave them a wave and then went back to chatting to Dewstow's town sergeant, who still looked like he might nod off at any moment.

Officer Thomas noticed Margery immediately, excused himself to his wife, Mary, and came strolling straight over, beaming at her. It took Margery a second to recognise him, and it wasn't until he was immediately in front of them that she realised he had shaved off his moustache.

'Hello, Officer Thomas,' Margery smiled back at him. 'I'm so sorry we're late.'

'You'd better call me Nigel now!' Officer Thomas said. 'I handed in my badge yesterday, it's all over.'

'Gosh, I don't think I could!' Margery laughed. 'Was it all worth it?'

Officer Thomas looked sad for the briefest of moments and Margery understood immediately how he must feel, sorrow for the past with a touch of relief. Time didn't wait for anyone, but it wasn't always possible to enjoy the present. As she got older, she realised all those tiny moments she had worried about something were easily forgotten. None of the little mundane events survived in her memory for very long, leaving instead only room for the big moments and the drama. She wondered if Officer Thomas felt the same looking back on all those cases he had been involved in, intermingled with the normality of day-to-day patrols and other small duties.

'I think so,' he said, his bare lip almost comically pale. 'I think it has to be. Forty-two years, God. When I first joined I never thought I'd manage one!'

Margery smiled, thinking of how she had only applied to work at Summerview School because Clementine had been accepted for a job there. That was coming up to just as many years now. They occasionally talked about retiring, but she felt privately that there was more left to do, though she didn't know what it was that kept calling her back.

'Well, congratulations,' she said, he held out his hand and she took it.

'Listen,' he said as they shook. 'My replacement, well… he's younger, a bit more determined.'

'Okay.' Margery wondered where this was going. Officer Thomas discreetly pointed over to a man sat at one of the tables. He had a cupcake and a glass of champagne in front of him. He was scanning the room, as if looking for trouble, his mouth pulled into a thin line, the cardboard party hat on his head looking very much out of place. He was the very opposite of what you would want as a party guest, and Margery briefly wondered if Officer Thomas regretted inviting him.

'I'm only telling you because, the thing is, even though you really helped us this time…' Officer Thomas said, his eyes meeting hers sincerely.

'Are you trying to tell me we need to stop meddling?' Margery asked with a smile. 'Because it's not only down to me, you know.'

She pointed to Clementine over at the bar and Officer Thomas smiled too.

'Just be careful,' he warned. 'I'm not sure he'll appreciate any help. You might get into trouble.'

'Don't worry,' she assured him. 'We really aren't planning to get involved ever again.'

They parted ways as Clementine came back with their drinks, Margery watched the ice swirl in the glass as the police officer sauntered over to the entrance. Even his walk seemed lighter, like he was finally free.

'What was that about?' Clementine asked, as they watched Officer Thomas greet another group of late arrivals at the entrance.

Margery turned to tell her at the same time as Officer Thomas's replacement looked up and caught her eye, glowering over at them both and causing the words to catch in her throat. He held her gaze for a moment before turning away, and Margery realised immediately that he knew exactly who they were. She was certain just from the look that he was not a big fan of theirs at all.

Acknowledgements

Firstly, as always, thank you to my family and friends for your endless support. Special thanks this time to Mum and Jim for double-checking the maths problem in the book.

Thank you to my wife, Robyn, for always being my calm oasis in a sea of bad punctuation and writer's block. You're always telling me that I can do it, and you haven't been wrong yet. I love you.

Thank you to my editor, Siân Heap, for everything you do, and for not cutting too many cat bits out!

Thank you to Canelo and Canelo Crime for publishing the Dinner Ladies stories and the team at Saga Egmont for their excellent work on the audiobooks.

A big thank you to Ami Smithson for another excellent cover! Thank you also to Kate Shepherd of Canelo.

Huge thanks as always to Matt Taylor and the Chepstow Bookshop. Thanks for continually stocking the series and letting me come in and scribble all over them!

There are several other people I need to thank for their support, so in no particular order; J Taylor and 'A Story Shared' Podcast, Fosters Little Bookshop, Jonathan Whitelaw, Sam Brownley and the UK Crime Book Club.

Thanks also to TikTok for stealing every last bit of attention span I had left after I downloaded the app for 'research'.

Lastly and most importantly, thank you to you for reading!

CANELOCRIME

Do you love crime fiction and are always on the lookout for brilliant authors?

Canelo Crime is home to some of the most exciting novels around. Thousands of readers are already enjoying our compulsive stories. Are you ready to find your new favourite writer?

Find out more and sign up to our newsletter at canelocrime.com